"Hello, Lisa."

She had intended to play it out, to ask if he had an appointment, to pretend she didn't know who he was, to pretend she didn't remember him. It wasn't unreasonable. It had been eight years. A lot had changed in that time. And they hadn't known one another all that long—the tail end of one dreary New York winter, and the blossoming of one perfect New York spring.

Yes, it was entirely plausible that she might not remember him.... Then she saw his face.

The square-jawed, strong-boned face, softened only by a mobile mouth and black-lashed blue eyes. She remembered it perfectly and decided that playing out the farce that she'd forgotten him would simply waste resources she feared she would need to keep control of this encounter.

"Detective Garrison."

One side of his mouth lifted in a half smile. "You used to call me Shane."

Dear Reader,

'Tis the season to ask yourself "What makes Christmas special?" (other than a Silhouette Special Edition novel in your stocking, that is). For Susan Mallery, it's "sharing in established traditions and starting new ones." And what could be more of a tradition than reading Susan's adorable holiday MONTANA MAVERICKS story, *Christmas in Whitehorn?*

Peggy Webb's statement of the season, "The only enduring gift is love" resonates in us all as she produces an enduring gift with *The Smile of an Angel* from her series THE WESTMORELAND DIARIES. Along with love, author Patricia Kay feels that Christmas "is all about joy—the joy of being with family and loved ones." And we are overjoyed to bring you the latest in her CALLAHANS & KIN miniseries, *Just a Small-Town Girl.*

Sylvie Kurtz shows us the "magical quality" of the holidays in *A Little Christmas Magic*, a charming opposites-attract love story. And we are delighted by Patricia McLinn's *My Heart Remembers* from her WYOMING WILDFLOWERS miniseries. For Patricia, "Christmas is family. Revisiting memories, but also focusing on today." Crystal Green echoes this thought. "The word *family* is synonymous with Christmas." So curl up with her latest, *The Pregnant Bride*, from her new miniseries, KANE'S CROSSING!

As you can see, we have many talented writers to celebrate this holiday season in Special Edition.

Happy Holidays!

Karen Taylor Richman
Senior Editor

Please address questions and book requests to:
Silhouette Reader Service
U.S.: 3010 Walden Ave., P.O. Box 1325, Buffalo, NY 14269
Canadian: P.O. Box 609, Fort Erie, Ont. L2A 5X3

My Heart Remembers

PATRICIA McLINN

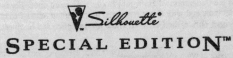

SPECIAL EDITION™

Published by Silhouette Books

America's Publisher of Contemporary Romance

To Dad, Joe and John
Topnotch technical consultants
and fixers of all things broken.

SILHOUETTE BOOKS

ISBN 0-373-24439-8

MY HEART REMEMBERS

Copyright © 2001 by Patricia McLaughlin

This edition published by arrangement with Harlequin Books S.A.

® and TM are trademarks of Harlequin Books S.A., used under license.
Trademarks indicated with ® are registered in the United States Patent
and Trademark Office, the Canadian Trade Marks Office and in other
countries.

Visit Silhouette at www.eHarlequin.com

Printed in U.S.A.

Books by Patricia McLinn

Silhouette Special Edition

Hoops #587
A New World #641
*Prelude to a Wedding #712
*Wedding Party #718
*Grady's Wedding #813
Not a Family Man #864
Rodeo Nights #904
A Stranger in the Family #959
A Stranger To Love #1098
The Rancher Meets His Match #1164
†Lost-and-Found Groom #1344
†At the Heart's Command #1350
†Hidden in a Heartbeat #1355
**Almost a Bride #1404
**Match Made in Wyoming #1409
**My Heart Remembers #1439

Harlequin Historicals

Widow Woman #417

*Wedding Series
†A Place Called Home
**Wyoming Wildflowers

PATRICIA McLINN

finds great satisfaction in transferring the characters crowded in her head onto paper to be enjoyed by readers. "Writing," she says, "is the hardest work I'd never give up." Writing has brought her new experiences, places and friends—especially friends. After receiving degrees from Northwestern University, and newspaper jobs that have taken her from Illinois to North Carolina to Washington, D.C., Patricia now lives in Virginia, in a house that grows piles of paper, books and dog hair at an alarming rate. The paper and books are her own fault, but the dog hair comes from a charismatic collie, who helps put things in perspective when neighborhood kids refer to Patricia as "the lady who lives in Riley's house." Friends, family, books, travel, gardening and sitting on her porch are among her joys. She would love to hear from readers at P.O. Box 7052, Arlington, VA 22207.

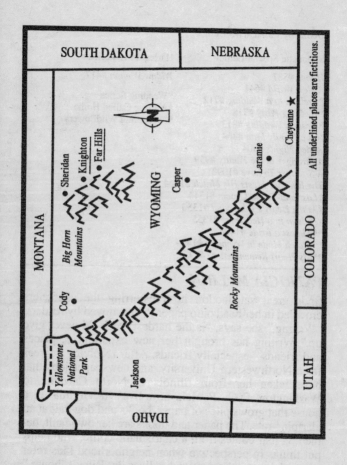

SOUTH DAKOTA

NEBRASKA

MONTANA

WYOMING

COLORADO

UTAH

IDAHO

• Sheridan
• Knighton
• Far Hills

Big Horn Mountains

• Cody

• Casper

• Laramie

Rocky Mountains

• Jackson

Yellowstone National Park

★ Cheyenne

All underlined places are fictitious.

Chapter One

"**Y**ou cut your hair."

There was nothing ominous about the words that came from behind Lisa Currick.

Except that with those four short words, she recognized a low, male voice she hadn't heard in eight years.

"I'll be with you in a minute," she said, keeping her back to him, buying herself time. Time to put the memories that came with this voice—this man—back in storage where they belonged. Except, if eight years hadn't been long enough, how could she hope another minute would be?

She slid into place the file she'd been holding. The corner was crumpled where she'd clutched it. She would replace it with a fresh folder later. Right now it was more important to put that sign of her agitation out of sight from the man standing just inside the door. If he was anything like he had been eight years ago, he wouldn't miss that sort of detail.

She closed the drawer and turned to face him.

"May I help you?" She crossed to behind her desk. From this desk she efficiently ran the Knighton, Wyoming, law office of Taylor Anne Larsen. It represented all that she was now—and had not been when she had last seen Shane Garrison.

"Hello, Lisa."

She had intended to play it out, to ask if he had an appointment with Taylor, to pretend she didn't know who he was, to pretend she didn't remember him. It wasn't unreasonable. It had been eight years. A lot had changed in that time. *She* had changed. And they hadn't known each other all that long back then—the tail end of one dreary New York winter and the blossoming of one perfect New York spring. Contrary to her fantasies at the time, she also hadn't known him *well.*

Yes, it was entirely plausible that she might not remember him…. Then she saw his face.

The square-jawed, strong-boned face, softened only by a mobile mouth and black-lashed blue eyes. She remembered it perfectly, yet it was different from her memory. Eight years had changed him, too. If anything, it had deepened the lines of determination etched in his face.

Seeing that, she decided not to play out the farce that she'd forgotten him. It would simply waste resources she feared she would need to keep control of this encounter.

"Detective Garrison." She gripped the back of her desk chair to give her hands something to do.

One side of his mouth lifted in a half smile. She used to see that as a challenge to win a full smile from him.

"You used to call me Shane."

"Your professional title seems more appropriate." The needs of his profession, after all, had been the bedrock of their connection—the reason it started and the reason it ended.

"Does that mean you want me to call you Miss Currick—or is it Mrs. something now?"

"Ms. will do."

He blocked her effort to sidestep the personal with a blunt "You're not married?"

"You're slipping if your detective work learned only that I had cut my hair." The tartness of that was a mistake. Bland was safer.

His left eyebrow—the one with the small scar above it—rose. "My powers of observation haven't slipped. I see there's no ring on your left hand."

She fought the urge to put her hands behind her back, winning that fight by curling her fingers into the chair's padding. His gaze focused on the motion, and his grin shifted ever so slightly. He sat on the chair across from her desk, leaning back, crossing his jean-clad legs, totally at his ease.

"Detective Garrison, I have work to do. If you would please—"

"You rent a house with your name alone on the lease, and your vehicle's registered in your name—but you could still be married and using your maiden name. However, I observed that you left home alone this morning, departing in the only car that had been parked there all night. You arrived at your place of business at 8:50 a.m., left at 12:08 to walk to the Knighton Café, where you sat at the back booth—again alone—until 12:53, when you—"

"You've been following me?" The accusation was clear, but she succeeded in suppressing the outrage into unemotional chill.

He nodded, not the least abashed. "Yup. And before that, I checked your public records."

"Then why ask if I'm married? You must have known the answer."

He hesitated less than half a beat. "I wanted to see what you would say."

"Why? No—" She held out a hand, standing straight, no longer gripping the chair. "No, don't tell me. It would be a waste of your time and mine, because there is no reason that could make me care why. And there is no excuse for following me. You've invaded my privacy enough. Please leave."

"Aren't you going to ask why I'm here?"

"No."

For half a second she thought she saw relief in his eyes—as if he didn't know what he would have answered if she'd said, yes, she wanted to know why he was here. But that was ridiculous, because Detective Shane Garrison had always known what he wanted—and didn't want—from Lisa Currick.

"With your help, Lisa, I can—"

"You're not going to get it."

She said those words just the way she wanted. Solid. Unemotional. Determined. And now she called on the discipline of the past eight years to return his look the same way. It wasn't easy.

Those dark-lashed, deep-blue eyes had once made her girl's heart quake like an aspen buffeted by a Wyoming wind. Her heart was no longer a girl's, but those eyes still held power. Beyond the innate sensual message of them was a probing intelligence that knotted her stomach.

"I need your help, Lisa—Ms. Currick."

How he managed to make a formal means of address somehow intimate, she didn't know. She refused to think about how easily she would have melted eight years ago at the idea of his needing her in any way.

"I believe the expression that covers this situation is, Been there, done that."

"I'm going to find the necklace, Lisa. You could make it easier—"

"No."

"It won't hurt his chances at parole. It might even help them."

He thought she was trying to protect Alex? A little late, wasn't it? Alex had been her dream mentor—no, more than that, he'd been another grandfather to her. Beaming with pride at her accomplishments, instructing her, introducing her into the realm of jewels and gems that a girl from Wyoming had dreamed about before going to New York City. The day she'd learned that she'd been picked for the plum internship with the man famed for restoring only the best pieces for only the best clients, had been the proudest of her life. And the months she'd spent in the Alex White Studio had been even better than she'd dreamed. She'd learned so much, she'd been given so many opportunities, and she'd formed a genuine bond of affection and respect with a living icon of jewelry design.

And then Shane Garrison had entered her life.

"I've put it—*all* of it—behind me, and that's where it's going to stay. I'd like you to go now."

He studied her. Once that concentrated regard would have driven color into her cheeks, flustered her into speech that sped ahead of her brain and set her heartbeat thundering.

But she'd outgrown blushing, she'd learned to guard her tongue, and her heartbeat was her own business. She gave him back look for look.

Slowly, he stood then advanced until the width of the desk separated them. This close she saw the flecks of black among the blue that gave his eyes such depth. She imagined she felt the heat of his body.

"I won't give up, Lisa."

"That's entirely up to you, Detective Garrison. As long

as you don't try to involve me in your quest." *As long as you go back where you belong, so three-quarters of a continent separates me from those memories.*

"Can't undo what's done."

While she tried to decipher that, he turned and walked out. As the door closed she concluded that it didn't matter what his cryptic remark meant as long as he was gone.

She heard his tread on the wooden sidewalk in front of the office. Not boot heels like most men around here, but thick-soled running shoes. Running shoes' soles were made for sneaking up on someone, unlike the straightforward here-I-come announcement of boot heels. But Detective Shane Garrison might not have counted on the wooden sidewalks most Knighton businesses had in front of them. On wooden sidewalks, even running shoes made plenty of noise to give warning. He wouldn't take her by surprise again.

"Lisa?"

Her employer and friend, Taylor Anne Larsen, stood at the door of her inner office, looking at her quizzically.

"Do you need something, Taylor?"

Taylor shook her head. "I thought I heard voices. And you look a little…distracted. Is everything okay?"

"Someone came in the wrong door, and he took some convincing to see his mistake. As for distracted, I'm thinking about that project for my management topics class that I told you about."

"I thought you had that almost done."

"I decided last night that it needs another layer. I was reading at lunch about how management styles need to adapt to the new economy."

"That doesn't mean you'll miss the Book Pass does it?"

"No. I said I'd come, and I will."

If she felt a twinge as she steered the conversation toward the day planned to celebrate the library addition that Taylor's husband Cal Ruskoff had funded, it was because Taylor's question had reminded Lisa of how many times she'd begged off a social function with friends and family because of schoolwork.

The twinge was not—definitely not—because she'd lied. Because she hadn't. Shane Garrison had come in the wrong door if he thought she would help him. And he had needed convincing of that.

It wasn't that she couldn't trust Taylor. She could—she did. But she hadn't told anyone in Knighton—not even her family—about what had happened after she'd left home thinking she could conquer New York and instead had learned just how unprepared she was for anything beyond quiet, sleepy little Knighton. If it had been something really serious, something dangerous, something they could have helped with, of course she would have turned to them. They wouldn't condemn, they wouldn't play I-told-you-so. But it had been her mistake and her failure. She would keep both to herself.

She'd believed in two men back then, and she'd been wrong about both. One had disappointed her hopes. The other had disappointed her heart.

She wouldn't take that risk again.

She would keep the door closed to Shane Garrison.

You cut your hair.

It was a damned stupid thing to say. He hadn't meant to say it. It had just come out, which made it even worse.

At least he'd kept his mouth shut about her hands. They used to bear nicks, bruises, burns and scrapes like the badges of her vocation. The hands that had squeezed the back of that chair today had been smooth and blemish free.

One of his rules of dealing with witnesses or suspects was to think through everything he said to them ahead of time.

Only, he remembered her hair so well. Maybe because of that day in late April—a Wednesday, he remembered that, though God knew why. They'd come out of the coffee shop, and a gust caught her hair. He'd raised his arm and let it wrap around his hand like a silk scarf. She'd looked at him then, eyes widening with possibilities.

Or so a fool might have let himself think

He stretched his legs in the rented SUV he'd parked under a tree that gave him a view of both the front and back of the law office, as well as Lisa Currick's parked truck.

He wasn't a fool now. He'd learned a lot since that first year as a detective. Learned enough to get offered a damned fine job. Of course he hadn't let Assistant District Attorney Anthony Prilossi know he considered it a damned fine job.

First, it would have broken a basic rule of negotiating. Second, it would have broken his personal rule of not giving Tony the satisfaction, since his friend tended to be too satisfied with himself as it was. And third…well, third was the reason he was in Knighton, Wyoming.

"It's a good offer," Shane had acknowledged.

"*Good* from you, Garrison, is practically a back flip from most people," Tony had said, sitting behind the stacks of files that obscured his desk. "So why aren't you saying, yes, I'll take it? Yes, I'm abjectly grateful to you, Tony, for your confidence in my investigative ability and your tolerance for my surly disposition?"

Shane snorted. "Yeah, right."

"What would it take to make you say yes, Shane?"

His head came up at the direct question. He met Tony's eyes for a moment and saw they were equally direct. He looked away, out a window that showed a cityscape through a haze of grime that returned within days of the window washers' visits.

"I don't want to leave things hanging at the department."

"You'd have time to wrap up some cases. Besides, cases get handed off all the time, so...?" Tony stopped in midstream. "Ah, this isn't about cases, plural, this is case, singular, isn't it? The Case as far as you're concerned. The Alex White Case."

"I just want to find that one piece—the necklace."

"Yeah, that's like Ahab saying he just wanted to go fishing." Tony shook his head. "I don't understand it, Shane. We put the guy away. So what we didn't find out where he stashed one necklace. It's not like Blanchard's destitute for lack of it. It's too damned gaudy a piece for us to have missed if it's gone into somebody else's possession. Plus, it's not like White is going to get out soon and enjoy his ill-gotten gains. And even if the parole board lets him out tomorrow, he's not going to start a crime wave. He's got to be near eighty."

"Seventy-nine. But if I'd handled it differently—"

Tony responded concisely, though profanely. "I hate to swell your head any more than it already is about your investigative abilities, but if it hadn't been for the way you handled that case, there wouldn't have been a case. Nobody else thought the renowned Alex White might be doing anything wrong."

Shane ignored that. "I'm not ready to give up on it. Not yet."

"Not *yet?* It's been eight years. Are you sure this one-that-got-away obsession is about the case?"

"It's not an obsession, I j—"

"You sure it's not about that girl—what was her name? You know, the wide-eyed one who was neck deep in the case—the one working with White?"

"She was never working with him, not that way. She was his intern. And she wasn't involved in the case, except as a witness. We went over all that back then."

"Yeah, yeah, so she said. I never quite bought that innocent-from-the-heartland act of hers. Where was she from? Nebraska? One of the Dakotas? Somewhere like that. But what was her name?'' He shrugged, dismissing her as an unimportant detail in a life overflowing with important details. ''Nope, don't remember. Guess you don't, either.''

Shane knew exactly what Tony was doing, but he couldn't let that particular detail be dismissed as unimportant. ''Lisa Currick.''

All vagueness in the other man's manner evaporated. His eyes were sharp, but his voice was soft. ''That's right. Lisa Currick. The one who got away.''

''Don't be ridiculous. She was a kid.''

''You weren't exactly Methuselah yourself...'' Tony let the pause build. ''...then.''

Shane shook his head, not in denial of the comment but of the whole conversation.

''Are you telling me someone at the department's been pushing you to find the necklace? That they'd be unhappier with your leaving than they're already going to be because you don't mop up that detail.'' He didn't answer. That didn't stop Tony. ''So, it *is* the girl.''

It was the tone of voice Tony Prilossi used in court to persuade a jury he was absolutely certain of what he was saying. Was he right now? Were memories of Lisa Currick what kept eating at him?

Sure he wanted to know how she was. She'd been a good kid, and they'd been...close. Not as close as his body had been urging him to be that spring eight years ago. But close enough that it was natural he wanted to make sure she was okay.

''I just want to find that last piece,'' he said doggedly.

''Right. You dream of finding that necklace.''

No, I dream of—

He shut off the thought. No court of law could hold his dreams against a man. But that wouldn't stop Prilossi from making use of them if he sniffed out what Shane dreamed about all too often.

"I want to find the last piece," he repeated.

It was Tony's turn to look out the window.

Shane sat still, giving him that time. Unlike those over-the-top cop shows that TV viewers seemed to think were so realistic, he'd found that silence and patience were among the most useful investigative skills he possessed. Skills that had helped him rise quickly to detective, where he'd first encountered Prilossi on the Alex White case. Skills Tony now wanted him to put to work as a special investigator.

Working for the D.A.'s office wouldn't be any walk in the park, but more of the going-nowhere cases would be weeded out, he'd have a little more time with the cases that remained, and he'd have fewer bosses to answer to. As long as the result was giving Tony the whole truth and nothing but the truth, he'd be left to work his own way. All that was very appealing.

But he didn't like leaving something undone. His police department bosses said he'd done all he could—a couple times a year when he revisited the case they said that. But he knew that wasn't true. There was one thread he hadn't followed as completely as he could have.

That's why he needed to talk to Lisa Currick again, face-to-face. Not because of one spring. Not because of a pair of wounded eyes staring at him across an institutional hallway outside a nondescript courtroom. But because she might have an answer.

Tony shifted in his chair, the movement pulling Shane's gaze to him.

"Tell you what," Tony said, with a look that Shane would have called concern in somebody else, "you take some time and give this case your full attention. If nothing comes of it, then you agree to let it go and start working here.''

''How much time?'' Shane's question set off a break-neck round of dickering.

''And if you haven't found out anything after two months,'' Tony said, wrapping up the negotiations, ''you let this case go.''

''Right.''

''I mean it, Garrison. I want you obsessed with the cases we're working on now. Not the ones we've already won. And sure as hell not obsessed with the girl you lost.''

That's what Tony didn't understand: Lisa Currick had never been his girl to lose.

Shane had known that coming out here to Wyoming. What he hadn't known was that she would no longer be anybody's girl.

More than Lisa Currick's hair had changed. She was a cool, reserved, unflappable woman, judging by today.

A couple things about that bothered him.

First, why had the openness, the daring, the joy disappeared?

He'd noticed the change from that first glimpse this morning of her coming out of that little house set off the road as if it had drawn back to avoid passersby. When he'd known Lisa in New York, she'd moved like she was ready at any given moment to open her arms and embrace anybody or anything that struck her heart. Now she seemed to move simply as the practical way to get from here to there.

And that job of hers. Last thing in the world he would have expected her to end up as was an office manager, following a routine, making details her life.

Maybe she'd needed the money. He didn't suppose there were many jobs available in a small town like this. But that didn't explain why someone who'd loved the unregimented world of creativity would drop all that and get a masters degree in business, as he'd discovered she now possessed.

He suspected she'd say the chin-length haircut was practical, too.

His gut told him something deeper than practicality was at work here. And that same rarely wrong organ was urging him to find out more about how and when and why Lisa had changed.

Which brought him to the second thing that bothered him.

As much as she'd changed, as clear as she'd made it that she was not one bit happy to see him, he'd felt a tightening somewhere south of his gut at first sighting her, and it hadn't let up.

That state had clouded his judgment before. He couldn't let it do that now. He had minimal time, and one mission: to find the antique diamond, platinum and emerald necklace that Alex White had stolen and that had never been recovered. Start his new job with a clean slate by wrapping up loose ends from his old one.

If accomplishing that also happened to lead to finding out why Lisa had changed, it couldn't hurt to satisfy his curiosity.

A letter from Alex was waiting in her mailbox when Lisa got home that night from class. She'd been deeply disappointed by Alex, but he'd hurt himself much more than he'd ever hurt her. She'd made her peace with him even before he was found guilty. He'd been writing to her and sometimes calling from prison ever since.

Today, though, she could have done without another reminder of the past.

Pulling the catalogs, flyers and other mail out, Lisa looked out into the Wyoming dark and saw nothing.

That didn't mean Shane Garrison wasn't there.

He'd made no secret of the fact that he was following her earlier. He'd been sitting in an obviously rented four-wheel-drive down the street from the law office when she came out at closing time. He'd trailed her to campus in Jefferson. He'd been there when she came out of class, and he'd trailed her back home.

Her first instinct had been to march over to him and tell him where to go. Second thoughts recognized the futility of that. The temptation to try to lose him she'd also shaken off as foolish. He knew where she worked, where she lived and where she went to school. What was the sense of trying to lose him when she would just go to one of those predictable spots?

When she'd pulled into her driveway, he'd slowed, as if to be sure she went in the house, then sped off. She'd waited twenty minutes without any sign of his vehicle before heading out to the mailbox.

Back inside the house, she consciously followed her routine, setting water to heat for caffeine-free tea, opening the bills first and filing them by the date they would be paid, tossing the junk mail and the charity solicitations that poured in year-round even though she contributed once a year. A waste of money and effort on their part. You'd think they'd have a computer program that would tell them if someone didn't respond to being inundated...which might be an idea for her end-of-term project for her Using Computers for Business course.

Only after she'd made a note of the idea in the notebook assigned to that course did she fix her tea, sink into the corner of the overstuffed jade-green sofa and begin to read the letter from Alex.

Alex had been a robust seventy-one-year-old when she'd last seen him. But clearly the years—and prison—had taken a deep toll. At first his letters were almost like Alex himself, full of sureness—some would say arrogance or even obsession, as the prosecutor had said—that he would get out, that he had been right to remove those glorious pieces from unappreciative owners and replace them with fakes, that he knew better than the rest of the world. They had also been full of his expectations for her. Nothing she'd written to the contrary had changed his view on that.

More often now the famed Alex White non sequiturs edged toward disjointedness.

Tonight's letter, though, sounded like the old Alex. He'd included a sketch, along with notes for his design of a pendant of amber set in gold, and the comment, "To look like that marigold you resemble."

It was an old joke between them. During her interview for the coveted internship at his studio, Alex had asked her the Barbara Walters question about which tree she would be if she had a choice. He'd clearly meant the question to flummox her, but she'd shot right back that she didn't know much about trees, coming from Wyoming and all, and she'd rather be a bur marigold, because they got around, and brightened up everywhere they went.

He'd roared with laughter, and that had been it—she had the internship. He'd taken to telling people that she was like the bur marigold—a bright, sunny flower also called sticktight because its seeds had a knack for sticking to passersby and ending up in the most unexpected places, like a girl from a Wyoming ranch ending up in the workshop of Manhattan's most revered and sought-after jewelry designer and refurbisher.

"I was going to pass you by after the first interview, with the hayseed still in your hair, but somehow you stuck to me," he'd said. "Ah, I do like a person who knows herself, my little bur marigold."

The smile born of those memories faded as Lisa sipped her tea. She hadn't known herself at all.

She'd thought she was ready for anything. She'd been proved miserably wrong.

Shane Garrison had stepped into her life one sleeting day in late March when he came into the studio, accompanied by Alex. In fact, Alex had introduced them, seeming to harbor secret amusement as he did so.

She realized why two days later, when Detective Garrison had asked her to have lunch with him, had told her he suspected Alex of fraud and wondered if she'd answer a few questions. Alex White—committing fraud? It was laughable—the kind of joke Alex most loved. She'd laughed at it, too, but Shane Garrison had never wavered.

She'd told Alex the whole thing, and he'd insisted that as long as she enjoyed Shane's company, she should keep seeing the detective and answer all his questions. Looking back, she supposed it had been a kind of game to Alex.

But as she and Shane continued to meet day after day while the weather slid out of misery toward delight, he had stopped talking about his suspicions. Instead, they'd talked about everything else under the sun. Books, records, movies. Her ambitions, his love of sports, her childhood, his fast-rising career and, of course, the amazing city around them. With the warmer weather, they'd started walking during their lunches. When lunch break wasn't long enough for their conversations, they began to meet on the weekends.

Not once did he touch her more than any man might the woman he was escorting in public. Not once did he kiss her.

But he'd looked into her eyes, and she was so certain...

She was so wrong.

It was June when she had marveled to Shane about the beautiful work Alex had shown her on a commission he'd just completed. She hadn't known that the bracelet's owner had asked only to have it cleaned, but Shane had known.

She hadn't known that Alex had duplicated the piece with false gems, but Shane had suspected. And with that small bit of information, he'd persuaded the owner to have the bracelet Alex had returned officially examined by the police.

It was a fake.

It was like pulling the joker out of the foundation of a house of cards. Alex's reputation was no longer impenetrable, and other customers soon had their pieces examined.

Of course, she hadn't known that at the time. She'd known only that Shane suddenly was around so much less and seemed distracted when he did come.

Then he'd arrived unexpectedly one glorious June midafternoon, talked her into taking off an hour early, and it had been like before. They'd spent hours walking and talking, looking in store windows and sitting on park benches.

The next day he and the others came to the studio to arrest Alex.

That was the worst day of her life. Worse even than being called to testify against Alex at the trial three months later. Alex had pooh-poohed her distress over that, saying of course she should tell them everything she knew—he was going to.

By the time the trial came, she knew Alex had been doing what they'd accused him of, fully convinced that he was right to do it. And she knew Shane Garrison had used her to find the proof against Alex.

She put the letter in the box in her closet with the others.

As soon as the trial was over, she'd left New York for good, returning to Knighton. At age nineteen she had put aside childishness and constructed a life based on the principles her experiences in New York had taught her.

And she would keep living that life, even though the experience that had taught her the hardest lessons had shown up in the last place on earth she would have ever expected to see him.

Chapter Two

Lisa adjusted her shoulder bag to a more comfortable position as she pushed open the door of the Knighton Café. Two textbooks weighed it down, but she didn't mind.

She was more than ready for the peace of note taking. The morning had not gone well.

Not the work; she'd handled that without a hitch. It was the chorus of "What's wrong with you" that had pounded this headache into the region behind her eyes.

She'd been nursing a headache when she'd arrived at work. She hadn't slept well. When she woke the second time, she decided it must be having that project for her Using Computers in Business class on her mind. When she jerked awake the third time, the lingering images from a dream informed her the subject had not been her class, but Shane Garrison striding straight toward her, reaching out— to embrace her or to shake her or to put his hands around her throat?

Given those options, apparently her subconscious had decided waking up was the best idea.

As she'd left, she'd scanned the area beyond her house for a deep-green SUV. None was in sight. And if he'd followed her to work this morning, he should double for the Invisible Man.

Not seeing him didn't make it a certainty that he'd left. And lack of certainty made her edgy. So, perhaps she was a little short when Taylor had asked if she was feeling all right.

"I'm fine. And I'll be even better when you stop cross-examining me and let me get these filing instructions completed so they can be submitted."

Taylor raised her hands in mock surrender, and beat a hasty retreat to her office. Lisa strongly suspected Taylor then placed a phone call, because not fifteen minutes had passed before the phone rang, and the female voice on the other end launched into a monologue that had left Lisa's sleep-deprived brain reeling.

"Matty," she'd implored her sister-in-law. "Please, give me the headlines on this—not the full rundown."

"Boy, you are cranky this morning," Matty Brennan Currick said. "The headline is that you've been looking tired, so Dave and I want you to come spend the weekend with us at the Slash-C—some riding, some lying around and a lot of eating. Say you'll come."

"My house isn't even twenty minutes from the ranch, why would I come for a weekend?"

"So we can pamper you."

"I don't need pampering."

"Everybody needs pampering—that's something Dave's taught me." Her voice changed slightly, the way it always did when she talked about Lisa's older brother, Dave, Matty's lifetime love and now her husband.

"What I need is to get work done this weekend on a class project."

"You work too hard. That's probably why you're cranky."

"I am not cranky, and I don't work too hard." She heard her sister-in-law drawing in breath to dispute that and quickly added, "Gotta go, Matty. Business calls."

An hour later, as she was relaxing into the calm of her routine, her brother showed up.

"You don't have an appointment," she informed him briskly, "and Taylor has a full schedule this morning."

"I'm not here to see Taylor, though you could ask her when we can get together to pick a mediator for the Johnston divorce."

She made a note, then started to turn back to her computer.

"I came to see you, Lees."

Dave, six years her senior, had that big-brotherly look. "What's up?"

"Apparently not you. You've seemed down lately, even more than when you first came back—" the flicker of his eyes acknowledged he'd reached forbidden territory, and he intended to come in anyhow "—from New York."

His pause, she was sure, was to give her a chance to object or to pour out her heart to him. She stayed silent.

"You look tired, Lisa, and you seem edgy."

"I'm not edgy. I simply have a lot of work to do and can't afford interruptions."

He didn't even blink at that broad hint. "Well, Matty and I want you to get some rest this weekend. Drive out to the Slash-C after work Friday, and you can get back in plenty of time Monday morning. It'll be like one of those spas, except we won't suck your bank account dry. How 'bout it? You need peace and quiet."

"You and Matty are both out of your heads. I am not

going to spend a weekend at the ranch doing nothing so you can get in good with your wife, who already adores you to a disgusting degree.''

''She does, doesn't she,'' he said with a besotted grin. But he wasn't sidetracked for long. ''Aw, c'mon, Lisa. It'll be fun. And we can plan something for Mom and Dad— you know they're coming home for a while later this month.''

Ever since Ed and Donna Currick had turned the running of the Slash-C Ranch over to Dave, which he did in addition to a part-time law practice, they had been indulging in almost nonstop traveling, from exotic to more run-of-the-mill locations. Their most recent foray had been a course offered in Williamsburg, Virginia, followed by visits to many of the colonial plantations along the James River. Now they were working their way vaguely westward in a customized mobile home.

''Let's let Matty plan something. She's really good.''

''We should help her get started,'' Dave said, implicitly acknowledging that his wife would most likely end up handling the details. Still, he had a point—she supposed Ed and Donna's kids should be involved.

''If I make enough progress with my project Saturday, I'll come by Sunday and we can talk.''

''Come all day Sunday no matter what.''

She glared at him. ''I know your negotiating techniques, Dave. I'm sticking to what I said.''

He shifted strategies. ''What's the deal with this course, anyhow? You have your MBA—I distinctly remember attending your graduation.''

''You should remember, since you and your wife insisted on giving that big party. As for the course, I'm taking a few additional ones that could be helpful.''

''Helpful to what?''

''A career in business.''

"What kind of career in business?"

"I haven't decided yet."

"When are you going to stop taking courses and start doing?"

"When I feel I'm ready."

"Ready for what?"

"Go away, Dave. I have a headache and a lot of work to do, and I don't need you going all big-brotherly on me."

He drawled, "No, you're not edgy, not a bit."

"Dave—"

"I'm going…as soon as you promise to think about the weekend—the whole weekend."

"I promise to think about it."

"Okay, then I'm leaving." He paused in the open doorway to say over his shoulder, "Take care of yourself, Lisa Lou."

That childhood nickname, combined with his accepting at face value her promise to consider spending the weekend at the Slash-C, added a sharper pounding to her headache—guilt.

Unfortunately, it didn't replace the sense of being pursued by her friends and family, it simply joined it.

So lunchtime came as a relief. She looked forward to sitting alone at the café, immersed in her books, yet subliminally aware of the comforting mumble of familiar voices talking about the same things as last week and last month and last year.

It was all so familiar that as she passed the stool sitters at the counter on the way to the last booth—*her* booth—she barely raised her head while automatically answering to "How'ya'doing Lisa" down the line of the same backsides that had sat there last week and last month and last year.

Until she came to a set of jean-clad knees at the second-to-last stool. Above and below stretched legs long enough for their owner to rest his running-shoe-wearing feet flat on the floor.

Her feet stopped and her head rose.

Detective Shane Garrison had his elbows propped on the counter behind him, managing both to look supremely relaxed and to emphasize the breadth his shoulders occupied.

"How're you doing, Lisa?" He'd never had a New York accent, but now he'd caught the local inflection, so it sounded like the other greetings. Except for a faint undercurrent of ironic humor.

Her gaze snapped to his mouth, to see if it might be quirking with similar humor, then jerked away. She directed a glare at the vicinity of his left ear.

"What are you doing here?"

"Now that don't sound friendly, Lisa," complained Hugh Moski, who sat beside the detective in his customary spot on the last stool.

"I didn't intend it to."

"Why'd you say a thing like that to this nice fella? He was telling us how he knew you in New York, and how you didn't meet in the best of circumstances."

Not in the best of circumstances? Was that how he thought of it? Was that his view of what she'd considered idyllic months? Was that how easily he dismissed the chilling end?

She pushed down those questions. What mattered was that for all these years she'd said nothing about her time in New York, and now he came to her hometown and started spreading her business all over.

"She's trying to make me feel at home," Garrison filled in, "greeting me like a New Yorker would."

His comment drew chuckles down the line. All the way down the line. They were all listening and all watching.

Her jaw throbbed, and she realized she'd clenched her teeth. She forced herself to breathe in through her nose and out through her mouth, before she spoke in a low, no-nonsense voice.

"I want to talk to you."

"Yes'm," he said with a duck of his head, trying to make it seem as if he were a student ordered to the principal's office. But she'd seen the glint of triumph in his eye he hadn't been quite quick enough to hide.

She gave a curt nod and continued toward the booth, not bothering to see if he followed. He would, because this was what he'd wanted. But that didn't mean he'd get anything else of what he wanted.

"Be gentle with him, Lisa, he's not broke to halter yet," someone down the line called, and more chuckles followed them to the booth.

She ignored them as she slid into her usual spot with her back to the rear wall. She also ignored the looks thrown their way. Some people wondered why she didn't sit with her back to the room, to cut down on the distractions to her studying. They didn't understand that the comings and goings, the talk and laughter out in the center of the café were no distraction to her.

Besides, it was what could come up behind you unexpectedly that could knock your life for a loop.

From his half second of hesitation before he slid in opposite her, Lisa knew he also would have preferred to face the room.

Good. Let him be at a disadvantage. See how he liked it.

Bolstered, she made her opening question starkly cold. "What do you think you're doing here?"

"Having lunch."

"Have lunch somewhere else."

"There aren't that many choices in Knighton."

"Try another town. Better yet, another state."

The lift of his eyebrows told her she was not being the

sweet young Lisa he remembered. The sooner he realized that the better.

But all he said was a mild, "Seems like a long way to go for a sandwich."

"Not if you're on your way back where you belong—New York."

"Ah, but I'm not on my way back to New York. So, having lunch here is much more convenient. And I heard they make a great burger."

She cut to the core of what was between them. "I told you I wouldn't help you."

"I heard you."

From the corner of her eye, she caught movement, and looked up to see Rainie Lester bearing down on them, carrying a tray.

"Here's your plate, Shane."

Rainie tended to size up newcomers slowly, yet here she was already calling him Shane. If Lisa had needed any reminder, this example of how easily he manipulated people into dropping their guard provided it.

"Thank you, Rainie." He took the plate, which held the remnants of a hamburger, about a third of a helping of fries, and two pickle slices. He rested his right forearm on the table, his relaxed hand encroaching into the half of the table that should have been hers.

"And here's your salad, Lisa," Rainie added, placing a Cobb salad without egg yolks in front of her.

"How'd you know what to bring her?" he asked the waitress with the same smile and natural curiosity Lisa remembered him using so many times to find out things.

"It's Wednesday."

Someone called the waitress's name, and Rainie headed toward the kitchen. Shane looked across the table and said, "You have the same salad every Wednesday?"

She shrugged. It made life more orderly to have the same

lunch from one week to the next, and she was always certain of being waited on quickly, leaving more time for studying.

Not that she was going to explain any of that to him.

"Detective Garrison, since you acknowledge having heard me say that I won't help you, and giving you credit for the intelligence—"

"Thank you." He bit off one end of a french fry, holding the rest between the blunt-tipped fingers of his left hand.

"—to know I mean it, you should also know the smart thing to do would be to leave."

"Now, Li—Ms. Currick." He'd done it again, adding a twist to the title that made it sound more intimate than her first name. "You of all people should understand about the charms of Knighton. I remember how you talked about it. You'd get this little smile on your face, and your eyes would glow, and you'd talk about the people and the town and your ranch. If you hadn't been just as enthusiastic about New York back then, I'd've wondered why you ever left here. Listening to you talk about Knighton was better than any travel ad I've ever heard. Made me want to see it for myself."

Her hand curled around her fork where it still lay on the table. "So now you've seen it. Now you can go."

"Oh, I haven't accomplished half of what I want to get done here."

Those blue eyes focused so intently on her that they seemed to want to look into her soul. Something sounded inside her head, but so faintly that it stayed just below an identifiable level.

He was reaching with his right hand. Coming closer to her hand. Perhaps he'd wrap his fingers around hers the way he had that day he'd said he'd give her the best lunch in New York, then led her away for vendors' fare on a bench in a tiny tucked-away park she'd never seen before.

Alarm bells—that must be what she was hearing. A high-pitched refrain of *Don't be a fool. Don't be a fool,* ringing in her ears over and over. Because only a fool would abandon the cautions that had gotten her safely and sanely through the past eight years.

She picked up her fork and stabbed a tomato.

His hand shifted course immediately, wrapped around the salt shaker and added a day's worth of sodium to the remaining fries on his plate. She kept her head down and her attention on her salad.

I haven't accomplished half of what I want to get done here. It was exactly the kind of statement he'd used eight years ago to tie her into knots. It seemed to imply that what he wanted to accomplish had something to do with her—something more than her cooperation in finding a necklace. Eight years ago she would have given the words exactly that sort of personal interpretation. No more. She'd learned that with Detective Shane Garrison, the correct interpretation was the one that had the most to do with his job and advancing his ambitions.

Not recognizing that had contributed to a great deal of heartache. She wouldn't forget it again.

"Here." The tips of two pickle slices entered her sphere of vision. "You do still like pickles, don't you?"

"Yes."

"And I still don't. So these are for you."

"Thank you," she muttered as she watched him transfer his pickles to the plate under her salad bowl. After all these years, he remembered her liking for pickles? Did he also remember how many times they'd made this transfer?

So what if he did? It was a prosaic action, an effort to not waste food. And possibly an effort to soften her up in order to get what he wanted—the necklace.

She didn't know where it was. She didn't want to think

about where it might be. She just wanted to forget it all
and live in peace.

"I wondered."

His words broke into thoughts that had gone off on such
a tangent that she couldn't pretend she knew what he
meant.

"About?"

"The pickles. Wondered if that was something else
you've changed. Like not sketching at lunch anymore."

She kept her head down. "I have other things to do now.
I have to make good use of my time at lunch."

"The sketches were a good use of your time. I liked
them." Before she could respond, he shifted gears. "You
know, one place I haven't seen yet is the ranch where you
grew up."

"Stay away. It's posted for trespassers. You'll get shot."

"Nice to know you care." His tone was impossibly neutral.

"I'd hate to see any of my family or our ranch hands
caught up with law enforcement and the criminal justice
system. Even around here that's something to be avoided."

His expression tightened ever so slightly. Ah, he wasn't
as neutral as he wanted to pretend he was. But his voice
gave nothing away.

"You know, when you used to talk about where you
grew up, I never bought your saying that everybody in
Knighton was friendly and easy-going. But I don't think
I've met one person who hasn't been friendly. And they're
all ready for a little chat, especially when it comes up that
I knew one of theirs in New York."

Chill seeped into her skin.

"Don't you dare pump my friends about me. Leave the
people around here alone. These are good people. They're
not used to dealing with someone like you. They'll never

forgive themselves if you get them to say something they didn't mean to."

"I can't decide if you're giving them too little credit or me too much."

"And I won't have you go around telling people about my time in New York. That's my business. Just leave, Shane. Leave."

"The faster I find out what I need to know, the faster I'll go. If you'd work with me, help me—"

She gathered up her books and her purse, sliding out of the booth. "I already helped you send one man to hell, I won't ever help you again."

She had let him get to her. But Lisa was confident that no one watching her as she walked out of the café would have an inkling that a ghost from her past was doing his best to rattle her out of her hard-won serenity.

Once out of view of the café's window, she slowed her pace.

It was going to take more than simply asking to get Shane Garrison out of her town and out of her life. Her dealings with him had taught her that nothing stood between him and the pursuit of what he wanted. But her neighbors wouldn't know that. They could be hurt by his relentless pursuit of this necklace. She might not see exactly how he might hurt them, but that didn't negate the potential.

So he thought he could blackmail her into helping him by obliquely threatening to use her friends in some unspecified way? Or maybe to tell them about how easily he'd manipulated a wide-eyed, trusting girl?

She could play tough, too.

At the second cross street, instead of turning left to head back to Taylor's office, she turned right. And went straight

to the Knighton sub-office of the Clark County Sheriff's
Department.

Shane sat at the café's back booth for a long time after
Lisa left, though he did switch around to the back seat.

*I already helped you send one man to hell, I won't ever
help you again.*

She made it sound like *he* was the one to blame, instead
of White. Alex White had reaped the consequences of his
actions. And White wasn't exactly in hell, not even much
of a prison. As for her *helping* him, if he hadn't been so
tied up in knots over her—

"Want any more coffee before I go off duty, Shane?"

Rainie's question jerked him out of his thoughts. He saw
with shock that he'd been sitting here for an hour. The café
was empty except for a young mother with her toddler having an ice-cream cone at the far end of the counter.

"No, thanks. I better get going."

As he headed out into the early-August afternoon sunshine after paying his bill, he thought about Lisa accusing
him of pumping her friends. He didn't need to pump them;
he was learning a lot about her simply from seeing the place
and the people who'd nurtured her.

He also thought about the fact that the one time she'd
called him by his first name was to tell him to leave.

As he fished for his sunglasses, he shook his head at
himself. Unraveling one more of Alex White's mysteries
was his reason for being here. Returning the real necklace
to its rightful owner was his reason for being here. Not
letting someone get away with thumbing his nose at the
law and thinking his position would protect him was his
reason for being here. And Lisa Currick… Well, Lisa was
a side issue. A detective never got anywhere if he let himself be distracted by side issues, no matter how tempting.

He'd mastered that lesson in his first go-around with the White case.

"Are you Shane Garrison of New York City?"

Shane blinked into the sun to see the uniform of a sheriff's deputy.

"Yes, I am, Deputy—" he squinted at the nameplate riding on a narrow chest "—Jessup."

"I have a report that you've been following and harassing a citizen in my jurisdiction."

Lisa hadn't wasted any time, had she? He'd have grinned if he hadn't seen from the deputy's serious demeanor that that would be a mistake. "If we can go somewhere to talk about this, I'm sure we can straighten it out."

The skinny deputy didn't listen. "We won't stand for stalking here."

"Stalking? That's—"

"And," Jessup went on with ill-contained triumph, "impersonating an officer of the law. Even the NYPD."

"I am not impersonating—"

"Oh, yeah? I contacted NYPD, and they say you tendered your resignation."

"It's not effective yet. I'm using vacation time and I'm still on the payroll."

"That's a fine distinction that might do okay for New York City, but not out here. I'm telling you to leave my town, Garrison. I want you out before sunset."

Shane was on his way out of town well before sunset—how long had Deputy Jessup dreamed of saying those words?

Recognizing the futility of trying to reason with the younger man, Shane left. He made a point of passing the law office where Lisa worked. She was standing in the doorway, her arms crossed at her waist, watching his SUV depart.

If she'd looked triumphant or smug or even angry, there was some chance he might have left for good. Instead, when he slowed to a crawl in front of her, he saw a cold, almost vacant look in her eyes.

In that instant he decided...

No, he didn't decide, he accepted.

He wouldn't have left for good no matter what her expression, because Tony, damn him, was right.

The girl had haunted him. Sure, he wanted to know where the necklace was, but it was wondering how Lisa was that had made him check the faces of so many dark-haired women who came up to about his cheekbone, and who had a certain innocent openness in the way they moved. The necklace might have kept him awake at night, but it was Lisa who'd slid into so many dreams.

Seeing her so changed should have ended that. She was no longer open and sunny. But his gut told him that would make the haunting worse.

I've put it—all of it—behind me, and that's where it's going to stay.

He'd had enough people lie to him to know that was a lie, even if she believed it. It wasn't behind her. So he'd be doing her a favor—both of them a favor—if he found the necklace to officially close this case, along with whatever lingered between the two of them.

He drummed his fingers on the steering wheel.

She was still his best lead to the necklace. Besides, spending time with her would get him over this once and for all. A sort of exorcism, without the incense. Remove the mystery, and she'd be just another female he'd once known.

So the first order of business was to get around Jessup, the fly she'd deliberately dropped in his ointment.

Just outside of town he pulled to the side of the road, got out his cell phone and started working his contacts.

Twenty hours later Shane was back in Knighton in as near to a blaze of glory as he expected this town got.

He followed Sheriff Kuerten's car along the main road, letting everyone in Knighton who cared to look out a window—which was everyone—see that the sheriff was personally escorting back into town the man the deputy had shooed out.

As they approached the café, Shane saw Lisa step out right on time to be heading back to work from lunch. When he'd asked the sheriff to plan on arriving at one o'clock, he'd hoped it might work out this way, but he hadn't expected it to be this perfect.

All the phone time, the calling in of favors and the schmoozing with the sheriff into the wee hours were rewarded in that instant. Because he saw, clear as day, a flash of the younger Lisa's passionate approach to life in the flare of pure, unbridled irritation as their eyes met.

Maybe irritation wasn't what he'd once aspired to arouse in Lisa Currick, but it was an honest, unchecked emotion. That was a start. He couldn't wait to start unearthing more.

Chapter Three

He was going to make her come to him.

That was clear by the next morning.

Lisa had half expected him to show up at the office before the end of the business day. She'd braced for him to be waiting outside. She'd been almost certain he'd patrol past her house. She'd steeled herself to get the confrontation over with when she opened her kitchen door the next morning.

Instead, he'd made himself at home in town. *Her* town. *Her* home.

She'd received the first phone call yesterday not more than five minutes after Sheriff Kuerten left the law office. The sheriff had stopped by, he'd said, on his way out of town to set her mind at ease. Apparently she'd been under a mistaken impression that Detective Shane Garrison wasn't the fine, upstanding law enforcement officer that he, Sheriff Kuerten, had ascertained that he was. But now that he, Sheriff Kuerten, had checked out Detective Garrison's bona fides—why Garrison was trained by the son of Sheriff Kuerten's old mentor and a finer man never lived than Boots Radkin, so if Boots's boy said Garrison was a fine man, that's all he needed to know—she should rest easy knowing that all was well and not bother her pretty little head about a thing.

He hadn't actually said that last phrase, but that had been the underlying message.

So when she'd picked up the phone and heard Deputy Jessup on the other end she wasn't surprised that he said in an aggrieved tone, "You could've told me the guy's connected to Kuerten's old-boy network."

She didn't point out that she'd had no way of knowing—in fact, she strongly suspected Shane Garrison hadn't known it, either, until he made it his business to dig up a connection. Neither did she point out that Jessup had jumped at the opportunity to strut his stuff by tossing a New York City detective out of town.

What was the use? She'd apologized and got off the line.

She soon regretted her speed, because it left the line open for calls from folks who had heard about Garrison's arrival, departure and return, and wanted to know the whole story. She'd fended them off at the office by insisting the line be left open for business. At home she let the machine take all calls with the volume turned down.

But this morning Ruth Moski, the gray-haired organizational whiz who ran Dave's law office, had arrived with papers that could have easily waited to be delivered, sat in the same chair Shane Garrison had occupied the day before yesterday and said, "We're not tying up the line now, so tell me about this fella."

Lisa had wriggled out from under the older woman's direct stare by pleading piles of work, at the same time feeding Ruth only the most basic information. Since Ruth's husband, Hugh, had been Shane's stool-sitting companion at the café, the woman surely knew every word Shane had uttered.

Ruth informed her that everyone already knew he was a detective in the New York City Police Department, that they'd met when Lisa had been in school there, and he'd stopped by to say hello since he was—improbably—passing through town.

"Looks older than you," Ruth said.

"He's thirty-five. I, uh, believe," she added, too late to do any good.

Taylor appeared then, requesting that Lisa come into the inner office to help find an older version of a file on Taylor's computer. Since that version was clearly labeled on a disk sitting on Taylor's desk, and since Lisa caught Taylor watching her with sympathy and concern, she knew luck had nothing to do with that rescue.

But she couldn't count on Taylor being around all the time.

When the office phone rang again and she recognized the number ID as Joyce Aberdick's extension at the bank, she flipped on the answering machine and made a decision. Since he wasn't coming to her, she would go to him.

She expelled a long breath through her nose, gripped the arms of her chair and stood. She rapped on Taylor's office door before opening it.

"I'm going to be out of the office for a while, Taylor. I have a—an errand to run."

Taylor had no kind of poker face—there was that sympathy and concern again. "Take as long as you need."

Lisa headed directly to the café. That took no detective work. Three-quarters of the phone calls this morning had mentioned that Shane Garrison was at the café.

The usual café sitters were lined up in their usual spots. With one important addition—a driven, ambitious New York City detective masquerading as just one of the boys who'd stopped by for a cup of coffee and the latest news.

Every head turned toward her, every face showed curiosity. With one important exception. Sitting at the same stool he'd occupied yesterday, Shane Garrison kept his broad-shouldered, narrow-hipped back to her.

She refused to allow her steps to falter.

"I want to talk to you."

"Okay." He spun off the stool ahead of her, leading the way toward the back booth.

They made the trip in silence. There were no comments from the other stool sitters today—probably afraid they might miss hearing something.

Noticing that made her a half second slow in recognizing Garrison's intention, so he was already sliding into the far seat of the back booth—*her* seat—before she could protest. He'd left her no choice, short of making a scene, except to slide into the opposite seat, with her back to the rest of the café.

"Are you happy now?"

"Happier than I was about twenty hours ago," he said. She'd meant about taking her seat, but he'd extended his answer to the entire situation. "I think my sheriff trumped your deputy."

His faint, wry grin invited her to see the humor. She resisted.

This was going to be tricky enough without giving in to emotion, even wry amusement. Confronting him had already meant leaving the haven of her placid routine.

"I have a question for you."

"What I want? I told you yesterday, I need you…"

He let it die as she shook her head. Maybe she made the gesture more vehement than it needed to be because of the flush of warmth that had threatened to overtake her. It had caught her unaware.

I need you… That sentiment from Shane Garrison had been a major part of her fantasies eight years ago. But she'd traded in fantasies for reality. The reality was he needed her only to find this necklace.

The only way to get him out of her life was to cooperate. But to come out the other side of cooperating with her orderly life in one piece she needed to keep a firm hold on reality.

"Okay, what's your question?" he asked.

"What is it going to take for you to leave?"

He didn't react. Not at all. And a perverse element in her interpreted that very lack of reaction to mean that her question had hurt him. She told that element not to be an idiot—no reaction meant no reaction. That was pretty simple.

"Finding the necklace."

"How could I possibly guarantee you're going to find the necklace?" Something hot and prickly bubbled through her, something like panic. If he truly meant to stay until he found a necklace that might never be found... "I can't."

"Then let's put it this way—what it's going to take for me to leave is to be convinced that there is nothing else you can tell me that might help me find the necklace. Nothing. Not a quarter of a syllable. *Nothing.*"

She'd once tried to convince him to share her belief in Alex's innocence. She hadn't succeeded. The fact that he'd been right that time made it even less likely that she would convince him that she had nothing to tell him.

"Why can't you just let it go?"

"Have you let it go?"

"Yes." She said it with all the discipline she'd learned.

"It remains an open case until I find that last necklace. You know Alex White. You know his work. You know that necklace."

"I swore in court—I have no idea where it is. I told you everything I knew about all that...before. It obviously didn't help you find the necklace. Why would it now?"

"Maybe everything you knew you knew. But you don't know how much you know. Not yet. But I'll find out."

Such confidence. It made her want to shudder.

"You can ask your questions. But—" she held up a hand to stop him from speaking "—there are conditions."

"I'm going to ask what I have to ask."

She returned his warning. "And I'll answer what I can answer."

His look searched her face. She quelled the instinct to shutter her expression. Instead, she let him see that she didn't believe there was a single thing she could tell him that would help him, and she saw his answering conviction that there was.

"Okay," he agreed at last. "I can live with that condition."

"There are more. You will not talk to my friends and neighbors—"

"Hey, that's everybody around here. You want me to take an oath of silence?"

"You know what I mean. You will not use them or manipulate them or pump them for information. If you do—or if you ever again use that threat—the deal's off."

He shifted his focus from her face to the wall beside their booth. The seconds drew out before he released a breath that might have been a sigh, then met her gaze.

"I never did that, and I never threatened to do that, Lisa. When I talked to people here it was to get to know them, and a little to find out what's been happening in your life."

For a slice of time so small it would take a scientist to measure it, she believed him. Then she remembered. He'd wanted to find out what had been happening in her life because it would contribute some mite toward his professional goals.

"Besides," he picked up, "it would be real hard not to talk to anyone, since I'm renting an apartment from Ruth and Hugh Moski, and I'm going to be eating breakfast and dinner with them."

"You're staying with Ruth and Hugh? How...? Where...?"

"Simple. I needed a place to stay. Nearest motel's way out by the Interstate. And it didn't seem like I'd get to experience Knighton or Wyoming staying in a chain motel that looked like any other. When I mentioned my problem to Hugh, he took me to the apartment—a studio up a flight of steps over another apartment.''

''That's Taylor place.''

''Your boss, Taylor Anne Larsen? I heard she got married last fall and she's living with her husband at their ranch at the north end of the county.''

She was shaking her head before he was halfway through. How had he gathered so much information about Taylor? If he dug up Cal's real identity, could Shane use that as leverage? Cal and Taylor both seemed to feel he'd tied up the loose ends of his previous life, but she'd have to warn them about Shane. That meant telling them how she'd first encountered Shane.

And pulling one thread from her past might lay bare the entire tangle of her mistakes and failures.

But she'd deal with that later. Now she had enough to deal with—Shane Garrison making himself at home smack dab in the middle of Knighton.

''She is—living with her husband, I mean. But she was the first person to rent it after Hugh fixed it up, and she lived there two years, so folks still call it Taylor's place.'' He was watching her with interest, and she realized she was letting herself get detoured. She leaned back, keeping her shoulders straight. ''Hugh's goofed. Fred Montress has been renting the place since he and Betty separated three months ago.''

He nodded. ''Hugh said a guy had moved in after his wife kicked him out. Said they'd been married thirty-seven years, and she finally got tired of him being more interested in livestock breeding lines than her.''

''Sounds like Fred and Betty,'' she admitted

''But Fred has moved back in and domestic bliss rules again.''

''Betty took Fred back?'' Before he did more than part his lips, she held up a stop-sign hand and looked to the ceiling. ''Why am I asking you?''

He kept a generally straight face, but the right corner of his mouth ticked up, and she knew he was fighting a grin.

She had to watch herself. She didn't want to make him grin. Not like before. Then she'd decided he needed to smile more, and it was her duty to see to it. Duty, hell, she'd loved what a smile did to that face. It didn't rob an iota of strength, yet it lightened its lines and sparked his eyes. Just that and her skin would blossom into goose bumps as if she were cold, while her insides melted from the heat.

That was why she had to watch herself now.

No trying to make him grin. No drinking in the sight if it happened by accident. No goose bumps and heat.

"I can't swear to it that Fred went back to Betty. Although, the evidence points that way. All I know is Hugh is renting me the place week to week, saving him the trouble of painting it and looking for a new tenant."

Week to week. She didn't know whether to be distraught that he planned to stay as long as a week or relieved that he hadn't taken a six-month lease.

"The condition still stands—no pumping Hugh or Ruth for information."

The stillness was shorter this time. "Okay. You want me to write this in my blood?"

"Don't tempt me." She looked away from the quirk of his mouth as she added, "You wouldn't have much blood left, because there's more."

Shane strode along the sidewalk away from the café, fully aware that he was the object of considerable interest. Movement inside the drugstore across the street resolved into two women in pink smocks hurrying to the front window to stare at him. A man who'd pulled up in front of the bank nearly tripped as he came around the back of his pickup because he was watching Shane instead of the curb. Inside the bank, a petite woman in a pale-blue dress pivoted her chair to look out the window. And down the street a teenage couple who had been skirting a construction zone near an old-fashioned stone building stopped dead and stared at him.

He had the oddest urge to wave to them all and shout, "Howdy."

This had been Lisa's best reaction so far.

When he'd said he was staying with Ruth and Hugh, she'd flared up, full of indignation and sass, the way she used to over some wrong she'd spotted.

He'd watched her cheeks flush, her eyes flash, her spine straighten. And he'd practically seen the indignant words shooting up her throat. He'd found himself waiting for the first one to come tumbling out like a kid waiting for Christmas morning. She'd reined it all in after barely uttering a word. But there'd also been that flash of her old humor, with that look to the heavens and that "Why am I asking you?"

But a lot of desert surrounded those oasis moments.

She'd set out "parameters" for their "meetings." Not during business hours. Not to interfere with her classes. Not in full view of the town.

When he'd grumbled that all those rules made finding a time to meet more of a mystery than the whereabouts of the necklace, she'd said that was his concern.

He spotted a sign that identified the old-fashioned stone structure as a library. He strolled onto the grounds, idly surveying the construction of an addition that added space with the least intrusion on the parklike setting.

He'd taken some pleasure in pointing out to Lisa that the longer it took for him to pick her brain, the longer he'd remain in Knighton. The haunted look that fell over her face then, however, had given him no pleasure at all.

He found a bench under a tree and sat.

It was human nature not to like the sense that somebody wanted to get rid of you. But he'd gotten what really mattered—her pledge of cooperation.

Her straightforward approach would make this all a lot

easier. Fewer shadows or might-have-beens from the past to interfere in what was, after all, an investigation.

So it had to be his investigative instincts that had him wondering why she disliked him so. Alex White was the criminal. Alex was the one who'd fed her lies, who'd put her in a perilous situation—hell, she'd risked being charged as an accessory. But she still reacted to Alex White like a beloved uncle.

Her response to Shane was considerably cooler. Like maybe one of the poles. She couldn't wait to get him out of town, and was putting up with his presence to speed that process.

It was one more element of Lisa he was determined to probe—as a matter of investigative curiosity.

A poster by the library's main door advertised an upcoming event called a Book Pass and a celebration to follow. His eyes automatically took in all the information, while his mind remained on Lisa.

She hadn't appreciated his taking her seat in the café. Clearly, she hadn't realized he'd done her a favor, because if she'd sat in her usual spot, all the interested townspeople would have had a wide-open view of her face. Not that her face was wide-open. No, she kept her expression as well guarded as Fort Knox.

What if he'd driven into Knighton to discover that Lisa Currick was the same bright, happy, creative person she'd been when he'd met her? That she'd settled into life in her hometown and made it her own, just the way she'd seemed to make all of Manhattan her own. What if she'd been married, even had a couple kids. After all, she was a beautiful woman, and it had been eight years…

He'd never given that possibility a thought.

He knew that for a fact, because if he had given the possibility any real thought he would have experienced this churning in his gut before, and instead it was a brand new feeling. A feeling he didn't like.

You sure it's not about that girl?...Lisa Currick. The one who got away.

Was that true? Did it matter?

Not as long as the necklace was out there. Because until he'd turned that necklace in he would never be totally free of this case. And only when he was free of this case could he stop wondering if he would have recovered everything if the witness he'd been working eight years ago had been anybody other than Lisa Currick.

He stood and headed toward his rented vehicle to reread the file—maybe the thousandth reading would turn up something new—and make notes for his first session with Lisa.

The sooner they started, the better.

"Two weeks after you started as White's intern, he took in an antique ruby bracelet from Constanza Rizzoli, with instructions to convert the stones into earrings. Do you remember that?"

"Yes. Fifteenth-century Italian. It was a shame to dismantle it the way she wanted."

"Did you and White talk about it?"

"Yes."

"What did he say?"

"I was the one who said it was a cri—*wrong* to take apart a piece of art like that. I was the one who said she was a vandal—even though I was just an intern. Because Alex White was the kind of teacher who encouraged me to express opinions."

He did not react. "What did White say about the antique ruby bracelet from Constanza Rizzoli?"

She rubbed at her forehead. She'd followed her routine last night, but maybe she'd somehow used caffeinated tea, because she hadn't slept well. They'd been going at this for more than an hour in the small café at the student center after her class. At first she'd been very aware of the interested looks they'd been getting from students—especially the female ones focused on Shane Garrison. But his relentless questions had pushed everything else out of her head—except this pounding ache.

More than an hour, and they had barely started on the time she'd spent at the Alex White Studio. And the questions were becoming more and more detailed. This could take all night.

All night... They'd talked all night sitting across from one another at the far back booth of a narrow little place on Fifty-third Street off Fifth Avenue. There'd been flurries of activity at the front, but they'd hardly noticed. Buffered from the outside world by their distance from the comings and goings...and by their fascination with each other. At least, that's what she'd thought at the time.

"You haven't answered."

He leaned back, hooking one elbow around the finial protruding from the top of the chair's back. The position twisted his torso, highlighting the broadness of his shoulders and chest. The gap from the open top two buttons of his shirt revealed a cord in his strong neck as it stretched down to connect to the hard line of his collarbone. But his eyes never left her. Those eyes that once had made her think she was seeing as deeply into him as she'd allowed him to see into her.

Another element of her self-delusion.

With the perspective of hindsight, she now saw that their all-night conversation hadn't been the result of fascination with each other. It had been a masterful interrogation cloaked in a velvet glove.

"Is there a special reason you don't want to tell me what White said about that bracelet?"

"He said very little about it. Noted the workmanship and described the commission. That's all," she said mechanically.

"That's hard to believe with a historic piece like that, and her wanting to take it apart. Come on, Lisa. What else did he say?"

Frustration bubbled up in her, and along with it came words. "If you think I'm not telling you the whole truth, then you must think I know where the necklace is, too. You probably think I've been parading around in diamonds and platinum with an emerald pendant around—"

"That thing would be hard to miss. If you or anybody had worn it in public, we'd have it by now."

She ignored that. "And you must think I've known where it is all along—even when I swore in court that I didn't. That would make me some sort of accessory wouldn't it? And a perjurer?"

In frustration she shoved at the stack of small notebooks he'd been consulting, tumbling them across the table. He reached out—she thought to catch the notebooks, instead he pinned her wrist to the table.

"I don't think you know where it is—not consciously."

I told you everything I knew about all that...before.

Maybe everything you knew you knew. But you don't know how much you know. Not yet. But I'll find out.

Now she understood why those words had made her want to shiver—because she had agreed to let Shane Garrison find out all the memories that resided in her head.

And what about the memories that belonged only to her heart?

No, she couldn't allow that.

She twisted against his hold. He let her loose.

"I can't do any more tonight. I'm tired, and even if I had something to remember, I wouldn't remember it tonight."

"We've barely started."

"I know." That was what scared her. "Just not tonight."

Shane shifted the knobby bag of groceries on his hip and knocked louder on Lisa Currick's front door.

"Just a minute!" came a voice from inside. Despite the door muffling the sound, impatience came through clearly.

The door swung open sharply.

Lisa had her hair turbaned in a rich green-blue towel and wore a similarly colored robe that zipped up the front. It was zipped all the way to the upper limit of the stand-up collar, but the speed with which she'd put it on was betrayed by one side of the bottom being caught up on itself, revealing her leg up to just above the knee.

Detectives were trained to notice details like that.

So were men.

The leg was bare. Two droplets of water trailed down it. One speeding down the front of her shin bone. But the other, visible because he stood slightly to the side of her instead of straight-on, was slower, taking its time following the curve where her thigh dipped in to that sweet hollow at the back of a woman's knee, where a man's mouth could surprise her into unexpected responses, that—

"You—what do you want?" Lisa demanded.

The part of him clamoring to answer that was definitely the man, not the detective. He kept the man quiet, but all the detective got out was, "Uh…"

Apparently she noticed things, too. Like a man standing outside her door just this side of drooling.

She shook the material of the robe slightly, and it fell to the top of her bare feet, closing off his view. It didn't matter. He knew—*knew*—she was naked under that single layer of fabric. So fresh from a shower she was still wet.

Wet… He nearly staggered under the image.

"What are you doing here?" she altered her demand to a safer one this time. With one hand she held the collar's fabric against her throat, as if to close off an extra half inch of flesh from his view.

Too late. Too damned late to stop the images hotly churning deep in his gut. They should have a course in this at the academy—How to Keep Your Mind on Your Job When Your Body's Rioting. He'd never have passed that one. Not with Lisa Currick standing in front of him fresh from a shower—or did she take baths…?

"Detective Garrison? We don't have an appointment to-day."

Even more than her use of his title, the faintest hint of discomfort in her voice snapped him out of it.

"No, but since we didn't get very far with our first appointment, I figured we'd try something different." He twisted the screen door's knob and pulled it open. She backed up three steps. Once inside he frowned at her as he pulled it closed and slid the lock home. "You should keep the garage door down. Don't open the main door without knowing who's out there. And keep this screen door locked. It's not much but it might slow down somebody trying to get in."

"Too late," she muttered.

Her unintentional echo of his thought about her covering an extra half inch with her robe brought his head around. Their eyes met, and the look held for a burning heartbeat. She looked away, backing up more as she spoke.

"Detective Garrison, I have work to do today."

"It's Saturday. You don't work Saturdays."

"I reserve Saturdays for working on special projects for my classes."

"Saturdays should be for fun, not working." He headed past her to the kitchen and started unloading the bag.

He stopped with a package of bacon inches from the counter and whistled when his gaze met a view of the snow-tipped Big Horn Mountains revealed by windows and a pair of French doors stretched across the back of the house. "Some skyline."

She refused to be detoured. "That's a change of attitude. You used to work Saturdays."

During the time they'd known each other in New York, he'd spent a high percentage of Saturdays with her—and it required a stretch of imagination to classify what he'd done those days as work. But before he could remind her of those long, warm days spent walking and talking, she was continuing.

"Besides, I don't consider another interview with you fun."

So much for images of showers and naked flesh and *wet*. "You've made that clear, Lisa. But even if you're going to work all day, you have to eat. And I brought breakfast."

She picked up a potato as big as her hand, put it down, then picked up a packaged steak. "This isn't breakfast, it's an orgy."

It was the first time she'd sounded like the Lisa he remembered. Amusement bubbling through her voice, sparkling in her eyes.

God, he wanted to take her in his arms. He wanted to feel her naked body against his through that robe and his clothes. And then he wanted to feel it with no clothes at all. He wanted—

She took a step back, as if she'd read his wants like a ticker tape across his forehead.

Damn. He better get control over his libido or she'd be running so hard and so fast that he'd never get her to open up.

About the necklace. About other things.

"I asked what ranch folks around here eat for breakfast," he said, keeping his attention on pulling the onions and eggs out of the bottom of the bag, "and this is what they told me in the store."

"That's for ranch hands who've put in half a hard day's work before 9 a.m.—and steak only on special occasions. In case you haven't noticed, I'm not a ranch hand."

"I've noticed." All the things he had noticed about her warmed and deepened his voice. "You go get dressed while I'm cooking, and we'll talk while we're eating. That won't cut into your working time."

When she hesitated, he gave a theatrical sigh. "All right, all right, I'll clean up, too."

He knew that she was going to give in a second before her expression changed. That knowledge felt better than getting the commendation he'd received last year. Only question was which part of this moment was better—reading her responses or knowing that she wasn't going to try to kick him out.

"Fine. For as long as it takes to eat breakfast."

"Sure," he lied. "And I promise it'll be a good breakfast," he added as she started to pivot away.

Then he added one more thing. Loud enough that she would almost surely hear it. Low enough for her to pretend she didn't.

"Although an orgy wouldn't be bad, either."

She hesitated half a beat, then kept going.

He caught a glimpse of the side of her neck as she turned into the hallway that led to the back of the house. It was beet red.

He whistled while he cooked.

Chapter Four

The second time she yawned he said, "You're beat. Let's call it a day."

She glanced up, but the pencil she'd been using to fill the sheets in front of her didn't lift. And her attention soon returned to where lead met paper.

"I don't know why I'm so tired."

He did. After last night's less-than-success, he'd taken a different approach this time. Surprise, food, few direct questions but lots of leading comments. It might have seemed like just talk. But once she relaxed, she'd been much more forthcoming than yesterday.

When her pencil first started moving across that legal pad it was as if she'd slipped into a talking trance, the memories of her time working with Alex White being pulled out without regard to chronology or topic. That was okay. Once everything was out on the table, then he'd start reassembling it.

"So we're done?" She hardly sounded interested.

"Almost—for today." He'd like to get out of here before she realized she'd been talking for the better part of four hours. "I just want one more thing."

She looked up, her hazel eyes wide and a little vague, as if they were still seeing something other than what they were looking at now. Since that happened to be him, it cooled the heat in his blood a few degrees.

"This." He tapped two blunt-tipped fingers against the pad.

"My notes from class?" Her brows and voice rose with disbelief.

"No. What you've been drawing."

Her eyes changed immediately. They had a look in them he'd seen twice before—when he'd arrested Alex White and the day the verdict came in.

Dazed incomprehension.

He understood why she'd had that look the first two times, but why now over a few drawings on a couple pieces of paper? She'd told him at the café that she had better uses for her time, sure, but that didn't explain this reaction.

Another half second and she dropped her gaze to the pad in front of her. She stared at it for two beats, then began flipping the pages over, using sheets of neat notes to cover what she'd drawn. They also covered his hand, which he hadn't moved.

"Lisa—"

"It's nothing. Just doodling."

"Then you wouldn't mind my looking at it."

Pressing down with his fingers allowed him to pull the pad toward him. She tried to tug it back. Stalemate.

"It has nothing to do with the case—nothing."

With his free hand, he flipped the covering sheets out of the way. Sketches of jewelry. Strong, firm strokes showing rough designs, but no hesitation or doubt. Yet he was certain she had done them unconsciously.

He looked at the drawings again, then at her. She was looking away—away from him, away from the pad.

"These are jewelry, aren't they?"

"Not the ones you're thinking of."

"Then what are they?"

She gave a dismissive wave with both hands. "I told you, doodles."

He took advantage of the wave to draw the pad close enough to see the drawings in more detail.

One was a swirl. A few deft tracings, yet the motion of it made him think of power and energy. He traced the curve with one fingertip. A bar drawn across it might have been the pin for a brooch—indicating which way it would be worn, which would put the open-wide end of it toward the top. Another started from what he recognized as the wire mechanism for pierced earrings, then dropped in a line of seemingly unrelated textures and shapes that somehow made a pleasing whole.

"Since they're just doodles, you won't mind my keeping them." He tore off three sheets.

"What? No!"

She pivoted in her seat and grabbed for the sheets, but he had them out of reach, and calmly finished folding them and put them in his shirt pocket.

"You think I'm lying," she accused him.

"No, I don't." The pieces Alex White stole were nothing like these drawings.

"Then give them back to me."

"Why?"

"Because they're mine." She hesitated, then added, "Please, Shane."

He retrieved the sheets from his pocket, unfolded them and spread them flat on the table with the weight of his hand.

"That's all you had to say."

Her gaze snapped from the paper to his face, then shuttered. But he'd seen the doubt in her eyes.

Doubt beat the hell out of cold certainty. He could live with doubt.

He allowed his index finger to again follow the curve of an earring she'd drawn, as if his fingertip could absorb some of her along with the trace of graphite. Then he took his hand away and straightened.

"See you round, Lisa."

She followed him to the door—making sure he left, he supposed. But as he backed out of the long driveway, he had a clear view through the screen door of her standing near the table, with her head bent. Just the way it would be if she were looking at those pages.

The inherent strength from the creases Shane had folded into the paper asserted itself, and the edges slowly rose. Instinctively, Lisa placed her hand over the page, as Shane had done a moment ago.

As Shane had done.

The image of his hand spread over the drawings she had made seemed more real at the moment than the sight of her own hand. So real that she felt a warmth, as if his hand rested over hers.

"Oh, Lord!"

She snatched her hand off the paper and backed up two quick steps.

That brought her calf hard against the chair Shane had occupied. The blow made her stumble. She sat down. Her muscles tensed to spring out of the chair, then relaxed.

From this angle, she could see things as Shane had. Maybe that would help her understand the expressions she'd caught on his face. Infinitesimal slices of expression. So small it had been almost like another fleck of color in the blue of his eyes—but definitely there.

She looked around the room. And saw nothing unexpected, out of the ordinary or new. Well, what did she expect? A big sign that said, "Read here to understand Shane Garrison?"

Besides, his strangest expression had been the one when

she first opened the door. And that one had been pretty clear.

She stood up abruptly.

That was biology. Had nothing to do with them as individuals. It was simply and solely a male-female issue.

She pushed her left hand through her hair and realized she'd used one hand because her right hand was otherwise occupied.

Her right index finger was tracing one drawing on the paper...just as she had watched Shane do. He'd repeated the motion over and over as if learning the shadings by heart. Yet, at the same time his touch had changed the drawing from its original.

Was that what would happen if Shane ever touched her with such deliberate concentration? Would he learn her at the same time he changed her?

She dragged her curled fingers across the pages, crumpling them into a ball.

There was seeing things from the other person's perspective and then there was being crazy.

Her hand tightened around the paper balled in her fist.

She headed toward the kitchen door that opened into the garage.

She lifted the lid on the garbage can, holding the fist with the wadded-up paper over the abyss.

Her hand had betrayed her into a relapse into her former life. Her hand and her unconscious mind.

And your talent.

The voice that said those words should have been Alex's, but the seductive whisper in her head was Shane Garrison's.

That didn't make sense. But then neither did the prickles up the back of her neck and along her arms.

She looked around the garage—empty except for her car and neatly stored supplies. Beyond the open garage door, the driveway was also empty. No sign of the rented SUV or of a certain black-haired man.

Nothing but her and three pieces of paper and the choice she'd made about how she would live.

She threw the wad of paper into the can and marched back into the house.

But triumph eluded her. If anything, the disconcerting sense of Shane's presence grew stronger.

So Lisa Currick battled it with her most reliable weapon—detailed, concentration-demanding and energy-draining work.

The figure in the black jeans and sleeveless sweatshirt holding a pair of pruning clippers stepped out of the way as Lisa pulled into her driveway Sunday.

"What are you doing?" she demanded, getting out of the car.

"Afternoon," Shane said.

His dark lashes lowered, but not enough to keep her from knowing that he'd surveyed her from head to toe...taking extra time for the portion of her legs beneath the knee-length skirt she'd worn to church. In a compromise with Dave and Matty, she'd agreed to go to the ranch for brunch after church to talk over what they might do to celebrate the senior Curricks' approaching homecoming.

The sapphire skirt and pearl-white blouse were entirely unspectacular. She'd worn each dozens of times without their making her feel anything other than adequately clothed. Now she had to curb the urge to pull down the skirt hem with one hand and close up the collar with the other.

"I asked you what you're—"

"Did you enjoy the church service?"

"—doing here, and I want— What?"

"Church. This morning. Did you enjoy it?"

"How did you know— No. Don't tell me. You were spying on me again."

"Actually, I was sitting in the back row, right-hand corner. Cops go to church sometimes, too. A few of us even sing.''

"Detective Garrison, I asked what you're—''

"Aw, c'mon, you can't be going back to Detective Garrison. I thought we got past that.''

"What,'' she started again, spacing each word, "Are. You. Doing. Here?''

"Doesn't take a detective to figure that one out, Lisa.'' His grin was impudent. "Trimming the bushes.''

"Why?''

"Improving the sight lines.''

She looked around, as if the view from the front of her house might have changed in the five hours since she'd left for church. Nope, it was still the small area she struggled to keep watered enough so grass would grow, the natural area beyond the fence, the road, then a halfhearted hill rising up. The view of the Big Horns that had kept her sane more than once wasn't visible looking this direction.

"There *are* no sights to be seen.''

"And that's the way to keep it. You want open sight lines—'' He waved toward the evergreens beside the garage door at the corner of the house. He'd reduced them to half their previous size. "—so you can see anyone hiding. With those bushes so overgrown, a basketball team could have hidden and you'd have missed them when you drove in, or when you opened the kitchen door—which you promised you wouldn't do anymore until you know who's on the other side.''

"I promised no such thing.''

"You're right—it was the front door we were talking about. You—''

"I made no promise about either door!''

"—should get a bar grid on each screen door, too. Those screens are too damned easy to cut. A grid will slow them down.''

"Them? There are no thems. This is Wyoming, not Manhattan.''

"Indulge me."

"This is ridiculous." She threw up her hands, and for no reason she could fathom he grinned. "You're a cliché! A paranoid Irish New York cop."

"Not true."

"You are paranoid. Do you have any idea when the last time anything like a crime happened around here?"

"Not the paranoid part. I probably am paranoid—a lot of cops are, though I'm not sure it's paranoid when it's based on experience. Still if you want to call me paranoid for wanting to make sure that the next time anything like a crime happens around here it doesn't happen to you, go right ahead and call me paranoid."

She planted her hands on her hips. "Thank you, I'll do that—you're paranoid. And with a name like Shane Ford Garrison—"

"You remember my middle name?"

Oh, yes, she remembered it. She also remembered teasing him about it when they'd ducked into a basement bookstore to avoid a spring downpour. *I suppose Ford is a family name—your patrician connections carried on in names. Are your siblings Rockefeller and Vanderbilt?*

He hadn't answered. Instead, he'd stared intently at the crown of her head. When he'd raised his hand, she'd followed its motion until the bookcase behind her stopped her from tipping her head back any farther.

He'd brushed raindrops from her hair. And brought his hand down to show her the moisture gathered on his fingers. He'd started to raise his hand toward his own face, and for one blood-sizzling instant she'd thought he might carry the moisture to his lips.

Then the motion changed, and he'd wiped his hand dry on the side of his jacket.

"Don't try to tell me," she said, ignoring his interruption, "you're not a New York Irish cop, so—"

"I'm a cop, and my family tree's mostly Irish. But not from New York by birth. Wisconsin."

"Wisconsin?" she repeated, straightening. "You're from Wisconsin?"

"Yup."

"But… Then you lied to me. I remember clearly—we were sitting…" Lord, something else to ignore—it didn't matter that they'd been sitting side by side, close enough that she'd felt the heat of his leg from hip to knee along hers. "We were talking, and I commented on your not having a New York accent, and you said you'd worked really hard to get rid of your accent."

"I did. My Wisconsin accent. When I first got to the city, I was pretty young and I got incredible grief about being a naive hick. I couldn't do much about my age, but I made sure I didn't give any New *Yawkers* clues to where I was from. So you can't hold it against me for being born a New Yorker."

"What makes you think I'd hold it against anyone for being born a New Yorker?"

"You lit out of New York like it had a bad smell. It's not unreasonable to think you're part of the legions who bash New York."

"Never. I'd dreamed about New York my entire life. The day I arrived it was even more—" she gestured widely to try to convey the scope "—more New Yorky than I'd ever imagined."

He straightened, the mischief gone. She half turned and looked away, as if the halfhearted hill across the road had done something interesting.

"So you started out excited about the city, but after a while you got tired of New York and—"

"Tired of New York?" Astonishment turned her back toward him. "How could anyone get tired of New York? That would be like getting tired of the universe. There's everything under the sun there." She chuckled. "Along with some things that I'm sure never see sunlight. Sure it's the theaters and the libraries and the art galleries and the museums. But it's all the life that's outside those buildings, too. You can hear every language, and taste every taste and smell every smell, just walking down one street.''

"You like all that about it. But you left and you haven't come back.''

Cautious once more, she said, "I'm better suited to life in Knighton.''

Once she would have thought his lost-in-thought expression came from mulling over what she'd said simply because she'd said it. Now she could practically hear the gears of his mind grinding her words into the fine powder of evidence.

"Sometimes the city wears on you after a while.''

Despite her intention to remain wary, she made a small sound of amusement.

"What?''

"Remembering how everyone there called it 'The City.' Like there's only one.''

He shrugged. "It can wear at people after a while—the toughness, the noise, the busyness.'' He cut a look at her. "The crime.''

That skated too close to their past. She looked back toward that hill that still wasn't doing anything interesting.

"After being here I can understand how the city could overwhelm somebody,'' he said. "Even Wisconsin to New York wasn't as big a jump as from here to Manhattan. I can't imagine anywhere more different from what you were used to.''

She shrugged. "I suppose. But there are similarities.''

"To Wyoming?''

She chuckled at his patent disbelief—it felt good to surprise Shane Garrison. "Sure. There's the fact that everything's on a large scale, the grandness, the never-ending variety. And the people who are real characters. There are just fewer of them here.''

"After spending time at the café, I'm not so sure of that,'' he said dryly. "But you had to have been nervous about living in New York.''

"Sure. Nervous and exhilarated and—" abruptly aware that her mouth had started to form a smile, she erased it "—out of my depth. Completely and totally out of my depth."

He nodded as if she'd confirmed something for him. "'Course now you'd have an MBA behind you. Are you expecting somebody? You keep looking toward the road."

Heat rushed up her throat and into her cheeks—could color be far behind?

"Let's get back to the point—I don't want you trimming these bushes." Actually she'd meant to do the chore her-self…sometime.

"I'm done, anyhow."

The appeal of primal-scream therapy became obvious to her in that moment.

"And I am not answering any more questions today or tomorrow. Or," she continued ruthlessly when he opened his mouth, "talking about Alex or the studio or anything else. I have a lot of work to do, and between you and my brother and sister-in-law, I am way behind."

"No problem. I'm taking the day off from the case. Helps give you a fresh perspective when you come back to it." He slanted a look at her as he grabbed the bag of clippings and slung it over his shoulder. "You should try it. See you, Lisa."

Shane followed her into the café at noon Tuesday.

Since she'd agreed to let him ask questions during her lunch hour—just this once, because she needed all her time after work if she was going to attend the library dedication this weekend—she couldn't complain. But did he have to follow her so closely that his heat radiated all along her back?

"Hi, Lisa," called Rainie. "I'll have your soup and salad coming right up."

"That's right," Shane's voice came from behind her, "it's Tuesday."

She took three more steps before stopping in the aisle. "No, wait, Rainie, I'll have a—"

That was all she got out before Shane ran into her, his chest hard against her back, his arms closing around her, and his hips snug against—

"What was that, Lisa?"

She couldn't catch her breath. She tried again. "BLT. I'll have a BLT."

Every stool sitter's head turned to face her. Rainie goggled. "BLT?"

"Bacon, lettuce and tomato. It's on the menu, right?"

"Sure, but..." She shook her head as if she couldn't finish.

"I think she's trying to say, It's Tuesday."

Shane's words, coming as they did from a mouth that was whisper-close to her ear, reminded her that he was still snug against her back. She jerked away.

She used all her discipline to make her next words even. "I'd like a BLT, Rainie."

"Sure, sure, Lisa. Coming right up. And you, Shane?"

"The usual."

Lisa glared at him over her shoulder, sure he was mocking her with that order, and even more sure of it when he smiled blandly. She forgot that, though, when he tried to pass her in order to get to the back bench.

She jettisoned the glare and beat him to the spot. He sighed, but slid into the other side without a word.

He slid all the way across, into the corner, and half turned so his back rested against the wall and his arm stretched across the top of the seat back. A position that let him see her while opening the rest of the café to his peripheral vision.

He wasted no time in opening the questioning. "Where did White go when he was angry?"

"Alex didn't get angry."

He looked at her steadily. "Upset, then."

"He rarely got upset, either. But I suppose he'd have

gone to his private workroom, and you already tore that place apart.''

"Happy?"

"His workroom. Or his apartment, I suppose. He'd lived there for years and loved it—but you tore that apart, too.''

That's where they'd found most of the pieces. A few had been at his country place. None particularly well hidden. Appreciation of the beauty had been Alex's motive, not greed.

"Which of his friends might he have given a package to for safekeeping?''

"You already checked all the ones I could think of eight years ago. And I know people from the studio gave you more names—and none of them had the necklace.''

"Tell me again.''

She pushed her hands through her hair in frustration as she recited all the same names.

"Did he ever give anything to you for safekeeping?'' Shane asked with relentless calm.

Her hands dropped, her palms making a faint slapping noise on the table. "Never.''

"Did he ever visit here?''

"Once. We'd gone to a show in San Francisco—first major I'd attended. He arranged for the stopover on the way back as a surprise. But it was only one night. Besides, that was in the early fall and that necklace didn't come into the studio until Thanksgiving.''

"Did he ever ask you to send something to someone for him not through the studio's regular delivery channels.''

"Never.''

"Did he ever tell you where he hid things?''

"Never. And you've asked all this before.''

Rainie arrived with their plates. After she'd set the BLT in front of Lisa and a burger and fries in front of Shane and walked away, he responded, "Sometimes people remember more later. Don't worry about it. There are other ways to help you remember.''

"I'm not worried. And I can't remember what I never knew."

He shrugged as he transferred his pickle slices to her plate. "We'll see."

Ignore him, she ordered herself.

It wasn't easy. He seemed to fill her field of vision, with his dark hair, wide shoulders and powerful hands securing the hamburger. That left one safe place to look—her plate.

She concentrated on her lunch in a way she hadn't done since…well, she couldn't remember when. Lunch was usually a side dish to studying. This time it was the only course. And it was delicious. She polished off half the sandwich in record time.

She'd forgotten how much she loved BLTs. Starting the second half, she relished the ripe homegrown tomato, the cool lettuce, the crisp, warm bacon, and the café's thick bread absorbing all the flavors and juices. No, not all the juices. She could feel juice from the thick tomato slice sliding down the valleys to either side of her middle knuckle, heading for a confluence before the combined forces would slide over her wrist and down her arm.

"Darn."

She couldn't put down the remnants of her half sandwich without having it disintegrate, so she'd lose the last two perfectly blended bites. She bent her head and raised her arms, planning to stem the flow with a well-aimed lick— and the hell with manners.

"Lisa."

Shane's tight voice brought her head up in surprise. He'd shifted around so his back was to the rest of the room, and his face was just as tight.

He reached across the table, wrapped a lengthwise folded napkin around her wrist, absorbing the juice, and growled another word.

"Finish."

Unhesitatingly, she obeyed, trying not to look at him, and not succeeding.

When she had the last bite in her mouth, he released a breath along with his hold on the napkin around her wrist. She used two more napkins to wipe her hands.

"I, uh, better go wash my hands."

She put her purse strap over her shoulder and started to slide out of the booth.

"Lisa."

She stopped. But he said nothing more until she looked at him. His face still had that taut look, and his voice came out strained.

"Don't ever eat one of those sandwiches in front of me again, unless you want—" His gaze dropped to her mouth, then to the base of her throat, where she could feel her pulse jump. When his gaze came back to her eyes, her pulse jumped again at the heat she saw in his. "Unless you want what you've made very clear you don't want."

He was in deeper trouble than he'd thought.

Watching her pleasure in eating a simple BLT had made him hard.

He swore, consciously easing his pace as he jogged up the hill beyond Ruth and Hugh's house.

The fact that the BLT was a change in her routine had snagged his attention first. He'd felt the oddest little charge at her defiance when Rainie and the others were so surprised.

Hell, who was he kidding? The charge wasn't odd and it wasn't little, and it had a hell of a lot more to do with coming up behind her so the rounded curves of her buttocks brushed against him. So her hair brushed against his cheek, like sun-warmed silk. So his arms encircled her below her breasts.

The slightest move, and he could have brushed across the tips of her breasts and seen if they responded. Opened a hand and found the weight and curve with his palm. So close...

He'd done his damnedest to keep his face blank. If she'd

seen what was behind that mask she would have run the opposite direction.

And that would have been a shame, because then he would have missed the BLT.

Her defiance. Her concentration. Her enjoyment.

She'd nibbled at a length of bacon sticking out of the sandwich. Then she'd licked a dab of errant mayo. And he'd felt the heat rising—along with something else.

Then, just when he thought the torture of pleasure might end, he'd seen pale juice sliding between her fingers. A solitary round seed carried by the flow tracked down the back of her hand. She'd moved…and if her lips had touched her skin, there might have been no stemming another flow.

Better focus on something else. Like Sunday. Her standing in her driveway in her church clothes with the sun lighting her hair like a halo and him thinking decidedly unangelic thoughts.

Think about the conversation. Words. Focus on words.

She still loved New York City.

When she'd stayed away after Alex White was convicted, he'd figured she'd soured on New York. It could happen that way. Especially for someone as open and optimistic as Lisa had been. They weren't used to being kicked in the teeth, so when kicks came they reacted more strongly than those who were used to it. She'd come back here where she felt safe, where everyone knew her and loved her and protected her.

And if she'd been the same open-to-the-world person who could outshine Broadway that he remembered, simply transplanted back to Wyoming, he might be satisfied to find the necklace and leave her in peace. Sure, he'd seen flashes of feelings from her, but he didn't see one bit of peace in that careful, serious demeanor she'd cultivated.

It was as if she'd closed herself up. He'd seen people do that—crime victims mostly. Their sense of security got shot to hell and they pulled in tight. Like Lisa had.

What she needed was a confidence boost. A refresher in believing that she could take on the world—including New York.

Not that he would expect anything to come of it if she returned. Hell, you could live years in Manhattan and never run into someone who lived a couple blocks away. On the other hand, the chances of running into her there were a lot better than if she kept living in Knighton, Wyoming.

Maybe he'd even see her eat another BLT someday.

Yeah, he was in a lot of trouble here.

Lisa should have been reading management case studies right this moment.

Instead, restlessness had pushed her out of the house. The nagging memory of those sketches she'd thrown out had sent her to this corner of the Slash-C she hadn't visited since before she'd left for New York. She'd jolted over a track barely visible yet so familiar that she never hesitated at its twists and turns.

The fence she'd talked her father into erecting to keep cattle out of this narrow draw was in good repair. Lisa had told Dave she'd lost all interest in what the wind and rain might unearth from the rock face, and to let the whole area be ground into dust for all she cared. He obviously hadn't taken her at her word.

The angle of the evening sun was perfect. She'd look for a moment...

The sun's angle had lowered, and she was straightening from determining that a glint was not a fifth find to add to those on a flat-topped boulder behind her when a jolt of instinct and adrenaline hit her, pushing out a gasp as she spun around.

"God! Shane, you scared the living daylights out of me! Don't sneak up on people like that."

He had his back propped against the trunk of a solitary cottonwood tree, his athletic shoes filmed with reddish dust and a baseball cap shading his eyes.

"Always pay attention to what's around you and no one can sneak up on you."

"I was…uh, thinking."

"Interesting place to come, uh, thinking." Pushing off from the tree, he looked around at the striated cliff face, the littering of rocks at their feet, the stunted vegetation hoping the creek would come back to life, and the lineup of items on the flat-topped boulder. "Come here often?"

Suspicion overtook surprise. They had no scheduled meeting this evening—the whole purpose of letting him ask questions at the café at lunch was to leave her evening clear. There'd been no sign of him when she'd left work. Or when she'd impulsively left home.

"It's my family's ranch. What are *you* doing here?"

"Following you. Didn't think I'd found this place on my own, did you? And considering the dust a vehicle kicks up out here, you should have spotted me a mile off." He shook his head, his expression stern. "You couldn't have looked back even once or you'd have seen me."

"I wasn't looking over my shoulder because no one had a reason to be behind me." Unless he thought she would lead him to the necklace. Did he think she'd been lying? Did he—?

"Bad guys don't need reasons. So the first rule is be aware. Always. Second, try to block a grab." His large hand shot out and circled her wrist. "But if it happens that he gets ahold of you, that's not all bad. One of his hands is occupied and you know where it is."

His grip around her wrist opened, and she pulled back, rubbing her wrist against her hip to eradicate the tingling.

"Shane, what is this?"

"So, if an attacker grabs you, don't wait for him to hit you first, you kick him. You can—"

"Kick?" She didn't bother to mute the scoffing. "Like martial arts on TV?"

"No. Those require expertise. Aim for the knee or below—and bring your foot back to solid ground fast for balance. Landing a kick isn't worth losing your balance and ending up on the ground. You're too vulnerable.''

"I'm very good at keeping my feet on the ground and keeping my balance. I've learned that lesson.''

His eyelids lowered for a second. But his voice was as even and calm as ever.

"If you're grabbed by the wrist, use that hold to draw him in at the same time you kick him in the knee. With enough enthusiasm behind her kick, a woman can break almost any man's knee. A lot relies on the shoes. Not those strappy little sandals you wore that froze your feet and—''

"Something like these?" She raised one leg and bent her knee, pulling the hem of her jeans up for him to see her no-nonsense boots. Chunky heel. Sturdy sole. And as a bonus, the metal piece around the front of the toe that had a number of impolite nicknames.

"You didn't wear those in New York.''

It was almost an accusation. For some reason she wanted to laugh.

"In case you haven't noticed, we're not in New York anymore, Toto. Besides, I was hiding my Wyoming roots then—like you hid your Wisconsin roots.''

"Wasn't trying to hide my roots. Just trying to do my job the best way I could," he said. "You'd have felt a lot more secure wearing these than those little sandals you always had on.''

Who cared about secure?

"I loved those sandals. They were a knockoff of a knockoff, and the height of fashion. Okay, they were probably past the height of fashion by the time the knocking off got down to me, but I loved them. They made me feel sex—special. I was sure they were perfect—not too arty, but not too career womany, either.''

Just right for a young woman who would take the jewelry design world by storm any day.

Even with all the knocking off, they'd stretched her budget until it shrieked, but she'd had to have them. And she'd loved them every time she put them on...until the day she'd realized they were not at all the right thing to wear to court to testify against Alex White.

"What you've got on now would do a hell of a lot more damage to a man's knee than those sandals."

Shane's voice jerked her back to the present.

Something wicked pushed her to say, "There is one man around here I'd like to kick."

"Contain yourself a little longer." The ghost of a grin twisted his mouth. "Don't waste oxygen by sucking in air in a gasp the way you did—push it out in a yell. Yell *fire*, yell somebody's name like they're around the corner or just yell—they'd rather go for the easy, quiet type." He looked her full in the face before adding, "And you were never that."

There was no mistaking his tone. But she didn't know what to do with his approval. So she was grateful when he broke the moment by looking around them.

"Looks like there's plenty of room here. You want to try it?"

There had been a time when she would not have needed a second invitation to kick Detective Shane Garrison in the knee—or elsewhere. The most recent time was thirty seconds ago.

But even thirty seconds ago she wouldn't have kicked him *here*. All the work keeping the fence repaired to keep cows out would be wasted if a couple of two-legged creatures started shuffling around. But telling him that would lead to more questions—about this place, about what she'd been doing—and she'd told him enough about herself to last a lifetime.

"I'm not going to kick you—not with it getting dark." She strode to the flat boulder, using tissue from her pocket to wrap her finds as well as she could. "I might miss and hit something vulnerable."

"That's exactly what you want to do—kick the attacker

in the most vulnerable spot possible. Kick him right in the—''

"Okay! I get the idea." She did not need him calling attention to that portion of his anatomy.

"Go ahead, take a shot at my leg, to get the feel of it."

The feel of it… The phrase alone had her nerves on alert.

"I'm leaving. And you better hope you paid close attention to how you got here from the highway, because I'm not going to slow down to lead you out."

"Don't worry about me. I'll stay right on your tail."

Turning on her sturdy boot heel and heading for her car, she refused to even consider that phrase.

Chapter Five

Lisa arrived at the library grounds after the line for the Book Pass had formed. It wasn't like her to be late, but it had taken a ridiculous amount of time to finish reading those case studies.

However, her late arrival produced one major benefit. Matty and Dave were already stationed near the door to the addition, so she could steer clear of them. They both had that I-want-to-talk-to-you look, and she wasn't in the mood.

Instead, Lisa slid into a spot at the opposite end between Taylor and Joyce Aberdick in time to pass on the first book making its way down the line. The collie belonging to Taylor and Cal, Sin, was lying a few feet away in the shade, holding court like a furry monarch to adoring kids.

"Where's the man of the hour?" Lisa asked. Taylor's husband, Cal Ruskoff, had donated a chunk of the proceeds from selling his family's business back east to the addition.

"After the second person thanked him, he got that

hunted look and decided he preferred unpacking boxes in the basement to being out here in the sunshine.''

"Still not exactly a social animal, is he?"

"Nope." Taylor lowered her voice and leaned close with a wicked grin. "But that's not the kind of animal that matters, if you know what I mean."

Lisa chuckled, knowing from Cal's incendiary looks toward his wife that she had no concerns in that area.

"You don't mind an extra pair of hands, do you?"

The deep voice from over her right shoulder brought Lisa spinning around and right into a blue gaze.

Before Lisa could utter a word, Taylor had her hand stretched out to Shane Garrison.

"Mind? We're thrilled. We can use all the hands we can get. I'm Taylor Anne Larsen."

"I know." He shook Taylor's hand and gave his best smile.

Taylor's brows rose slightly. Lisa knew her friend and boss well enough to know she was assessing him carefully. "And you're Shane Garrison, the famous detective from New York City."

"Famous? Not hardly."

"Oh, around here you are, Mr. Garrison. Although perhaps notorious would be a better description."

Neither looked at Lisa, which didn't hide that they were talking about her.

"Then a stint of community service might be what my reputation needs. Mind if I get in here next to you?"

"Not at all," Taylor said, still without looking at Lisa.

As soon as the line adjusted to the addition—all the adjusting done on Taylor's side, since Lisa didn't budge an inch for him—Shane turned to her.

"Afternoon, Lisa."

"What are you doing here?" she said so only he could hear. "There's no way I'm going to answer questions here."

"I wouldn't think of asking them here. I'm here to help. This is pretty ingenious."

His nod took in the human chain. It was based on the old fire-bucket principle, that an object could cover a distance faster being handed person to person than by having one person carry it. Instead of buckets of water, their line was to move books.

"We don't have much money and we do have people, so that's what we use."

"That's why it's ingenious." She received a book, handed it to him, and he sent it on down the line. "But I admit to curiosity about where the books are coming from and going to."

"They were put in boxes to be stored during construction of the addition. Now, there's a librarian at one end taking them out of the boxes in the right order and a librarian at the other end putting them up on the shelves where they belong."

"Not always easy to tell where things—or people—belong, though, is it?"

"That's why it's important to have a good system," she said before blatantly turning her shoulder to him and addressing Joyce.

"Think we'll finish today?"

That's all it took, and Joyce was off. Lisa tuned out the rambling monologue without guilt. Joyce was happy to be prattling on, and Lisa had her own problems.

The most immediate was that each time she held out a book, Shane brushed his hand against hers. He had to be doing that on purpose. If she held the books any closer to the edge, she would drop them, and she'd be damned if she'd give him the satisfaction of knowing he'd gotten to her.

Right now he was talking to Taylor. Not loud enough for her to make out words. Just loud enough for his deep voice to rumble through her nerve endings.

She extended a thick book in his direction, and his palm

cupped the back of her hand. At the same time he must have turned toward her, because his words came through clearly.

"The element of surprise can knock a guy flat."

The book fell to the ground with a thud.

"Be careful there!" someone scolded from down the line.

"Sorry."

"It was my fault," Shane said, then before Lisa could respond, he continued to say to Taylor. "Attackers are braced for a guy to fight back, but if a woman who's cornered starts by acting weak and frightened, getting the guy to relax, then unleashes solid blows, it can catch them off guard. Or throw something at them—but don't give up anything that could be a weapon."

"Like keys?"

"Keys are a last resort. Think how close someone has to get to make keys a good weapon. Now, an umbrella, or a cane—"

"A cane?"

He smiled at Taylor's tone. "Okay, so you aren't going to carry a cane. But even a tightly rolled newspaper, jabbed in under their ribs, can stun them."

Taylor looked up. "Lisa, Joyce, I'm glad you're paying attention to this. This is important for women to hear."

Lisa braced for Shane to gloat that she'd been caught listening. But he seemed too intent on his subject.

"You could use a newspaper to hit him upside the head." Joyce's eagerness drew Lisa's head around to look at her.

"Better to jab it into his face. The face is more vulnerable than the skull. Always go for the vulnerable spots."

Remembering all too well which vulnerable area he'd mentioned prominently the other evening, Lisa jumped in to prevent a return to that subject. "Every female over the age of six has heard about where to kick this mythical attacker, so—"

"Yeah, the groin is good."

She tried. She truly tried. But her gaze went to the region of his snug jeans under discussion as if her eyes were the needle of a compass and it was true north. What snapped her out of it was the sensation of Shane's look touching her face. She dragged her gaze up, met his eyes, then looked away.

Too late.

In that fragment of a minute, she'd seen recognition ignite to flame.

He cleared his throat.

"And the knee…kicking from the side can break the knee. A kick from behind can take a guy down. From in front, stamp down. If you hit it right, you might dislocate the kneecap. If you miss and it scrapes down his shin and lands on his foot, that helps. Especially with heels. Stiletto heels are great."

"Stilettos!" Taylor chuckled. "Not many women torture themselves with those these days."

"Maybe Shane's been working vice," Lisa muttered as she passed him a book.

Not only did Taylor and Shane laugh, but chuckles arose along the line in both directions. Lisa realized most of the women within earshot were listening. Or maybe earshot was less important than eyeshot, considering how Shane looked in a University of Wisconsin T-shirt and jeans.

She blinked, catching up with talk of going for the eyes or the base of the nose.

"Use your elbows. Especially if you can get a good swing and drive it into him. Here, let me show you. Lisa, turn around."

"No." She scrambled for an excuse to give in front of this audience. "There'll be more books."

"Joyce can pass directly to me," Taylor said.

He already had his hands on Lisa's arms, turning her so her back was to him.

"No, Sin!" Taylor's command stopped everyone, including the dog, now standing on alert not four feet from Shane and Lisa. "It's okay, Sin. He's not hurting her."

The dog's ears flicked toward Taylor, but his eyes stayed pinned on Shane. And he did not relax.

"You better tell him it's okay, Lisa. He's protective of his people."

The temptation was there. She could use the dog as an excuse, and Shane would stop touching her, and she'd stop feeling this way...wouldn't she?

"If you all had a dog like that you wouldn't need to know the stuff I'm telling you." Shane's comment drew chuckles at the same time as it covered her hesitation, but it also reminded her that the other women were interested.

"It's okay, Sin."

The dog relaxed, going to Taylor for a pat before returning to the shade and the kids.

"You've all got a weapon that can't be turned against you—your elbow." Shane's hand cupped her elbow. "It's hard, pointed and bony—that's tough to beat."

Warmth transmitted from his hand to her elbow, from his skin to her skin. Then sank deeper, into the muscles, tendons and bloodstream, where it traveled to regions far removed from that mundane joint. Somehow it even made her sensitive to the brush of his breath across her ear and the side of her neck. His fingers flexed, and his palm rubbed ever so slightly against her flesh.

Her elbow—every hard, pointed and bony millimeter of it—turned to mush.

"Someone comes up behind you—" Shane reached around her and placed his left forearm in front of her throat, illustrating the potential for the hold without touching her. His breath crossed her face, bringing a shiver of warmth. "—you react. Especially with choking, because you can start to lose consciousness in seconds, and then you don't have options. So act first and get explanations later. You swing that elbow with everything you've got."

Another brush of breath—this wasn't her sensitivity alone, was it? His breathing had changed. Hadn't it?

His grip on her elbow tightened enough to start her pivoting toward him.

"The throat or face aren't bad targets, but they're small. Go for the gut or the chest."

Lisa completed the motion, her elbow connecting with his chest, though without force. He transferred his hand from her elbow to her wrist, holding her arm in place so everyone could see the end of the move.

"If you happen to hit him around the heart you can do some damage."

Lisa turned, met his eyes, then wished she hadn't.

Calling on eight years of discipline, her mush-for-muscles had just enough oomph to step away from him.

"And that's the next step." He held her wrist an extra beat before releasing it. "If your blow makes him loosen his hold, get free. Then immediately follow with another blow."

"Running away would seem wiser," she said. Sometimes what looked like cowardice was really self-preservation.

He held her look. "If you haven't disabled your attacker, he can come after you. So you'd have to be a very good runner. They can catch up with you when you're least expecting it."

"That's the mistake characters always make in horror movies," said Joyce. "Just when they think they've gotten away, the bad guy grabs their leg."

As Joyce offered examples, Shane's gaze skimmed down Lisa's legs, and it felt not only as if he could see through the tough, no-nonsense denim of her jeans but simultaneously had touched the skin beneath it.

Did those characters in horror movies feel any thrill of warmth at the clasp around their ankle? No. They'd be nuts to feel that way.

"Grabs their leg and drags them to their doom," she said.

A shadow of Shane's grin appeared, as if he'd followed her thoughts. "Doesn't have to be that way. Your legs—" another flicker of a glance toward her legs "—have some of the most powerful muscles in the body. Use them. Kick. If you don't have room to maneuver, use short, stamping kicks to whatever you can reach."

Joyce's eyes glittered. "That's great! Anything else, Shane?"

"Sure. There's an area on the side of the thigh halfway between the hip—"

Before Lisa saw it coming, he'd skimmed his fingertips from her hip to the middle of her thigh.

"—and knee that if you hit it hard, you'll give the guy 'dead leg.' If a guy's bothering you at a party, you can give him a good knee there. Nothing permanent, but it'll stop him temporarily."

Lisa looked from Joyce to the other absorbed faces and had a horrible premonition of what the next party in Knighton might be like. This had gone far enough.

She grabbed a fistful of sleeve and pushed Shane out of the line as she said over her shoulder, "Taylor, will you fill the gap for a minute?"

"Sure."

"Do I get a say in this?" He might have succeeded in sounding plaintive if he hadn't so clearly been on the verge of laughter.

"No. I want to talk to you."

"You know, you keep saying that, and you keep getting my hopes up, but you never do."

"Get your hopes—" Oh, no, she wasn't going to ask him about hopes. Hopes were definitely off-limits for discussions between them. "Never do what?"

"Talk to me. You set down rules, you give edicts, you order me out of town, tell me to leave, and insist I stop trimming bushes, but I don't call any of that talking to me, do you?''

Hands on her hips, she fought the twinge of guilt with a tart reply of, "It's the best you're going to get."

"Making the most of what I get is the detective's lot." The challenge in that segued into a sigh. "What is it this time?"

"Stop all this self-defense stuff. You're making Sin nervous, and you're creeping everybody out. With talking about gouging elbows and breaking knees and…" Her gaze flicked away. "I don't know why you're doing this."

"Like Taylor said, it's stuff women should know. So they don't restrict themselves from going wherever they want." He held up his hands in promise as he took two steps toward the line. "No more lessons for today."

She could have disputed *today* but it would have been in the full hearing of their neighbors in line. She took her spot with a quick thanks to Taylor.

Taylor simply nodded. But Joyce looked from Shane to Lisa and demanded, "Isn't he going to do any more?"

"No. This isn't the time or place."

"I suppose it was slowing the relay." Joyce sighed. "But it sure was fun to watch. Like one of those really hot videos on MTV—you know, the ones where you can tell there's even more going on between the two people off the screen than they're showing on the screen."

Joyce watched MTV? That concept so boggled her that Lisa's reaction to the rest of what Joyce had said was delayed—then it hit. Joyce thought she and Shane had a history—a physical history.

"No." It came out a croak. Lisa cleared her throat to try again, but Joyce was already talking to Annie Gatchell on her other side. Lisa would have to tug at her arm to get her attention and declare that she and Shane had never had anything going on "off screen." Talk about making a bad situation worse.

He'd never embraced her or caressed her or kissed her.

There'd been so little physical contact between them that the fleeting touches of a man guiding a woman along a crowded sidewalk had burst across her starry-eyed imagination like fireworks. And the one time there'd been more than those polite contacts...

They'd been walking through Central Park. They'd skirted a group of people flying kites and started down a long slope dotted with couples on blankets. To her eyes they'd all seemed to be making out.

From that observation it had been a leap that a flea with a sprained leg could make to imagining what it would be like to kiss Shane like that couple on the blue blanket. Or to be wrapped in each other's arms as closely as the couple on the bright quilt. Or, there under the tree, to have Shane touch her like that with his hand on her—

She never knew if she tripped over a root, her own foot or her imagination. But she pitched forward, stumbling in a desperate effort to keep her footing. Shane grabbed for her, caught her sleeve, but not her arm, and that took him off balance, too.

They tumbled in a tangle of arms and legs, coming to rest with her legs straddling his hips and the rest of her spread across his chest. She'd raised her head.

Now. At last. He was going to kiss her—finally! She saw it in his face. She knew it in every millimeter of skin that touched his.

She waited. Not trying to hide how much she wanted this.

And then his lids dropped over his eyes for three counts—not even long enough for her to fully take in the significance—before he gripped her shoulders and rolled them a final time. For an instant, his lower body pressed against the yawning ache at the top of her legs, and she thought...

But if he'd wanted her, he had one strange way of showing it. He levered off her, drawing her with him. He had to do all the work because she was limp. But in seconds he had them back on their feet. And he was chuckling. *Chuckling!*

"That was a pratfall worthy of Dick Van Dyke."

She'd wanted to throw herself at him. She'd wanted to shake him. She'd wanted to disappear into the earth of Central Park never to be seen again. Instead, she'd brushed herself off, and they'd continued on their way. As if nothing had happened.

Because nothing had.

Nothing ever happened between them. Except in her imagination. He'd simply and solely been working a case.

It wasn't until the first day Alex had appeared in court that the full reality of that had sunk in. Before they brought Alex in, she'd been talking to Alex's attorney behind the defense table. Shane came in wearing a suit and tie. He'd glanced toward her, gave the barest of nods, then went directly to the prosecutor, exchanging quiet words with him before taking a seat on that side of the courtroom. The opposite side from where she sat.

That was the real Shane Garrison. Perhaps at some level he'd liked her, but the reason he'd spent all those hours with her that spring was because he'd wanted something from her, something that would advance his career.

That hadn't changed. But she had.

"Last book! Last book!"

The cheer came down the line ahead of a slim volume. As it passed from hand to hand, the line broke up into pockets of conversation.

"Ice cream will be ready in ten minutes" came the next call as Joyce took the book and handed it to Lisa.

"Ice cream?" Shane's eyes burned with blue fervor.

"It's to celebrate the new addition, and to reward the helpers," Taylor said. "Cal told the mayor he didn't want any speeches or formal dedication, so this is what she came up with. Looks like you approve, Shane."

"Ice cream's the best food ever invented, just ahead of nachos."

Taylor laughed. "A nutrition nut, huh? Come get some before it melts."

"Thanks, I will."

"You, too, Lisa."

Having packed her water bottle and cardigan into her tote bag, Lisa slung the strap over her shoulder. "See you later, Taylor."

Her friend waved as she walked toward tables spread with tubs of ice cream. Lisa waited another second, then turned the opposite way.

"You're heading the wrong direction, Lisa." Shane said. "The ice cream's over there."

"I'm heading the right direction to go home."

Shane's left eyebrow rose. "Don't let me scare you off from the ice cream."

She stopped and looked him straight in the eyes. "You don't scare me." Able to sustain that only so long, she added, "But your interrogation sessions have put me behind. I'm going to study. With no interruptions."

It would have been a more triumphant moment if she hadn't felt shivers all down her neck and back at the knowledge that he was watching her every step of the way to her car.

Shane opened the hood of Hugh Moski's thirteen-year-old sedan Sunday afternoon. Somewhere among the wires, hoses, belts and spark plugs would be the answer to why, as Hugh had said at breakfast, "its get-up-and-go's gone-and-went on me." The solution to this mystery would be logical and reasonable.

Gather the symptoms to narrow the field of inquiry. Methodically work through the possibilities until he found the right one and fixed it. Afterward drop the hood into place with that satisfying clang, wipe off his hands and know he'd set things right.

Sometimes he wondered why he'd been so damned set on police work instead of following in his father's footsteps. Because people weren't clear-cut, because methodical didn't always work, even though things still needed setting right.

So, where was he on this case?

He'd already known most of what Lisa had told him, and none of the new details gave him any clues to the necklace's whereabouts.

No obvious clues, he corrected himself. Sometimes what you heard didn't reveal itself as a clue until you added it up with another fact or two or three or ten. The patience to unearth each of those gems—along with dozens of duds—was what set apart a good detective.

He absently tested the give in the fan belt.

Unearthing gems…could that be what Lisa had been doing the other evening at the Slash-C?

He'd heard from Hugh and Ruth that Lisa used to go hunting for materials for her jewelry designs. Kind of a hobby. She needed that.

She looked so tired after each session from considering every word she spoke that he wanted to pull her into his arms and tell her to rest her head on his shoulder and go to sleep, the way he would a child.

He grimaced as he cleared leaves caught up in the engine.

Okay, *not* the way he would a child.

Memory hit: that evening at the Slash-C his hand encircling Lisa's wrist, the bones hard, knobby, yet delicate, and covered by skin so soft he'd wanted to stroke it over and over, never letting go. But he had let go.

And she'd rubbed her wrist against her jeans as if to wipe off his touch.

Even so, his blood had heated and headed south like snowbirds when she'd started on about how those sandals she used to wear had made her feel sexy.

They'd made her look sexy, too. Trouble was, she looked sexy in scuffed cowboy boots, too. But it didn't take a detective to figure out it wasn't footware that produced the effect on him.

A worried sigh jerked Shane out of those thoughts.

Hugh Moski was coming toward him. He was frowning, and the next second came another sigh.

"Sorry, Hugh, I got sidetracked. I'll get started on the car now."

"It's not that. Though I surely hope you can fix 'er. I'm here to tell you, I near as got flattened by a blue pickup when I went to pass a horse trailer yesterday. I gave 'er the gas, and she didn't give me nothin' back."

"So, what's the matter, Hugh? You look like a man chewing over a problem."

"That's it exactly." From admiration at Shane's perception, his face fell again. "It's my Ruth."

"What's wrong with Ruth."

"Not a thing. Fact is, she's smart as a whip. Always has been. Pop always said 'Marry what you ain't,' and that's what I done. Though it wasn't her brains I was interested in back then. It's our anniversary coming up. Fiftieth." He shook his head. "Can't hardly believe it."

"And you're wondering what to get her."

"Yup. Gotta be something special. I want it to be something she'll always remember. And I've been thinkin' and thinkin' but haven't got an idea in the world." His gaze sharpened suddenly. "Say, you're a smart fella. You gotta have ideas about such things."

"Sorry, Hugh. Anniversary gifts aren't my area."

Gloom folded deep lines into his face. "Suppose not, seein' as you haven't even got yourself married. How would you know what to give a good woman after fifty years of livin' and lovin' together? That's how desperate I am, askin' you for help."

Shane was certain Hugh had meant to make no more than a statement of fact, with no judgment attached. Yet, as the older man walked off, Shane felt a lingering sting.

How would you know what to give a good woman after fifty years of livin' and lovin' together?

He wouldn't. He wouldn't know what to give a good woman after five years of living and loving together. And even though he and Julianne had practically lived together and had talked of marriage, he couldn't honestly say the two years before she'd left this past spring counted as loving.

He shook his head and stuck it back under the hood, where it might have a chance of doing some good.

Lisa had a dilemma.

To get to Ruth and Hugh's back door to deliver the Johnston mediation papers, she had to either walk past where Shane Garrison had his rear end sticking out of a car engine, or along the far side of the car, where he would see her if he happened to lift his head.

She considered the front door for about fifteen seconds—exactly the amount of time it took to imagine Ruth asking why on earth Lisa had come to the front door for the first time in her life.

She chose the far side of the car.

Moving slowly and silently, she'd passed the trunk, rear passenger door and was working on the driver's door.... She might just get past—

"Hi, Lisa."

She squeaked a word that might have been his name. He hadn't even looked up.

"How'd you know it was me?"

Now he did look up. "How'd you know it was me?" he retorted. So apparently her squeak had been recognizable as his name.

"I—" She stopped dead. What could she say? She'd recognized his butt?

"I'm glad you're here."

You are? "I don't have time to play Twenty Questions with you today."

"Fair enough. That's not why I'm glad you're here, anyway."

Oh.

"I was hoping," he continued, "you'd do me a favor. Actually, do Hugh a favor, since it's his car."

"What?"

"Turn over the engine—the keys are there—and rev it up. I can't do that and see what's happening with the engine at the same time."

"Okay." She slid behind the wheel and turned the engine on. She couldn't spot any catch in the request...but she hadn't anticipated what sort of havoc he could produce at the Slash-C or at the Book Pass, either.

Through the open passenger window she heard him clearly, "Rev it up, Lisa."

She would *not* let her unruly imagination imbue that prosaic phrase with any other meaning. Absolutely not. She pressed on the accelerator.

"Again."

A slice of his shoulder and back were visible beneath the edge of the raised hood. He was leaning into the engine compartment. He had his hands in there and what if—

He twisted his head around to make eye contact through the windshield. "Hit the gas again, Lisa."

It was his hand, and he should know what he was doing.... She hit the gas. He looked back toward the engine. She let out a breath.

"Good. One more time.... Okay. Thanks. That's good for now."

She climbed out, aware that the inside of the car had been warmer than she would have expected.

He was fiddling with something, but she couldn't see what it was. Even if she could have seen it, she wouldn't have been able to identify it.

"What's wrong with the car?"

"Hugh says it's lost its pickup."

"And you think you know what's causing that?"

"There're a few possibilities. Could be that the diaphragm in the spark advance is leaking. Or it could be that the distributor housing isn't rotating the way it should. That could be caused by a couple of things."

"Like?"

"No vacuum, so it's not being pulled around." He looked up. "That's why I needed you to rev the engine— I should have felt the vacuum at the end of the hose, and I didn't."

"So you're good at this, too?"

"Too?"

"Tracking down problems in cars and tracking down criminals." If that final word had a twist to it, so be it. "Nothing that makes you get really close to people."

He winced. He masked it well and quickly, but she'd seen it and felt it. She hadn't meant to hurt him...had she?

He looked over the engine, then turned toward the house, where she could hear Hugh's chuckle and Ruth's laughter rising like a syncopated chord of amusement. He glanced at her again before his gaze returned to the engine.

"Right now this is the only thing most people would say I'm good at."

Not his career? When she'd known him, he'd been so pleased to be a newly minted detective. Had he been disappointed in his career?

Had the failure to find that final necklace Alex had hidden somehow blighted Shane's career? His dreams?

She didn't care. She *wouldn't* care. But she could be fair without caring about his dreams.

"I shouldn't have said that—about you staying away from things with people."

He shrugged as if he didn't care. "You know some folks say duct tape is the most useful material on earth."

She was going to be fair whether he wanted to hear it or not. "It wasn't true, either. You have to be good with people or you'd never get anything out of witnesses, not to mention confessions."

"Don't you watch television?" With sure motions he wrapped silver tape around what looked to be a piece of narrow rubber hosing. "We yell at people until they tell the truth, except for the times we beat it out of them."

"I know that's not how you operate. You forget I have firsthand knowledge of how you conduct an investigation." His wrapping motion checked, then resumed.

"Plus, seeing how you've been with people here, it's clear you feel a connection. I'm sure you get the most valuable information from witnesses by that...that involvement."

He continued at his task, holding on to the silence like his ace in the hole. Finally his voice came, as unhurried as his motions.

"In my years of law enforcement, I've felt sorry for some witnesses. I've distrusted a good number of them. And I've liked a few. But connection? Involvement?" He cut the end of the tape, meticulously finishing off the repair before he raised his head and met her eyes. "Once."

The single word slammed into her ribs. No, that was her heart.

"I, uh, have to get this to Ruth." Not waiting for a response, she headed for the back door in a hurry.

Ruth answered practically before Lisa's knuckles touched the wood of the door.

"Oh, good, the Johnston papers." She tucked the envelope up by her purse. "Now, come have an iced tea. Looks like you could use it. You're flushed."

Ruth's look shifted to over Lisa's shoulder, aimed right at where Shane was working. Before Lisa could deny whatever it was the older woman might be thinking, Ruth went on, "It's a warm day. We could all use some."

Ruth drew her inside and had the tea poured in no time. She dispatched Hugh with a glass for Shane. A car engine revving outside informed Lisa that Hugh must have taken over her job, so there would be no reason for any further conversation with Shane. She relaxed, listening to Ruth's menu plans for an upcoming gathering at Taylor and Cal's ranch.

But when Lisa left the house, Hugh was nowhere in sight.

"Hey, Lisa."

She could keep walking, pretend she hadn't heard Shane. But why would she do that unless she was running away? Scared. She stopped.

"I could use more help."

She'd sworn she would never help him again. But here she was.

"So you didn't succeed."

"Not yet. But you should know by now that I'm a persistent man." Something about the way he said that strummed at the back of her neck. "If you'd hit the gas again…?"

She left the car door open, perched on the edge of the seat and stretched her leg to press the pedal.

"Good. That's enough." Before she was out of the car, he was adding, "If you could stick around, I'll need to check it again after I…"

The rest of it dissolved into muttering about resistance, a housing, rotation and an open-ended crescent wrench.

He could get Ruth or Hugh to hit the gas pedal. She didn't have to—

"Do you remember saying you thought my middle name showed my high-class connections?" He asked the question without raising his head. "That day we got out of the rain, remember?"

"Yes." Startled by the proof that *he* remembered, she left it at that.

"You want to know the real story? I believe I got that middle name from where I was conceived."

His delivery was so dry that it took her an extra beat to get it. "Ford? As in—"

"Back seat." He nodded. "Mom and Dad were married when they were both eighteen—a couple weeks after high school graduation. Now, Grandma Kenney would be quick to note that I wasn't born until a full eleven months later. You might wonder why they'd take to the back seat of a Ford when they were married, but they were living with Grandma Kenney, and if you knew her, you'd understand. Besides, with Dad working at the garage, they had access to plenty of cars. I'm lucky my middle name's not Buick or Chevy or VW Bug. Not that they admit it. Subject comes up and Dad chuckles, then Mom giggles, and you can't get anything out of them.''

His mouth curved with an easy smile, the creases at the corners of his eyes softened into laugh lines. And his voice... His voice was low and smooth. Even the hard glitter of determination that had stared out at her since his arrival in Knighton eased and softened.

It was the Shane Garrison she'd known one spring in New York. The Shane Garrison who had evaporated before her eyes when he'd clasped handcuffs on Alex and who had stared through her in court as if he'd never seen her.

All these years she'd believed the first Shane had been a sham. And she'd been a gullible fool for falling for it—for him. Yet, here was evidence of that old Shane back. Or were her hopes leading her astray again?

"But the theory fits the facts," he continued. "They didn't have another kid until we'd moved out of Grandma's place—after Dad started buying off the garage from his old boss and had a couple years of running it under his belt. I was six when we moved into our own house, seven when my brother was born.''

For the first time she empathized with Shane's drive to solve mysteries. A little information just produced more questions. And questions piling up in your head could make anyone want to search out answers.

"Your father owned a garage?"

"Yup. Outside Beloit, Wisconsin. And Mom worked a cash register at a grocery store for several years before she became a receptionist at a dentist's office. What you took for blue blood was blue collar."

"How did you—why did you…?"

"Become a detective?"

She nodded.

"There was a break-in at the garage one night. I was about ten. I remember the phone waking me up. When I heard what happened, I was thrilled—this seemed like real excitement. I sneaked out and rode my bike in the dark to the garage. Dad was so distracted he didn't even send me home. Just let me sit in the corner and listen.

"Didn't take long before it didn't seem like such an adventure. They'd ransacked the place. Took money, tools and a piece of new equipment. Dad had been saving for it for two years and he'd taken delivery of it three weeks earlier. It was a computer to diagnose engine problems—cutting-edge for those days, and he'd been talking about how it could really make a difference. I remember sitting in that corner and watching Dad. I'd never seen him look so…destroyed." He flicked a look at her, then immediately returned to the engine, squeezing goop from a tube onto a piece.

"Looking back, I can see it was a bad financial setback, especially with Mom pregnant with my sister by then and the insurance never enough. But at the time all I knew was it was unnerving to see my dad that way.

"The cop on the case was an old-fashioned type. Officer Bronski had lived in town all his life, had known my dad all his life. Couldn't have passed the physical required now to save his soul, much less to save his heart. He was way behind the times on methods even then. But he knew his town and its people."

She wanted to play back those words in her mind so she could try to capture the tone and uncover its elusive emotion. But he kept talking.

"Officer Bronski figured out pretty fast who'd done it—one of 'em had helped deliver that computer. The cops charged them, but they never found the stuff that had been stolen, and there wasn't enough to take them to trial.... I remember the day Dad came home from the courthouse. He didn't say a word. Mom just looked at him, and he shook his head.''

He put the top back on the tube of goop.

"It took the starch out of Dad. He'd been working eighteen-hour days, six days a week for a lot of years to make a go of that place.''

And ten-year-old Shane, his eyes already observant, his mind quick, had watched his father and put together the clues that would elude many adults.

"About three months after those boys got off, though, we got another call late at night from that same cop, telling my father something had been delivered to the garage and he'd better get it secured before somebody thought to take it.'' He straightened. "It was that diagnostic computer. A few scratches, but working.''

"The same one? But how—?''

"Officer Bronski. He'd put the heat on them so fast they hadn't had time to dispose of it—it's not the sort of thing that could be fenced around the corner. They would have had to get it to Milwaukee or Chicago. And he never gave them the chance. He was on them that first night, and he didn't let up. Kept busting them for every petty infraction he could find—jaywalking seventeen times for one. A cop doing that now would face harassment charges, but it was Bronski's way. He let it be known that if they wanted to lose him as a shadow, they better see that a certain piece of equipment got back to Garrison's Garage. You should have seen my father's face. It was like who he was and what he did was all secure again. What's the quote? 'God's in his heaven, and all's right with the world.'''

"Robert Browning.''

But her mind had jumped to another quote. This one spoken three days ago by Shane Ford Garrison. *You'd have felt a lot more secure wearing these than those little sandals you always had on.*

Security, sandals, cowboy boots, bad guys, Officer Bronski and a ten-year-old Shane all jumbled through her head. Was there a pattern or was she seeing things?

"So life got back to normal at the Garrisons'. But I'd decided I wasn't going to follow in my father's footsteps. I was going to be a cop."

"Because Officer Bronski was your hero."

"No." His eyes glinted at her. "I was ten, but I wasn't stupid. After the break-in, I went to the library and read up on law enforcement. Kids' books. But even so, I thought Bronski was a throwback who should have been left back with the dinosaurs—he broke about a dozen basic law enforcement principles, not to mention harassing those suspects right out of their civil rights. But he produced the one thing that came near to resembling justice for the victim of a crime. He set things right. I decided I wanted to do that—and I wanted to do it better than Bronski."

Set things right. She added that phrase to the jumble in her head.

"Why New York?"

"I didn't start there. I got a degree, joined the force in Milwaukee. I was young—they'd jumped me a couple grades in school—and I was gung-ho, and I got a bit of a reputation. I moved up real fast. Then I crossed paths with this guy pretty high up in NYPD, and he encouraged me to apply there. So I did, and I got the job, made detective. End of story."

Maybe this detective stuff was contagious, because she knew that might be the end of the story but it sure wasn't the whole story.

"How'd you cross paths with the guy from NYPD?"

His mouth gave that little quirk.

"His son and daughter-in-law's wedding gifts were stolen while they were on their honeymoon. I caught the case.

With the newlyweds in Europe, he flew in to check things out. He liked how I worked. And I got the job done.''

"Just like Officer Bronski."

"Better than Bronski. I got the stuff back in two days and I didn't stretch any laws or break any regs to do it." He looked up and sighed. "Go ahead and say it."

"Say what?"

"I sound like a bragging egomaniac."

Surprised, she laughed. "No need to say it when you know it." He laughed, too. And the sound of it had her searching for a distraction. If his grin was dangerous, his laugh was lethal. "So are you going to be able to fix Hugh's car?"

"It's fixed. He needs a new hose, but it'll run okay to get him to where he can pick one up."

He released the hood, letting it drop into place with a resounding thud, revealing his triumphant grin. And heaven help her, she grinned back.

Chapter Six

Shane reaped his reward for fixing the car in homemade chocolate cake. Two layers, with frosting thick enough to form another layer. If this had been the payment at Garrison's Garage, he might have joined the family business.

The envelope he'd seen Lisa clutching on her way into the house was propped next to Ruth's handbag on a shelf by the back closet.

"Lisa dropped off something from work for you?" Ruth made a noncommittal noise that he chose to take as a yes. "Does she always work seven days a week?"

"Between the office and her classes, yup, she pretty much does."

"Office and classes, but no social life?"

"I wouldn't know."

Hugh snorted, and Ruth daggered him with a look.

Shane tried another approach. "Working all the time's not good for someone."

Approval crept into Ruth's expression. "Haven't I told her that a thousand times? Balance is what that girl needs."

He shook his head in sympathy. "Everybody needs a hobby or pastime to take their mind off work. Working on cars helps me clear my head. But I don't suppose Lisa has anything like that to balance her life, like you said. A hobby…or…"

The nibble on that bait came from Hugh, rather than Ruth. "She used to make jewelry. Real good she was, too."

"But that was her job."

"Not when she was growing up," Hugh countered. "Just a little tyke and she'd be finding stones and polishing them, and putting them together. First she'd do a drawing of what she wanted it to look like. Real nice those drawings were."

"So drawing's her hobby."

"Said she used to. Used to draw all the time. Not anymore."

"Not even jewelry designs?"

Ruth rejoined the conversation. "Especially not jewelry. It's too bad, too. I have five pairs of earrings she made me, and they're things of beauty." His gaze flicked to the feather and bead earrings she wore. "Not these, I keep Lisa's for best. But she hasn't made anything, my goodness, must be since before she came back from New York City. Yup, not since she came back from New York City."

At Ruth's repetition, Shane met her pointed look. The words and look together said that she considered the two events cause and effect.

If she was right, it was one more thing to hold Alex White accountable for. Lisa's joy at designing and creating pieces had been strong and free that spring. Yet these people who knew her so well said Lisa hadn't done these two things she loved ever since.

Except she had. She had made those sketches at her kitchen table.

Maybe it was sort of like Pavlov's dogs. She'd spent so

much time sketching around him in New York that the old habit kicked in. Or maybe it was something else, something more.

Not that he thought he was a miracle worker. But it was a fact that after all these years she'd started sketching again after he showed up in town.

She hadn't even been aware of doing it. She'd been totally surprised when he'd pointed it out. His satisfaction dimmed a notch as he remembered her stricken look and its similarity to her expression at White's arrest. It hadn't been a pleasant surprise.

But her drive to create was another piece of the amazing young woman he'd known eight years ago. A damned big piece. And whether she liked it or not right this moment, having it stir to life was a good thing. Now, if he could help it along…

"Why're you grinnin' like a hyena, boy?" Ruth asked.

"I wouldn't say like a hyena."

At her husband's objection, Ruth turned her head fast enough to swing her earrings. "What's wrong with hyenas?"

"Nothin' wrong with 'em. 'Cept you and me never seen one 'cept in books or TV and such. Better to pick something closer to home."

"Like what? A coyote?" Ruth appeared to be intrigued despite herself. "Wait, I got it. Grinnin' like old Monica when she'd found a good tree limb to scrape a dude off."

"That's it! That's the bull's-eye. You hit it exactly. He was grinning just like that." He turned to Shane, beaming. "Told you my Ruth was smartest one around. Monica's an old mare of ours we rent to a dude ranch. Crotchety thing, but too old to do any real damage. When she unseats one of those dudes, she grins so wide you expect she'd break out laughin' any second. And that's how you looked—she got you to the life, my Ruth did."

Ruth tried to hide her pleasure, demanding of Shane, "So what were you grinnin' about?"

By this point he'd controlled his facial muscles.

"I was given a commission by a friend to come up with an idea, and I think I might have done that."

"What idea? What friend?"

"Can't tell—I'm sworn to secrecy."

She snorted, but pushed the matter no further. Shane figured it was fifty-fifty whether she did that out of a reluctance to pry into someone else's business or out of recognition that her husband's abrupt interest in hustling Shane out of the kitchen meant the idea had to do with her.

What mattered more was that when he told Hugh his idea, the older man whistled with admiration. Shane was genuinely pleased to have helped Hugh. And it didn't hurt that his solution fit his own agenda.

"Turkey club," Rainie announced as she put the plate before Lisa on Thursday. It was a return to routine, and it felt good. Really good.

"Thanks. Oh…Rainie, I wondered if I could ask you a question?"

"Sure thing." She propped her hands on her hips.

"I, uh, I wondered… It seems like you took to Shane Garrison right away, and I just wondered…" There didn't seem to be a subtle way to ask this. "Why?"

Rainie shrugged. "He's nice looking, polite, tips real good and he's your friend. I know folks say New Yorkers are cold, but that white-haired guy and Shane have been good people. Shows you got good taste, you know? Fifteen years and three kids ago, and I'd give you a run for your money for Shane."

"Oh, no, Rainie, it's not like that. You've misunderstood."

The older woman chuckled as she turned away. "Sure, sure."

Minutes later a shadow fell over Lisa's books. Her heart jolted once, then immediately settled.

It couldn't be Shane, because she couldn't have missed

his presence among the stool sitters on her way to her usual spot. And she would have sensed if he'd come in.

Couldn't have missed him? Would have sensed him?

She jerked her head up, hoping that the shadow caster would be Shane Garrison just to prove her foolish self wrong.

Hugh Moski retreated a step at her expression. "Didn't mean to bother you, Lisa."

She swallowed a slug of guilt. "No, no, Hugh. I was startled. Don't go. I'm sorry."

Her rush of words halted his retreat, but he didn't venture any nearer. Great. Now Shane had her frightening off people she'd known all her life.

"You sure? I know you don't like being disturbed when you study. I thought…well, I got something particular to ask you."

She didn't like to be disturbed. She certainly needed to study. And under the circumstance, she wasn't free to agree with either of his statements.

"Please, sit down, Hugh. And ask away."

She gave him a smile that must have looked better than it felt, because Hugh eased onto the opposite seat. "I'm hoping you'll help me out of a real pickle, Lisa."

That caught her complete attention. "Of course, I'll do anything I can to help. What sort of pickle?"

"It's Ruth. It's our anniversary. Fiftieth. And I—"

"Fiftieth!"

"Shh. Not so loud. I don't want the town knowing. Ruth and I talked it over, and what with Brenda's divorce and Jamey's middle boy so sick, we decided we're just celebrating the two of us. So don't say anything. Promise?"

"I promise." But then why was he telling her?

"Problem is, I don't want this to slide by without giving her something special, you know? Something that every time she looks at it, she thinks that saying yes to Hugh Moski fifty years ago wasn't such a bad idea after all. You follow me?"

She blinked back tears. "That's—" She swallowed adjectives that didn't do the sentiment justice, and settled for "I follow you."

"Good. Well, I was thinkin' and thinkin' and not comin' up with the first idea. Really startin' to wear me down, I'll tell you," he confided. "But then, uh…well *I* came up with an idea sure to make Ruth happy as a flea in a doghouse."

Lisa blinked at the image, but didn't let it detour her. "That's great, Hugh. You want me to help you shop for this present?"

"Naw. I want you to make 'em."

"*Make—?* Make *what?*" But the grinding in her stomach already knew.

"Earrings."

She felt as if she'd stepped onto a sheet of black ice. It looked normal enough, but a move in any direction could mean falling flat on her—

"Hugh, I don't do that anymore."

"Not regular, but you'd do this like a special commission wouldn't you? For me? For Ruth?"

That sounded like a line he had practiced. But Hugh had no such guile in him. Were her feet starting to slide out from under her?

"I haven't made jewelry in years. Not designs or—" A memory of the sketches she'd done so mindlessly while Shane questioned her rose up in time to stop her from telling a lie. "Much less producing a piece. I don't know where my tools are and—"

"Bet you could find 'em with a little lookin'."

"—there's finding the right materials."

An image of the agates she'd picked up at the Slash-C last week popped into her head. Two of them had been nearly identical. They could be worked into a design that—

She drew in a deep breath. It had no steadying effect, but it gave her the oxygen to say, "Hugh, I'd be happy to help you find someone to make earrings for Ruth. There are excellent craftsmen around, and I know you'd love their work.''

''Ruth loves *your* work,'' he said. ''Still wears every last pair you ever made her, even when you were knee-high. Lays them out on this piece of velvet she's got and covers 'em up like they're gold and wears them so proud.''

Lisa couldn't talk because the sharp sting in her eyes seemed to be attached to a lump in her throat. That left the floor to Hugh, who took it as a sign of acquiescence.

''I thought something fancier than usual for when she wears her best dress. Something with gold—I read that's for fiftieth anniversaries—and maybe polished kinda stones, you know, that look pretty? Something from 'round here like would mean something special to her. How's that sound to you?''

''Oh, Hugh…''

''Well, if you don't like the stones and gold, I know you'll come up with somethin' good.''

''It's not that, Hugh. Gold and stones would be good.'' Small stones, like the ones she'd picked up, and the gold spiraled, so there would be movement and shadow…. One of the sketches she'd done that day Shane was at her house might have given her a start, if she'd kept it. More likely, it would have been useless. Desperation pushed out more words. ''I don't know if I can do it. It's been so long.''

''You can do it. Known you all your life, girl, and you can do whatever you set your mind to.'' Hugh heaved a sigh as he pushed up on the table to get out of the booth. ''Sure am glad that's taken care of. Now I can quit worrying.''

And she could start.

Shane fell in step with her as she passed the library grounds on her return to work.

''Hi, Lisa. Got a minute?''

''I need to get back to work.'' She cut him a look. ''And

I do not want another self-defense lesson. I have better things to do.''

"Like what?" He put out a hand to stop her rejoinder. "Besides working. Or studying. What else do you find to do around here?''

"Boy, if that doesn't sound like a New Yorker! And when was the last time you went to a Broadway show, huh?''

"A cop's salary—''

"Museums? Even a cop's salary can stand a museum.''

"You dragged me to so many, I've been recovering.''

"For eight years? That's an awful lot of recovering.''

"For some things eight years isn't long enough to recover.''

She tried to shut it out, but that comment tripped her heart.

"We never went to enough museums that you would need eight years to recover. So are you becoming one of those New Yorkers who bemoan other areas' lack of culture and sophistication when they never bother to experience it themselves in their city?''

He gave a shrug, while a tiny grin pulled at his mouth. "Still doesn't answer what there is to do here.''

"It's not my responsibility to find fun things for you to do. You can always leave.''

"It's you I was thinking about.''

"Of course, because you're always working, so you're not interested in doing fun things.''

"A policeman's plight.''

Under the lightness there was an edge. Like he'd heard that before. Or like he wasn't happy about always working. Could she have been right about not finding the necklace causing trouble for his career? The owner was certainly rich enough and influential enough—all Alex's clients had been—to pressure the department.

But he was going on. "You used to talk about riding

and roping on the ranch. But I haven't seen you do any of that. All you've done is work, go to class and study.''

Had Shane's bosses made him come out here? That could explain the withdrawal she sensed from him sometimes. Maybe he'd resisted. Not wanting to disrupt her life again.... Or not wanting to see her again?

''I do other things.''

''Like?''

''Like go to Billings. I'm taking a half day off work and going up Wednesday.'' She'd retrieved two boxes of her tools from the old barn at the Slash-C. The trunk with mementos from New York and her childhood efforts was there, too. That she left, unopened. She'd found the tools in good condition, but she needed soldering flux, and she was low on polishing compound—not the sort of things the Knighton Food Stop carried. And if she ordered them through Tim Balder it would be all over town that she was making jewelry again.

''For?''

''Shopping.''

''Going to buy a pair of sandals?''

''No.'' She refused to consider a ridiculous warmth at the way his glance skimmed down her khaki-covered leg.

''Okay, one shopping trip. No sandals. What else do you do?''

''Get together with friends and neighbors.'' His skeptical look goaded her into continuing. ''For example, Saturday we're getting together to paint Taylor and Cal's house. They've been so busy getting the ranch in shape they haven't had a chance to do anything about the inside, and we're going to help them out with a painting party. It's the same idea as the old barn raisings. Not the sort of thing that would interest someone addicted to the sophisticated cultural life of the Big Apple.''

''Okay.''

''Okay, what?''

''I'll come with you.''

"You'll co—? I did *not* invite you."

"No, but you challenged me, and that's close enough for anybody from Wisconsin. And I'll drive you to Billings on Wednesday. I've been looking for a chance to see more of the country."

When she came out of work at noon Wednesday and found him waiting with his rented SUV already gassed up, she could have refused and driven her own car. But she wouldn't have put it past him to follow her. Besides, she had a better idea.

"Wait here. I'll be right back."

She returned to the office, picked up what she needed and was sliding into the passenger seat of the SUV in practically no time.

"What's that?"

"Notes for my class. I'm behind because of you, and as long as I don't have to drive I can make good use of this time."

"I thought you were going to tell me about the countryside we were passing through."

"And I thought I was going alone," she retorted.

That corner of his mouth quirked. "No history lessons? No local legends? No cattle lore?"

"No, no, and there's not much on this earth less lore-prone than a cow." The quirk bloomed into a grin. She turned away. "I'm going to work."

"You work too much," he grumbled.

"And you would be the pot?"

"Huh?"

"Calling the kettle black."

He gave her a sharp look, manufactured a smile she didn't buy, then lapsed into silence.

Now that was an interesting reaction, she thought as she arranged her project notes for her Using Computers course. Sort of the first cousin of his no-reaction reaction.

Maybe this was the way to deal with Shane.

She'd tried erecting a wall to keep him out, and he'd found ways to come over, around and through it.

But this way, instead of fighting to keep him out, she made his intrusion on her life work to her benefit. Why hadn't she thought of this before? It fit in with that article she'd been reading for her management class about using other people's energy instead of resisting it. Besides, she could keep a closer eye on him.

"Garrison!"

Tony Prilossi picked up the line almost as soon as Shane told the secretary his name. If it had been someone else, Shane might have thought the other man was worried about him.

"So, you calling to tell me you're going to start work sooner than scheduled?"

A vision of returning to New York formed in his mind, and even with plugging in the new job it fell flat. Something nudged him to add Lisa to the vision and see what happened. He ignored the temptation.

"There's still work to do here."

"No gaudy necklaces dropped into your lap yet, huh?"

"No." But he hadn't been thinking of the necklace; he'd been thinking of Lisa.

"Anything else drop into your lap? Like maybe that girl?"

"Prilossi—"

"I know, I know. It's strictly business. Like everything else with you. One-track mind."

"I work on cars." Ordinarily he would have ignored Tony's ranting—in fact, he realized with mild surprise, he already had ignored this rant from Tony several times. Maybe it was hearing it so soon after discussing Lisa's workaholic habits that spurred him to respond.

"You work on cars—and notice *work* cropping up again—when you're trying to figure out a case. That's no more getting away from your work than reading a law book is for me.''

Stung into defensiveness, Shane said, ''Yeah, you're not exactly Good Time Charlie yourself, Prilossi. You work long, hard hours.''

''Sure, but I also play—I play racquetball, I play poker and I play with people's minds. I even enjoy the company of a lady in a social setting now and then. You know, a date. Maybe a glass of wine, candlelight, a good dinner. The kind of relaxing evening that lets you unwind.''

''I'm not wound tight like you, Prilossi, so I don't need unwinding.''

''No, you're more like a machine running on batteries that keep going and going. Someday even those batteries run out.''

''So why are you hiring me?''

Prilossi paused before saying, ''Hell if I know. I suppose you'll be of some use until the batteries give out. Especially if you get your ass back here soon. When're you coming back?''

''I've still got six weeks.''

''So why're you bothering me now?''

''If anybody calls about what I'm doing out here, you can tell them I'm coming to work for the D.A.'s office, but nothing about the White case, understand?''

''Why would anybody call—''

''They might not. I just want this covered.''

After meeting Taylor, it had struck Shane that if she decided to do some digging on one Shane Garrison, she was plenty sharp enough to reach Prilossi and find out about the Alex White case. Lisa didn't want that—and sure as hell, she'd blame him if anything got out.

It was to avoid a setback in his relationship with a witness, he told himself after hanging up with Tony Prilossi.

The reason for finding a nice restaurant and making a reservation for two for that night was a little hazier.

* * *

Staying in Billings for dinner had seemed completely logical when Shane proposed it.

Lisa's stop at the supply store had taken longer than she'd expected—she'd fallen into conversation with the manager about innovations over the past few years—so waiting to eat at home would have meant a very late dinner.

His choice of restaurants had startled her. She'd been expecting fast food or a chain restaurant heading out of town. Instead, he'd driven to the historic area downtown. When she'd balked, he'd explained he'd asked someone for a recommendation of a good restaurant. Being a stranger in town he'd simply followed their advice, and that's how they'd ended up in a cozy, dimly lit corner booth. The specialty meat loaf was delicious, so was the glass of Cabernet Sauvignon he'd encouraged her to order. But she couldn't shake the feeling more was going on in Shane's mind than he was saying.

She thought about their talks the past few days. When he'd followed her to the ranch and again at the Book Pass, he hadn't brought up the necklace or Alex.

But that didn't mean he wasn't working on the case. As she knew from experience.

At the moment his attention appeared to be completely devoted to the piece of apple pie the waitress had placed in front of him. Warm apple pie with a wedge of cheddar cheese.

Shane had turned on the charm to persuade the waitress to add the cheese, which was not included on the menu. But from the moment he'd smiled up at the fiftyish woman, Lisa knew the cheese was a done deal.

"Mmm," he approved of the first bite.

His eyes were half-closed, the lashes casting shadows on his cheeks, and his mouth relaxing into a dreamy curve. He looked like a man who'd had his every need fulfilled. Was this how he looked after—

No, she wouldn't go there. U-turn. Think of something else.

Was this how he'd felt watching her eat her BLT, was that why he'd said—

Almost as bad. Something else, anything else.

"Just like your mother makes?" She tried to smile to ease the tension in her voice.

"Not as good as that—she makes the best apple pies ever—but it's good. Especially with the cheese. Can you imagine expecting to serve apple pie to someone from Wisconsin without cheese?"

"Horrors."

"Don't scoff until you've tried it. Here," he secured another forkful, along with a portion of cheese, "try some."

"No, I—"

The fork was already at her lips. Reflexively she opened them. Sweet, tart, sharp, flaky, warm, smooth flavors slid over her tongue.

"Mmm."

She felt the tines of the fork retreating, and opened her eyes to find the blue fire of Shane's gaze pinned on her lips.

She swallowed hard, teetering on the edge of choking, until she grabbed her water glass and took a sip. That helped nearly as much as escaping Shane's look.

"So, your mom is a receptionist in a dentist's office and makes the world's best apple pies. What else does she do?"

"She makes costumes for plays—it started with us kids in grade school, and she doesn't seem to know how to quit. She argues with her mother over recipes and the right way to make tomatoes grow and she worries."

"About?"

"Anything. Everything. It's one of her greatest talents."

"You," she guessed. "And what you do for a living."

Did this woman in Wisconsin whom she had never met—never would meet—worry solely about the physical dangers of Shane's job? Or did she worry that he didn't smile enough, that he didn't relax enough, that he needed more good things in his life to balance the pain that was part of the job description?

"I suppose. I keep telling her..." He met her eyes and let it trail off while he shrugged, as if he recognized that she wasn't buying it, either.

"So, with a mom who worries, of course, you became a policeman in the biggest, meanest spot around—what every mother hopes for."

"How about you?" he challenged. "You were nineteen, and you weren't a cop. Your mother must have worried about you."

"Not really. My father was the worrier about me being in New York."

"I remember—your mom spent time in New York as an actress before she met your dad while she was touring out West."

"You remember that?"

"I remember a lot."

Her heartbeat tripped...then steadied. Remembering details would be essential for a detective. It was an occupational habit.

Shane turned away, and only then did she realize he'd been watching her.

"The trick with parents is to keep reassuring them. Let them see you're fine. Do you go back to Wisconsin?"

"Every year—almost every year. Didn't make it this past year. Otherwise I've gone around the holidays. Sometimes we've celebrated in early January." His eyes lightened. "Mom leaves the tree up, no matter how late I get there."

Just thinking of those reconnections with his family had eased his face in a way that made the hard planes almost boyish.

"Just once a year?"

"Now you sound like Mom. It's not easy getting away. And it gets harder as you get older. You know how that is. You get caught up with your job, and..."

She waited for him to fill in *life*, but it trailed off into silence.

Of course, because his job defined his life. She'd had cause to regret his single-minded devotion to his job. Did he?

"Do they visit you?"

"They're not wild about the city," Shane said. "They didn't have problems when they visited—a grand total of twice—but they keep sidestepping the issue of coming back. I suppose the prices jolted them. They stayed in a hotel because I didn't have any place to put them up. But now I do, so I could..." His eyes narrowed as he considered her. "What's that expression for?"

"God, there were times I tried so hard—"

She drank from her water glass so she couldn't say more.

"Tried so hard to what? You mean when we knew each other before?" Then it hit him. His eyes turned opaque. "To get me to talk."

"Oh, you talked. Just not about yourself. Not anything truly personal. I thought maybe it was being a cop. I even— It doesn't matter. It was a long time ago."

"You even what, Lisa?" His cool, level challenge brought her spine away from the chair back.

"I even read books and articles about cops, trying to understand. I remember one article by a cop's wife who was also a therapist and she said no one who wasn't a cop could ever truly understand."

But the article had also said how desperately many cops needed a deep connection to a world beyond the police force to stay balanced. That had been her dream. That she could be Shane's anchor in that other world. A world with color and beauty and joy.

"That wasn't why I didn't tell you stories about my growing up, Lisa."

"I'm sure you had your reasons."

"I was on a case."

"Right." Her agreement sliced through the air. "You

kept it all black-and-white. Cut-and-dried. It wasn't your
fault...."

*That I fell for you. That I took your black-and-white and
mixed them up into the big box of 124 colors, all of them
bright and full of a future.*

"That Alex got arrested? No, that was his fault."

She didn't want to talk about Alex. And the alternative—
to talk about her feelings back then—was worse.

"It's late. If you don't mind, I'd like to go home now."

Back in his SUV, she announced she was going to try
to sleep, since she had to get up early. She squirmed against
the seat belt, turning her back to him, and found a comfortable position with the side of her head resting against
the seat back.

But she didn't sleep.

His hometown, how he came to be a cop, how he arrived
in New York, details of his family—all the things he'd told
her these past weeks.... How she would have reveled in
each sentence eight years ago. She would have seen it as
fodder for all her foolish fantasies.

Now she had her feet on the ground. She was a reasonable, responsible woman.

But, dammit, why did he have to go and open himself
up to her like this now?

Because even a reasonable, responsible woman could listen to him talk about his family and draw the conclusion
that there might be more than the New York criminal code
in his heart. And that was the path to trouble.

He pulled to a stop in her driveway, turned off the engine
and started to come around to open the passenger door. But
she was already out, heading through the garage toward the
kitchen door.

"Thanks for the ride and dinner. Good night."

"Lisa."

She stopped, one foot on the single step that led up to
the door, but she didn't turn around.

"Eight years ago, I..." From his voice, he was standing

at the open garage door. "Well, let's say I never succeeded in keeping it cut-and-dried in my own head."

The wind sifted through the leaves, brushing them against each other in a ragged sigh. It didn't fill the silence that stretched between them.

She felt as if her feet had sunk into tar. She couldn't move them forward to go into the house or back toward him.

The faint sound of footsteps moved away. The driver's door of his SUV slammed, and the lights arced across the garage as he drove off. Leaving her to wonder about so many things, even as she told herself that wondering was the road to pain.

"Lisa? Will you come in here, please?" Taylor called through the open door of her office.

Lisa took her notepad. It was probably a futile hope that Taylor had dictation in mind. Matty had gone in not five minutes ago, and Lisa had recognized the look in her sister-in-law's eyes. The look Matty got just before she interfered in somebody else's life.

"Close the door, please," Taylor said, "And sit down. We'd like to talk to you. We're worried about you."

"I'm fine."

"You're not fine," Matty said. "I don't know what happened in New York or what Shane Garrison has to do with it. No, don't bother to deny he does have something to do with it. That's not even open to debate, Lisa. But whatever happened it's past time to tell us—"

Lisa heard her familiar response coming from her lips. "I tired of big-city life, and wanted to come home to Knighton."

Matty let out a huff of breath, propped her hands on her hips and said, "Yeah, right. And you just happened to—"

Taylor stepped in. "Lisa, you're my employee and I don't want to cross a line that would make you uncomfortable, but you're also my friend. And I hope you know I would do anything I could to help you."

When Lisa said nothing to fill the slight gap Taylor left, the other woman sighed, while Matty scowled. Taylor picked up smoothly, "I also have to respect your privacy. And if you don't want to confide in us, we're not going to try to drag it out of you, so—"

"The hell we're not!" Matty declared. "Maybe Taylor will let you go around looking like the walking dead and pretend it's your own business, but we're family, Lisa Currick, and I'll drag if I have to."

Lisa giggled.

Not a laugh, not a chuckle, but a call-a-silly-sound-by-its-rightful-name giggle. She couldn't remember the last time she'd giggled. She'd never been the giggling type, not even as a kid. This giggle didn't even sound as if it came from her throat. Not her calm, rational, in-control throat.

"What are you laughing about?" Matty demanded suspiciously.

"I'm not laughing," she got out. "I'm giggling."

She pulled in breath to try to stop the giggles, and it became something close to a sob. Oh, God, she was going to cry.

This was exactly what she'd been afraid of when Shane Garrison showed up.

She'd worked so hard to keep her emotions under wraps, so her heart would obey her head. And now here she was giggling and weeping within half a minute and over nothing. Just a couple of friends caring enough to insist something was wrong.

"Here, Lisa, sit." Taylor's competent hands guided her to a chair. Her knees seemed to crumple, and she dropped to the seat cushion. "You've needed this for a long, long time."

She hadn't cried since...since...a pulse of panic hit her. No, no, not then. She'd cried at Dave and Matty's surprise wedding reception. She breathed again, and that, too, became a sob.

"Well, you can't pretend everything's fine after this!"

"Matty," Taylor's tone gently chided her.

But in an odd way Lisa found her sister-in-law's forthrightness bracing. Or maybe it was relief at not having to pretend she didn't have feelings.

"No, I can't." she agreed.

"Don't worry about that right now, Lisa. Go ahead and cry, you'll feel better."

"No, she won't." Matty said, dropping a box of tissues into her lap. "She'll feel like she's had a cold for a week and she'll look like hell. But it can't be avoided—sort of like sweating out a fever. Or watching the same movie over and over even though the memories hurt every single time."

Lisa looked up at that reminder of when she'd gone to Matty's house during an extremely painful time between Matty and Dave. Matty had been crying and watching a movie that had echoed her past with Dave.

"'You scream, you holler, you keep crying your eyes out. But don't you give up,'" Matty said softly. "Remember? That's what you said to me, Lisa."

She didn't remember the specific words. But she remembered the need to rouse Matty, to get her back to the fighter she'd always been.

But she wasn't Matty. She was practical, calm Lisa. She didn't scream, she didn't holler, she didn't cry her eyes out—despite the momentary evidence to the contrary—not anymore. Not since she'd resolved no more leading with her emotions, no more taking chances.

And she had succeeded in living exactly that kind of life until Shane Garrison barreled back into her life.

"Damn him," she muttered.

"That's better. Though it could use more firepower." Matty pulled a chair up near hers. "Now, I'd be perfectly willing to join in damning this New York detective on your say-so, Lisa, but you know how Taylor is, wanting all those lawyer facts and specifics. So, you better tell us what the no-good creep did.''

"How can you call him a no-good creep when I haven't told you anything?'' Lisa objected with a return to calm reason.

"That's obvious—''

"Because he hurt you,'' Taylor filled in, as she, too, drew up a chair.

So much for calm reason. Her friends' loyalty brought on another spate of tears. When it had ended, though, she did what she had never done before. It was only the broad outlines, not delving into details of what she'd thought she'd felt about Shane, but she told them about her last spring in New York City.

"...and that last day, after they convicted Alex, Shane didn't even say a word. It was so clear—even to naive little Lisa—that he'd used me to get to Alex. With the case over, he had no need for me anymore—not until he decided he needed to find the necklace and showed up here again,'' she concluded.

She turned to Taylor. "There's something else.'' She launched into an explanation of her concerns that Shane might dig up the details of Cal's past and somehow make trouble. It had seemed a lot more convincing in her head than it did when she said it out loud.

Taylor studied her a moment. "I'm confident that won't be a problem, but I'll mention it to Cal.''

But Matty's mind was on her tale of eight years ago.

"And you'd never told anyone this? Not even your parents?'' Something in Matty's tone suggested she saw a specific significance to that. "If they'd known you were involved in a criminal case—''

"They would have swooped in to protect me,'' Lisa picked up, "and to try to make everything right that I'd messed up.''

"Messed up? That's kind of harsh unless you're expecting perfect—"

Lisa talked over her. "And Dave would have been right behind them."

Matty gave an "Ah" of comprehension. She'd had her own battles with Dave's protectiveness.

Lisa nodded. "I couldn't let that happen if I ever wanted to be treated—to feel—like a grown-up. Besides, I'd made the mess—I took the internship with Alex, I naively trusted everything he said and did, and I even more naively failed to see what Shane Garrison truly wanted from me. So I was the one who needed to clean it up."

"But…" Matty's focus shifted away from her, and the tightness across Lisa's shoulders eased. "Taylor, you're awfully quiet."

"Just thinking."

"About?"

Instead of answering Matty, Taylor turned to Lisa. "Was there any talk about your being an accessory?"

"No. Of course not. I wasn't."

"There's no *of course* about it, Lisa. I'm not a criminal lawyer, but if I didn't know you as I do and with these facts in front of me—the way that New York A.D.A. had— I would have been inclined to charge you."

"What!" Matty started. "How can you say—"

"Maybe charged is too strong, but I sure would have investigated you closely. From what you said, others from the studio were investigated."

"But I never did anything."

"How would the A.D.A. know that?"

"Shane knew…."

That was as much as she got out before her own words opened the door in her mind to accept the import of what Taylor had recognized.

"The fact that the A.D.A. didn't investigate you, much less charge you… Well, I suspect Detective Garrison must have had a lot to do with that."

Shane had believed in her eight years ago, while she'd never even considered that he might have—should have—suspected her.

She stood.

"I...uh...I have to go." Matty reached for her, but she moved away. "I have to...I have work to do, and—"

Thinking to do. Hard thinking. About black-and-white swirling together into a confusing, frustrating, streaking mess of gray.

Chapter Seven

A thin man in uniform stepped into the middle of the aisle, preventing Lisa from reaching for the shampoo, which was her reason for being in Van Hopft Pharmacy. That and the overpowering urge to get away from the office, where her thoughts had swamped every effort to work for the past three hours.

Taylor thought Shane had looked out for Lisa's best interests.

Boy, that was an angle she'd never considered.

Perhaps, given her inexperience and her shock over Alex, she could be excused for not looking at other angles at the time. And immediately after, she'd packed away all thoughts about Shane and New York. When he burst back into her life what came out of her box of memories was exactly what she'd put in there—the pain and hurt and confusion of a nineteen-year-old. Maybe it was time to examine those memories in light of the mature, practical person she was now.

But right now she had another representative of law enforcement to deal with.

"How are you, Deputy?" He liked being called by his title.

"I've been better."

She stifled a sigh. Duane Jessup showed no sign of budging, and his look reproached her.

"I hope it's nothing serious."

"It's serious, all right, when a law enforcement officer gets taken advantage of when he's trying to help a citizen."

"I told you, I had no idea Garrison had friends who knew the sheriff. And I've said I'm sorry. What else do you want me to say?"

"You can tell me what I'm supposed to tell the sheriff when he calls up this past Tuesday and rides me for trying to run that fella out of town and blaming it on you when it's clear as day the two of you are seeing each other. You can tell me what you thought you were doing lying to a sworn officer, by saying he was bothering you. You can tell me what you thought you were playing at using an officer of the law in some lover's quarrel. You can tell me—"

"Lover's quarrel? You hold it right there, Duane Jessup. I never—*never*—lied to you. He was bothering me, and I truly wanted—*want* him to leave town. But...but..."

Lord, how was she going to explain this?

"It's complicated. There's some, uh, history he's trying to wrap up. It's not personal. His reasons for being here, I mean. I never intended for you to take any flak over this. And if you think my telling Sheriff Kuerten that you were entirely innocent of anything but good intentions might straighten things out—"

"Today?"

"I'll try. If he's in his office when I get to Jefferson for my class," she promised.

He was smiling as they separated. She had no inclination to smile.

Telling Taylor and Matty had been a relief. And reassessing what had happened might be in line. That didn't mean she wanted to turn her past into a spectator sport for the interested citizens of Knighton and the tri-counties area.

"Oh, I know all about the Alex White case."

Sheriff Kuerten had greeted her warmly when she'd arrived shortly before five-thirty. She'd covered the facts of Deputy Jessup's innocence and that she and Shane had no personal relationship, contrary to popular rumors. But when she'd started with vague references to a *situation* that Detective Garrison thought—erroneously—that she might be able to *provide additional information about,* he'd interrupted with his expansive declaration, and left her gaping.

"You do?"

"Sure. Didn't get much play out here at the time, of course—folks round here aren't interested in rich fellas in Manhattan losing their trinkets. We got our own worries. But I'm up to speed now. I talked to a friend or two, and they told me all about it. Professional courtesy, you know. Told me how this Garrison is fanatical about crossing every *t* and dotting every *i,* and how this situation he's hoping you can help him with is the solitary bent straw in his pack. Not even the owner's after him to find this gew-gaw, since the insurance paid off. But Garrison's got his own standards. Gotta admire a man who wants to leave a clean slate before he goes to another job—"

Another job?

"—especially when he could make that jump to the D.A.'s office and nobody would think a thing about this old case." Sheriff Kuerten nodded to himself. "Yup, gotta admire a professional like that."

Lisa felt the way she had once, getting off a horse that had bucked a blue streak. He hadn't unseated her, but when she dismounted, her head had felt like it was bobbing around on a pipe-cleaner neck.

Shane's career was not in jeopardy. Dissatisfied bosses

hadn't pushed him to come here to find the final necklace. It was his own doing to rattle and shake and dent her safe, sane life.

Including letting the notoriously loose-lipped sheriff know about the Alex White case, and that she'd had a role in it.

"Sheriff Kuerten, you do know this is all confidential, don't you? I mean what Garrison's doing here, and my, uh, cooperation."

"Don't you worry about that any, Lisa, I won't say a word. Professional courtesy, you know."

Shane Ford Garrison was going to answer *her* questions for a change.

And those questions were piling up faster than snow on Cloud Peak in January. Including the question of how she felt about what she'd learned. Not that she expected him to answer that. But with some answers to her other questions from Shane, maybe she could figure it out.

No one answered Lisa's loud knock at Shane's apartment, but the rented SUV was parked beside the steps, so he had to be around.

She was sitting sideways in the front seat of her car with her legs out the open door when he came jogging toward her in the golden twilight. A sweat-dampened T-shirt molded to his chest. Abbreviated shorts showed every inch of his muscle-curved thighs. His motion was rhythmic, controlled, measured.

His head came up when he spotted her car, and his motion changed, the muscles in his legs bunching more forcefully as he sprinted.

"Lisa? Why aren't you in class? Are you okay?" His big hands on her shoulders made her feel almost weightless as she started to stand. He looked her over as if checking for wounds.

"I need to talk to you."

He heaved a sigh and scrubbed at his face with a towel

left on the railing. "Geez, next time you skip class and give a guy a coronary how about a little warning? Come on up."

"No, I—"

"You can wait while I take a shower and—"

"No."

"I've got to take a shower." His mouth quirked. "I don't want Deputy Jessup citing me for polluting Knighton."

He hooked one hand around her upper arm and guided her to the stairs, giving her an encouraging nudge to start up. She should be saying something, objecting. She should at least be thinking something. Instead, every brain wave was devoting itself to imagining that body in the shower.

"And then you can tell me what's wrong," he added as he opened the door and ushered her in.

He pulled items from a stack of clothes on the dresser and went into the bathroom. "Make yourself at home."

The room hadn't changed much since Taylor had lived here. But it had changed.

A pair of his jeans sprawled across the corner of the bed. The legs held an almost lifelike pose, so she could imagine his muscled thighs still inside them. The shower turned on, and it was his muscled thighs out of the jeans that flooded her imagination.

She turned her back on the jeans, as if they were to blame.

A T-shirt had hooked on the arm of the rocking chair in the corner. A duffel sat on the floor beside the chair. Next to the clothes on the dresser, a spattering of change, a wallet and a utility knife gave evidence of a man having emptied his pockets. A laptop computer and papers were on the desk. A magazine lay open on the small sofa. A book on Wyoming history was on the bedside table, beside a mug holding the dried dregs of coffee.

The room wasn't dirty, not even particularly messy. But it had the air of a masculine presence.

That spring in New York he had never invited her to

where he lived, had never indicated the least interest in seeing where she lived—or in being with her in a room with a bed and privacy. Now...now she couldn't deny that he was giving her pieces of himself the way she'd once dreamed. His childhood, his family. But why?

If she had learned one thing from her history with Shane Garrison, it was that the only way to get to the truth was to ask the questions, wait for the answers, then check them out. Not to operate on faith. Or hope.

When he came out of the bathroom, his hair glistening with moisture, his body covered with another pair of shorts—longer than his running shorts, thank heavens—and a loose-fitting T-shirt, she had her focus back on target.

She moved near the desk to give him a wider berth as he passed by on his way to the dresser to return the items to his pocket. She'd started to turn away when a sheet of yellow legal pad paper caught her eye.

"What— Where did you get these?" She spun around, holding the papers—the ones with the sketches she'd made that first day he'd come to her house. "I threw these out. They were in the trash can. You went in my trash?"

"They were on top."

"On—on top?" she sputtered. "You went through trash—*garbage?* How could you do that?"

"Done it more times than I care to remember. A cop's job's a dirty job, but somebody's got to do it. But this time, I saw you toss them out, and—"

"You came back to spy on me because you don't trust me."

"I came back because you'd left your door wide open, and I wanted to see how close I could get without you knowing I was there," he said. "That's the reason I cut those bushes the next day."

"You're a trained professional, of course you could get close enough to see me put something in the trash. Why you could have been halfway across the county and—"

"I was standing not six feet from you when you threw those pages out, Lisa."

"That doesn't explain why you bothered to check what I'd thrown out or—"

"Call me naturally curious."

"Or to keep it when you saw what it was. The only reason to do that was because you didn't believe me that they had nothing to do with the necklace."

"I believed you."

She was shaking her head as he came across the room and opened the desk drawer. "Then why keep these? It doesn't hold together. You had to—"

"Adding to my collection." He pulled out a large envelope and dropped it on the desk.

"What?"

He tapped the envelope. "You were sketching all the time. I like your drawings. So anything you didn't pick up yourself, I kept. You want to look?"

She shook her head. She had not looked at the trunk of materials in storage in the barn, she didn't want to look at these, either. Even with that phrase *I like your drawings* thrumming in her head. Maybe especially not with it thrumming in her head.

"That's why I took these drawings—" He touched the sheet still in her hand, and she put it down on the desk as if it were hot. "When you said you wanted it... But you threw it out, so I figured I might as well take it."

He said it all so matter-of-factly, defusing her roiling reactions. Outrage? Flattery? Uncertainty? She felt them all, yet none fit.

"Let's sit on the steps and watch the sunset," he said. "Don't get to see many sunsets in Manhattan. Want something to drink? Soda? Water?"

"No, thank you. I want to ask you some questions."

"Must be important." He grabbed a bottle of water from the refrigerator and crossed to the outside door, holding it open. "For you to miss class, I mean."

Class. She stopped in the middle of the room. ...*next time you skip class...miss class...*

She hadn't really heard his comments before—now they crashed over her.

She had totally forgotten. She had driven from the sheriff's office to campus thinking only of using the Internet at the library. By the time she'd skimmed the news media mentions that came up under a search for Detective Shane Garrison of the NYPD, even more questions had piled up. Along with the need to find Shane.

"Lisa?" Shane jiggled the door he was holding open with his back. "You want to come out before all the bugs take up residence inside?"

She would make up the class. And she'd worry about how she'd forgotten her schedule later. Right now she would concentrate on getting answers. Feeling wobbly, she passed through the doorway and sat on the top step.

"I talked to Sheriff Kuerten today," she said. Shane sat beside her, leaving five inches between his bare thigh and her chino-clad leg. "He tells me he knows all about the Alex White Case."

"I didn't tell him." He looked directly at her and spoke with decisiveness. "When he talked to people about me he heard things, but it never came from me. When I found out he knew, I asked him to keep it confidential. He promised he wouldn't talk about it to anyone around here—I guess he figured you didn't count. And I've done what I could to keep information from getting back here from other sources."

She wasn't sure what he meant by that, but she believed him—about this.

"The sheriff also told me you've left the police department."

He muttered something that might have been a curse. She waited, but he offered nothing more.

"So, you're not here for your job... You didn't have to come here and make my life a misery. It's not like you have to find that necklace or you won't get the new job. It's already yours. So why do you even care?''

He stilled into that no-reaction posture. "I don't like leaving something undone."

"But you moved to homicide a few years ago and didn't worry about the necklace then."

"How do you know I was on homicide?"

"The Internet reaches Wyoming, too, and that means we can read archives from newspapers all over the world. Sixty-one hits on Detective Shane Garrison/NYPD/homicide. A lot of big cases." Her voice dropped. "A lot of horrible cases."

She'd read the crisp, dispassionate accounts and tried to imagine the horrific sights reflected through the blue of Shane's eyes. Even with the past and present littered with questions, doubts and pain, she had to order her muscles not to reach out for him, to comfort him. Even as he showed no sign of wanting comfort.

"It's part of the job." He cleared his throat and shifted on the step, straightening his right leg. "Like the necklace."

She believed that, yet something about it didn't quite convince her. "It doesn't sound like anybody else is worried about it."

He shrugged.

His bosses hadn't ordered him to follow up on the necklace—that didn't change that he was still here for his job. His vision of his job. Just like Officer Bronski doing what needed to be done to get that stolen diagnostic computer back to his father. What had he said about Bronski?

He set things right. I decided I wanted to do that—and I wanted to do it better than Bronski.

"So my sympathy for you was entirely wasted, thinking you might be having trouble with your job—"

He faced her, his surprise genuine. "Trouble with my job? What made you think that?"

She opened her mouth, then closed it. Her own imagination, that's what.

"You're right. You never said that. It was all my own doing. Okay?"

"Whoa, now you're mad at me because I'm not in the situation you happened to think I was in?"

No, she was mad at herself. But it was a hell of a lot easier to pretend it was at him.

She drew in a deep breath. "Tell me what this new job is about."

He listed the duties and the benefits with as much pizzazz as an IRS instruction manual.

"Why take this new job if you're not interested in the perks?" she asked.

"Who said I'm not interested in the perks?"

She considered his profile. He would still be setting things right in this new job, otherwise he wouldn't have taken it. But there was still something…

"But you're not taking it because of the better pay, more vacation, lighter caseload—and all the other things that would make most people take it."

"I didn't write up a pro-and-con sheet on the job. They asked. I said yes. End of story."

She stood so quickly that her knees felt a little wobbly. "I have to go."

Oh, yeah, she was a champ at getting to the truth. And he was a champ at giving it. The nonanswer shouldn't have surprised her—it matched the nonreaction—and it surely shouldn't have disappointed her.

He caught her hand. Not like the grip around her wrist a week ago at the Slash-C, but the way a man might hold a woman's hand.

"When we get together Sunday afternoon—"

She pulled her hand free of the warmth of his grasp at that reminder of their next scheduled Q. and A. session.

"—I'm going to take you for a drive."

She managed a laugh, a little harsh, a little brittle, but still a laugh. "That's better than being taken for a ride."

You didn't have to come here and make my life a misery. That's how she thought about his being here.

He swore quietly into the darkness beyond the top step. Then he sat up straight.

Well, dammit, if shaking her out of the damned rut she'd sunk herself into made her miserable, too bad. Because the alternative was leaving her tied by fear to only this one spot on the globe, denying herself creativity or fun or laughter.

He wasn't going to quit now. He was going to make things right with her, so she was free to be the person she had been—the person she was meant to be.

He'd find that damned necklace, too.

And then he'd leave.

The sound of someone at the back door the next morning had Lisa's heart hammering in triple time.

"Hey, Lisa."

Matty. Air whooshed out of her lungs as she turned back to cleaning the sink.

"Matty, what's up?"

"I was on the way into town and thought I'd stop by for a cup of coffee before you left for work."

"Help yourself."

"Thanks. I also wanted to see how you are. We didn't finish talking yesterday at Taylor's and— Are you okay? You look…" Her glance sharpened as she poured. "Were you expecting someone else?"

"No. Of course not. I just… It's probably carryover from…" She stopped, getting her thoughts in order. "I suppose you heard about the self-defense lecture at the library?" She hardly needed to make it a question. Matty had probably heard about it while it was happening.

"Shane's on this kick—talking about people hiding outside the door and fighting off attackers. I guess he's got me jumpy." Lack of sleep didn't help, either.

"Is that what he was talking to you about yesterday when he was holding your hand at the apartment?"

Lisa threw the paper towel into the garbage can under the sink and closed the cabinet. "Well, that was a record even for Knighton."

"Joyce was driving by."

"And she had to pick that exact moment, didn't she."

"Was that all it was? A moment?"

Wrapped in a quilt on the chaise longue on her deck, she'd spent most of the sleepless night staring at the moon-tipped peaks of the Big Horns. The sight was like a truth serum. She'd gone to Shane Garrison yesterday hoping he would say he'd come to Wyoming to find her, not the necklace. Despite all the evidence to the contrary, she'd hoped. Like a fool.

She couldn't blame Shane. He'd said from the start that he was here for the necklace.

"Less than a moment. An aberration."

If Lisa had been a gambling woman, she would put money down that Matty was about to start asking the questions clearly tumbling through her mind, and she wouldn't stop until one or the other of them fell over from exhaustion.

"So, the reason I stopped by this morning," Matty said, "was to let you know we heard from your parents last night."

"Which is why I don't gamble," Lisa muttered.

"What?"

"Nothing—so what did my parents have to say?"

"They're having a marvelous time, and they expect to arrive a week from Wednesday."

"That soon?" Was there any way she could get Shane out of town by then? "How wonderful."

Matty met her gaze. Her expression turned thoughtful.

"Did you know I used to feel sorry for you when we were kids?"

"Sorry for me?"

"Yeah, I know—how could I feel sorry for you? You were the one with the perfect family life—the loving parents, the successful ranch, the annoyingly perfect brother, the good grades, the artistic talent, the personality that made everyone like you—heck, you even had straight teeth without braces. It was a good thing there's three years between us or I might have been blinded by all that and hated you."

"Gee, guess I was lucky."

Matty ignored the wry sarcasm and nodded a solemn acknowledgment. "Yes, you were. And that's what made me feel sorry for you."

"Okay, now you've lost me."

"You had everything. And that meant you had no excuse for any mistakes. Some kids in those circumstances might have been real jerks. You took another route—you decided you had to be perfect all the time. That's a hell of a burden to put on a kid. Or an adult."

"Matty, you know my parents too well to think—"

"I'm not talking about Donna and Ed, I'm talking about Lisa. And what you expected—*expect*—of yourself."

Lisa opened her mouth to speak the words of protest bubbling up. But they didn't come out. Had she put a burden on herself by her own expectations? But weren't high expectations what made you strive?

"You know, I might not have been in Manhattan with you, but I spent some years in the big city, too. And I know there's an awful lot out there that can knock a person several pegs down from perfect. I'd be willing to bet that yearling colt of Juno and Brandeis's, that you've been beating yourself up for somehow not living up to your own expectations of perfection.

"Why else would you come back here and take the kind of job that you could do perfectly with one hand tied behind your back—the kind you'd avoided before because filing

and organizing and scheduling are about as far from drawing and designing and creating as you can get. And on top
of that, you become the next best thing to a professional
student. And look at what you've been taking—MBA
courses, for Pete's sake. Acing them, of course.''

"An MBA makes a lot of sense for an office supervi-
sor.''

"Right, and that's what Lisa Louise Currick always
wanted to be, through all those years of art and design.''

No! something in her shouted.

Lisa rallied, spotting an opening. "People change. Like
you have. Look at this turnaround. You were the one heading the committee to tar and feather Shane.''

"Actually, I'm starting to wonder if you've been beating
up on him along with yourself. But I'm holding off judgment for the moment,'' Matty said with great dignity. Dignity that eroded as she added fiercely, "But if he hurts you,
I won't need a committee. I'll do it all myself. Course I'd
have to fight your brother and parents, and probably Taylor
and Cal, and Ruth and Hugh and a dozen others for the
honor. But I'd win.''

Lisa chuckled. A real chuckle. No giggling. And no sob-
bing.

Matty's expression eased. But her voice was deeply serious as she said, "Think about what I've said, Lees. If you
think you've got to be perfect and anything less is failure…
Well, that could explain why you haven't told anybody
about Alex White and the trial and everything before—
because you felt like you didn't deserve sympathy or support or even understanding. Perfection's an awfully small
target. All I want—all any of us want—is for you to be
happy.''

Matty's theories about her being a perfectionist and
about her motives were all things Lisa had extreme doubts
about. But about the other woman's affection and loyalty
she had not a single grain of doubt. That's what tightened

her throat and stung her eyes as they hugged goodbye and her sister-in-law turned to go.

Lisa pulled herself together.

"Hey, Matty. Just so you don't think I've gone completely soft. What you said about being willing to bet the yearling colt from Juno and Brandeis? I do know that's not much of a bet, since you gave that colt to Dave for his birthday."

Her sister-in-law grinned unrepentantly. "Well, you don't think I'd bet this year's foal, do you? This one's mine!"

Shane was leaning against the front of his rented SUV parked behind her car when she came out of the kitchen door Saturday morning. After saying she shouldn't leave the garage door up, he announced he was driving her to Taylor and Cal's for the painting party. She said she was perfectly capable of getting there on her own. He asked if she didn't care about the environment—driving two vehicles when one would do. She threw up her hands.

This made keeping an eye on him easier. And it didn't bother her, not at all, now that she had her head straight again after that foolishness over the news of his job change. She had lost her balance temporarily, but just like Shane said, the important thing was to get both feet back on the ground and prepare for the next kick.

"Hello!" she called out as she opened the screen door at Taylor and Cal's house.

Taylor answered. "We're in the den, Lisa."

Lisa headed through the kitchen toward the den, fully aware of Shane directly behind her. If Taylor was alone, or with Cal, this might not be so bad.

Hope fled as she stopped at the doorway. Taylor was there, but so were Matty and Dave.

"Hi, Shane." Taylor gave him a warm smile.

Shane put his hands on her shoulders to move her out of the doorway so he could shake hands with Taylor. Lisa watched her brother's eyes narrow at the contact, while Matty's eyes lit up. Lisa didn't know which reaction was worse.

"Do you want me to do the introductions?" Taylor offered.

"Oh, no. I'll... Matty Brennan Currick, this is Shane Garrison." Matty bestowed a smile on Shane. He returned it, while Lisa added, "Matty's my sister-in-law. And this is my brother, Dave Currick. Dave, this is Shane."

Dave acknowledged the introduction with a clipped, "Garrison."

Shane stepped forward and reached out a hand to shake. "Nice to meet you, Dave."

If Dave didn't shake his hand... If Shane's gesture was left to wither...

"Shane's a detective from New York City," she added brightly. "We, uh, knew each other when I was in school. He's my friend."

Shane's head came around at that last phrase, but Lisa refused to meet his look. Or the looks she could feel beaming her way from Matty and Taylor. She was concentrating on her brother, mentally ordering him to shake Shane's hand. Dave's mouth took on a grimmer line, but he lifted his right hand from where it had been resting on a ladder and met Shane's still-outstretched hand.

"Good to meet you."

From her vantage point, Lisa could see the shake was hard and fast, with an undertone of challenge.

"I heard a New York City detective was in town. Didn't realize Lisa considered you a friend."

"Neither did I."

Lisa fought a groan.

"Dave, why don't you and Shane go and help Cal with the main attic room." Taylor wrapped a hand around each man's arm and turned them toward the door. "It's a big room, and we're hoping to get a couple coats on, so we need to get started."

The sound of footfalls in the hallway hadn't entirely faded when Matty propped her hands on her hips and said, "After everything you said, I can't believe you brought him."

"I didn't bring him."

"He's here, isn't he? So you must have brought him."

"You don't know Shane Garrison if you think those are the only alternatives."

Matty and Taylor exchanged a look.

"What?" Lisa demanded.

Matty squinted her eyes, as if trying to get her in better focus, then quoted, "'He's my friend.'"

"Well, I had to do something before Dave belted him. It was strictly so Taylor wouldn't have to clean blood off the floors."

"Right. I saw the way he touched you."

"He just wanted to get past."

Matty shook her head. "No *just* about it. He liked touching you. Clear as day. And the *way* he touched you—"

"That's ridi—"

"And the way you looked when he touched you."

"—culous. Absolutely ridiculous. It was nothing. Nothing. And I didn't look any way at all. Don't let your imagination run away with you, Matty."

Before Matty could respond, Taylor stepped between them, holding out a roller and a roller pan to Lisa. "Thank you for your consideration in keeping blood off my floors, Lisa. And since he's here, I'm happy to put him to work. We can always use an extra pair of hands."

"Could you manage to give him the very worst job?"

Taylor nodded. "That's already been arranged."

"Yeah," Matty said with an evil grin, "he's up there in a room alone with Dave and Cal, isn't he?"

As grillings went, it wasn't half-bad.

Not particularly subtle, but then what inquisition was.

Cal Ruskoff's few questions were plenty sharp, but it was Dave Currick who concerned Shane more.

He soon realized Dave was a man divided—trying to look out for his little sister and trying not to cross the privacy line because, after all, she was an adult…and she'd have his hide if she found out.

Out of empathy—he had a little sister who wanted to be treated as a grown-up, too—Shane made his life an open book to the other men, with one exception. Lisa.

Since that was what Dave wanted to know about, though, the rest of those open pages did little to satisfy him. Oh, he didn't lose his temper or anything that blatant. But he kept painting at a faster and faster pace.

Finally, Cal took pity on Shane or maybe on Dave, or possibly on the walls, and suggested Dave go see about getting each of them a soft drink from the cooler out on the porch.

Other than the swish of roller against wall it was quiet for a few minutes before Cal spoke.

"Glad you got Lisa to come."

"Can't say it was my doing."

"Taylor says it was." That clearly was enough for him. "Taylor also tells me Lisa's concerned you'll try to use my past."

Shane knew Lisa didn't trust him. This evidence shouldn't have even nicked his hide. But it did more than nick it. He'd told her he wouldn't use her friends—and she didn't believe him.

He looked up to find Cal watching him. He didn't try to pretend he didn't know what he was talking about. "My understanding is that your connection to your family's business has been lawyered and regulated up one side and down the other."

"It has."

"As long as there's nothing illegal—"

"There isn't."

"—it's no concern of mine."

"Good. I knew you couldn't do much of anything, but if you tried it would bother Lisa."

Shane cut a sharp look at the other man, but he'd resumed painting.

It was another minute or two before Cal spoke again. "I hear you've been spending time at the café. That's not a bad way to get to know folks around here."

"They're friendly, but I'm still an outsider."

Cal nodded. "You should come out here to the ranch and I'll show you around."

"I'd like that, depending on when we could work it out."

"Oh, daytime hours are fine. It's not a ploy to keep you away from Lisa."

"Didn't think my suspicions of your motives were that obvious."

"Maybe it takes one to know one. I'm a suspicious sort myself."

"Guess you know how hard it is being an outsider around here, too."

Cal's eyes were following something in the hall. Shane shifted enough to see it wasn't some*thing,* but some*one.* Taylor. The other man's expression eased, as if he were smiling inside.

"It's a hell of a lot harder staying an outsider around here if they decide they want you in. And they're generous about who they let in." His face changed again, wiping any hint of a smile away. "Unless you hurt one of ours."

"Come and eat!"

Shane recognized that holler echoing up the stairs at one-thirty, but turned to Cal. "Ruth Moski?"

"Yup. She and Hugh don't do ladders anymore, but nothing could keep her from organizing the food."

People had come by all morning. A few stayed only long enough to leave a covered dish or other sustenance for the workers, some for an hour or two of painting, and others,

like Jack Ralston, the foreman from the Slash-C, settled in
to work steadily.

When they reached the kitchen—among the last to get
there, since they'd been up two flights and no one on the
lower floors had dawdled—the need for organization became apparent. The table was loaded, with outposts of food
on the kitchen counters, with one devoted to desserts.

"Don't even think about it," Ruth instructed as Shane
drifted in that direction. "You and Cal get scrubbed up
first, eat some decent food and then we'll see about dessert."

Shane opened his mouth, but Cal nudged him hard
enough to make him stumble toward the door, as the ranch
owner said a meek, "Yes'm."

When they were outside, Cal instructed, "You don't argue with Ruth when she's between you and that kind of
spread."

They washed off a good portion of the paint in the yard
at a hose left over a tub to catch the drippings. Then they
piled plates high with chicken and beef and pasta and sal-
ads, tucking rolls and olives along the edges before returning to the porch to join the other painters.

Shane said hello to a few from the café, but deliberately
made his way to a patch of porch amid a group that included Lisa.

He soon had company.

Four-legged, furry and long-nosed. He remembered the
animal from the Book Pass at the library, and the way the
dog had prepared to come to Lisa's defense. He admired
that, though he did prefer the dog's significantly friendlier
attention now.

"Sin, don't beg."

The dog's ears flicked at Taylor's command, and he lay
down. But if pinning soulful brown eyes on Shane's plate
constituted begging, he didn't obey the command.

"Sin, huh? Is that name a warning?" Shane asked.

Taylor laughed, and several other people chuckled. He

heard the story of how Matty and Taylor had taken in an abandoned puppy as part of a Rescue League, then decided he should go to Cal, and how Cal had named the puppy Sincere—Sin for short—to yank Taylor's chain.

"And now," Matty concluded, "Sin thinks he's a cattle dog—just like I told Cal would happen. So, I was right."

Cal responded to her triumph with a nearly bland expression. "Sin does not think he's a cattle dog—he doesn't think he's a dog at all—so you weren't right."

"He's always trailing you around out with the herd."

"Exactly. He thinks he's a cowboy."

As the laughter faded, Taylor quietly said, "I saw that, Shane."

Not quietly enough because everyone else looked at him. He tried a bluff. "What?"

"The hunk of roll you slipped Sin."

"Oh-ho!" said Matty. "A cop who doesn't obey the rules."

"Laws I obey. Rules…?" He shrugged and openly tossed the dog a piece of beef.

"It wouldn't be so bad," Taylor said with resignation, "except everybody here's been doing the same thing and he's going to be waddling by the end of the day."

Dave put his empty dish aside. "I don't believe I've ever met a cop socially before."

Matty snorted in disbelief. "Are you kidding? The number of times you were stopped for speeding when we were kids?"

"That's not exactly a social situation," Dave said.

"Well, it sure wasn't sociable some of the things you called them," Matty agreed.

That drew muffled guffaws, though the offenders presented straight faces when Dave looked around.

When everyone headed back to work it didn't seem like an accident to Shane that where they assigned him to paint was nowhere near wherever Lisa was. Not that being in the same room would have helped—he'd still be left wondering what was going through her mind.

About four o'clock Lisa found herself back in the den, painting trim with Matty and Taylor.

She went on alert when she realized the desultory conversation had picked up steam.

"I have this theory—" Matty shot Taylor a look that Lisa intercepted. When Lisa raised her brows in question, Taylor lifted one shoulder, signaling ignorance. "—about romantic relationships."

Lisa groaned.

"Look at the bright side, Lisa," Taylor said, "a Matty theory is better than a Matty plan. At least you don't have her meddling in your life by sending you out in a blizzard on a wild goose chase."

"What are you complaining about?" Matty shot back. "You got a great guy out of the deal—a great guy and a great dog. Besides, I remember a couple women concocting a plan of their own that meddled in my life big time."

"Nothing was ever proven," Taylor said primly.

They all laughed.

"Anyway, about my theory," Matty started again.

This time Taylor joined Lisa's groan.

"Hey, it's a good theory. In fact, I think it would be the key to stopping the fighting in the Middle East, the ethnic wars in the Balkans and the troubles in Northern Ireland."

"This theory is going to stop war and cure romantic relationships? This I've got to hear," Taylor said.

"Good. My theory is everything would work out if nobody talked or thought about the past. Just get on with the future and stop raking up the past all the time. Because nothing anyone ever says or does is going to change the past, it's only going to change the present and the future."

"I seem to recall you and Dave doing a lot of thrashing out of the past," Lisa objected.

"We did. But that wasn't all we did. If we'd stuck with

trying to solve things in the past tense we'd still be stuck where we were when I first came back. What changed everything was when we started talking about *now*."

Matty gestured with her paintbrush. "The trick is that nobody can use anything from the past to justify what they're doing now or in the future. No saying, well, you did that to me then, so I'm going to do this to you now. That never works. Both sides—countries or religions or sexes—have to say 'we're here *now*, where do we want to go and how are we going to get there?'"

"And that's what you and Dave did?" Taylor asked.

"Yup. Anything and everything that had happened in our past wouldn't have made one bit of difference toward us having a future if we hadn't done that."

Lisa put down her brush.

"Something wrong, Lisa?"

"No, no, I need a break—bathroom break."

"Better use the half bath off the kitchen. Jack's painting the one off the guest room, and who knows what state the one upstairs is in."

As Lisa left the room, she heard Matty quietly ask Taylor a question that sounded like, "Do you think it helped?"

Lisa didn't return to the den. She found Jack Ralston backing out of the guest bathroom, having finished those walls, and told him she'd been sent to do the trim.

He nodded, and headed off—no doubt to find another solitary spot to work. At times in the years since he'd become foreman of the Slash-C, she'd wondered how—and why—Jack spent so much time alone. But right now she understood completely.

She stroked white paint across the top of the window trim with precision. Getting her hands to make the materials do what her mind envisioned had been one of her assets in making the jewelry she'd designed. These past weeks she'd been surprised—*pleased?*—at the return of her hand coordination and steadiness as she worked on the earrings for Ruth.

Too bad *coordination* and *steadiness* didn't apply to her mental processes.

Before Shane's arrival she'd been so sure of how she needed to live to be safe from making another life-exploding mistake in judgment.

And now? Her carefully constructed regimen was crumbling. Her schedule was shot to hell. She was behind in her course project. She'd missed classes. She'd indulged in more emotion in these past two and a half weeks than the previous eight years. Plus, she was sketching again. And Hugh's commission had her making jewelry again.

And what of Matty's "theory"? Was she returning to the past or shaking it off? She had no idea.

Sometimes what looked like cowardice was really self-preservation.

Maybe…but what concerned her now was what if what looked like self-preservation sometimes was really just cowardice?

Chapter Eight

The back screen door had already banged behind her, and Shane had spotted her, so there was no way to turn tail and return to the house without that particular piece of self-preservation definitely looking like cowardice.

She'd meant to talk to him. Perhaps she would have sought him out eventually. But not like this.

He'd taken his shirt off and was sluicing water over his bare chest.

She'd seen men's chests. No big deal. Even well-muscled chests. Even chests that started from strong necks flaring out to a sharply ridged collarbone. Even chests that continued down from that collarbone like a textured curtain of muscles. Dark hair sprinkled across from one brown nub to the other, then trickled down the indentation at the center.

"I'm done if you want the water."

He turned to grab a towel, and that was no better. His back was smooth and tanned. Muscle rippled over his shoulder blades with his movement. As he twisted, the shadow of his lower backbone deepened where it disappeared beneath the waistband of his jeans, down to—

"Lisa? You want to wash up?"

"Uh, yeah, thanks."

If he went inside…but he stayed put as she neared the tub.

If he put his shirt on…he kept rubbing.

"I'll have to wash up again after we finish that attic room after supper, but it sure felt good."

Everyone else had left, but Cal, Shane and Dave seemed to consider finishing the attic room a matter of honor.

She turned on the hose, filling both hands with cold water and splashed it onto her face.

"Hey!"

"Sorry!" She'd caught him with the spatter, and now he had to dry where he'd just dried. So the process would take even longer. Great. Just great. How long could she keep her face covered in water? Not that it did any good. Her memory was suddenly proving to be photographic.

"They're a great group of people," Shane said from the darkness somewhere beyond her closed eyes as she used her hands to rub at her face.

"Yes, they are."

Even if a few of them did talk a lot. During her hours alone painting trim, her mind kept wandering back to things Taylor and Matty had said, and things she'd said to them.

"Shane, I have something—I want to talk to you."

"Okay. Here, use this."

A towel came into her hand. She put it up to her face. It smelled like Shane. Oh, Lord. She refused to be sidetracked, even by her lungs' sudden failure to function properly.

"I know I've been, uh, prickly about the past. That's because I was only seeing it from my own angle—and through the eyes of a nineteen-year-old. And that wasn't fair to you. I've been looking back these past few days and seeing it from your point of view. And I know I should be thanking you for some things.''

''Like?''

Believing in me. ''Well, for starters, not taking me up on what I kept offering.'' Her chuckle sounded rusty but she hoped sincere.

He went still, sinking into that nonreaction mode faster than she could have believed. ''Sorry, you're going to have to explain that one.''

''There you were, trying to do your job, and you had this kid ready to fall at your feet. I'm sorry if I caused you awkwardness or embarra—''

''We better get inside.''

''I just wanted you to know—''

''You're grateful I didn't jump you. Yeah, I got it.''

She blinked. If there'd been something—*anything*—in his voice, or in his face, she might have responded. Instead, she was left with nothing to do but to follow him inside, her effort to square some things from the past falling flatter than Nebraska. Maybe Matty was right about just forgetting the past completely. But if Shane could do that, he wouldn't be here in the first place.

After they'd filled their plates from dishes that had barely suffered a dent from the earlier meal, they drifted to the same area of the porch as before and found the same people there.

As they sat—Shane again on the floor against the pole—Matty was saying something about pulling off the upcoming party without the guests of honor getting wind of it.

''You mean Hugh and Ruth?'' Shane asked.

''No.'' Lisa said quickly, hoping to nip any bright ideas he might have in the bud stage. A man who invited himself to a day of painting at the house of people he'd barely met was fully capable of inviting himself to a party for her parents even though they'd never met at all. The idea of her parents and Shane Garrison in the same room made her stomach clench.

"Our folks have been away for a while. We're having a get-together to welcome them home," Dave supplied as he speared potato salad from his plate. He met Lisa's gaze and frowned. "What?"

Brothers! Not only had he missed her signal to be quiet, he'd called attention to the fact that she was glaring at him.

Taylor prevented any sibling mayhem. "What about Hugh and Ruth, Shane?"

"It's their fiftieth wedding anniversary coming up."

"Fiftieth!"

The others exclaimed along with Taylor, but Lisa was following a different track of thought. She knew about the anniversary from Hugh asking her to make the earrings. But... "How do you know that, Shane?"

Shane gave her that twisted grin. "Would you believe because I'm a great detective?"

"He must be pretty good, since none of us knew it," Matty said. "Ruth hasn't said a word to me. How about you, Taylor? Dave?" Dual head shaking was her response. "And she obviously hasn't told you, Lisa. So how did you find out, Shane?"

"Hugh told me."

"Hugh?" came the chorus of incredulity.

"He knew?" Dave sounded impressed.

Lisa couldn't confirm that Hugh knew without exposing their secret, so she stayed quiet.

A crease appeared between Shane's brows. "Maybe I shouldn't have said anything. I thought, when you mentioned a party—"

"No, no, you did right to tell us," said Matty. And she patted his arm.

Patted his arm! Like a woman who would never even consider calling him a no-good creep.

"I'll call Brenda. That's Hugh and Ruth's oldest daughter," Matty explained to Shane. "And find out if they have something planned. But even if they have a family party set, we should do something for them." She snapped her fingers. "You know, if we told Ruth and Hugh we're having a surprise party for Ed and Donna, and told Ed and Donna we're having a surprise party for Ruth and Hugh, we could surprise them both!"

Dave said, "Isn't that going to get awfully complicated?"

"Sure, that's part of the fun."

Neither Dave nor Cal appeared convinced *fun* was the word they would have chosen. But they all knew that once Matty had an idea in her head, it took a lot more than a few complications to change her mind. Plus, she had a great track record for pulling off even the most complicated event.

So maybe it would be fun.

"And since you're the one who got us started, you're definitely invited, Shane," Matty said with a wide smile.

Or maybe not so fun.

One of those sudden silences hit the porch, and Lisa realized it was because everyone was watching her for a reaction.

No, not everyone. Cal was saying something to Taylor in a low voice. Only the abrupt quiet around him made it audible to anyone beyond his wife.

"No more painting for you. You've done too much already. You said you'd spend most of the day in the kitchen, away from the paint."

"The doctor said as long as the windows were open—"

"I don't care what the doctor said—"

"Doctor?" Matty zoomed in on the word. "Why would the doctor…? Oh, my God, you're pregnant! Are you? You are!"

"We weren't going to say anything yet…."

Lisa felt a clutch at her heart for both these couples she loved. It was understood that Matty and Dave would like to have children, too, and they'd married more than a year before Taylor and Cal. Knowing their news might stir disappointment, Taylor and Cal had held off celebrating.

But the joy Matty and Dave expressed was impossible to doubt. The excited congratulations and conversation about babies-to-be occupied the rest of the meal and the kitchen cleanup the three women performed while the men finished the attic room.

Only later, after Shane had taken her home, reminded her he'd pick her up at eleven-thirty tomorrow and left, did Lisa realize that she had let it stand that he was invited to the dual parties.

Shane wouldn't tell where he was taking her, even as they wound up the Big Horn Mountains on a road like the grooves on the inside of a bottle cap. Not until he'd driven to an area by a creek not far off the highway.

"Perfect," he said. "Wind's blocked by that higher mountain, the sun's warm, the shade's cool and the grass is soft. No vendors, but being the resourceful type, I can overcome that lack."

He pulled a duffel from the back of the SUV, gesturing for her to follow the short path to the creek. Out of the duffel he pulled a chenille bedspread worn to rows of nubs, a series of plastic containers labeled neatly in Ruth's handwriting and a thermos.

"I hope you got a receipt for all this," Lisa said dryly as she helped place the containers on the bedspread he'd laid out in the sun. At his quizzical look, she added lightly, "A business lunch—so it's a business expense."

"Lisa—"

"I know—that's what this meeting is for, so ask your questions."

He'd been kneeling on the spread, now he dropped back onto his heels, a container in each hand. "Roast beef or ham with mustard? How's that for a question?"

She laughed. "Okay, we'll eat first. Roast beef."

"Damn. I wanted the beef."

"Too bad." She took it from his hand, tugging when he

didn't release the container immediately. "You shouldn't play if you can't afford to lose."

"You're a tough one, Lisa Currick."

"I am now." She said it cheerfully. And took a bite from her sandwich. "Mmm."

He grimaced, but she could see the humor sparkling in his eyes as he started on the other sandwich. "And mean, too."

"Me? You ask anybody who's meaner, an office manager or a cop, and mean old cops'll win every time. And before I was an office manager I was even less mean. I was a cream puff. What's the old expression about witnesses singing?" She took a handful of cherries from another of Ruth's containers, grimacing at herself. "I did a whole opera all by myself—and all about me. My family, my past, my hometown, my hopes—God, by the end you must have heard about every skinned knee I'd ever had. Twice."

"Don't—" At the tightness in that single word she looked up. His eyes had changed, like a lake before a storm. Then they changed again, turning opaque. "Having somebody else's attention all zeroed in on you, it's flattering. That's human nature. And as cops we're trained to make use of that human nature."

"That's how law enforcement often gets criminals to confess, isn't it?" She nodded as she turned the sandwich around looking for the right spot for her next bite. "Playing up to their egos. Letting them think someone's interested in hearing them talk and talk and talk."

"I didn't mean that."

"But that's what I did. I lapped up all that attention."

"I wouldn't put it like that. Besides—" the faintest hesitation came, as if he was deciding whether or not to take a risk "—there was the male-female thing."

Heat seeped into her. Stronger and brighter than the sunlight around them. But she kept it light, adopting fake primness to say, "It might surprise you to know I was not a complete novice at 'the male-female thing.' I've had plenty

of attention bestowed on me, before and after meeting you.
Male attention.''

"It doesn't surprise me." That upped her thermostat.
Then he ruined it by adding, "Of course, some women find
the idea of being around a cop exciting. You should see
the turnout at bars the cops hang out at."

She pinned him with a disbelieving look. "Are you saying you think I spent all that time with you that spring
because I was a cop groupie?"

"Nothing to be ashamed of. You were a kid." He offered
her lemonade he'd poured from the thermos into a cup
formed from its top.

She took the cup, but didn't drink. "I was not a kid."

"At most, maybe you had a crush—"

"A crush? I was..."

"What, Lisa?" His voice was soft and dangerous. His
eyes were hot and dangerous. His mouth was just dangerous.

*I was falling for you so fast and so hard I was drunk
with it.* Was he baiting her? Trying to get her to say that?
Why? Stalling, she took a drink of lemonade and held out
the cup to him.

"You're right. I was a kid. What did I know?"

He hesitated before taking the cup and draining it in one
swallow. The muscles of his throat worked, the motion dis-
appearing into the vee of his collarbone revealed by his
open shirt.

He opened a container of brownies and set it between
them. "So, what kind of male attention?"

Despite the blandness of his tone she cut him a look.
Maybe *because* of the blandness of his tone. Why would
anyone who sounded that disinterested bother to ask the
question? His expression was also bland. It irked her.

She could goad, too. Yes, his first priority had always
been his work, and yes, she'd been foolish to think he cared
about her. But between strictly business and caring, there

were certain male responses. Her judgment had been lousy, but that hadn't stopped her powers of observation.

Detective Shane Garrison *had* been attracted to her. He wasn't entirely immune to her physically now, either.

A feeling flowed into her she didn't recognize, a sort of fizz in her bloodstream.

"What kind of male attention?" he repeated, not as bland this time.

"Lascivious, drooling, panting attention." She dropped back flat on the blanket, then caught his gaze skimming across the part of her body that in fact wasn't flat. She popped up again, as if struck by a sudden thought rather than a sudden awareness. "Oh, were you asking about before or after meeting you?"

"Before."

She nodded. "Lascivious, drooling, panting attention."

"And after?"

"Lascivious, drooling, panting attention."

His voice stayed light, but the line of his jaw shifted slightly, as if he might be clenching his teeth. "So you would have known how to handle it if I'd forgotten I was on official business and had lavished lascivious, drooling, uh…"

"Panting," she prompted.

"Thank you—panting attention on you."

"Of course I would have known how to handle it."

"How did you handle it with the panters before you came to New York?"

"They all knew I intended to leave for the big city, so there wasn't a future in it. And those who weren't interested in a future…well, most of them knew my big brother Dave."

"And after?"

"There was still Dave." This was fun—teasing, yanking his chain.

"How about those who wanted a future? You came back here, so you can't say there wasn't a future."

"I've been busy. Classes and work and—"

"Was that enough to satisfy him?"

The fizz evaporated. "Who?"

"The one who wanted to marry you."

"How do you know someone wanted to marry me?"

"Because there had to be at least one smart man around here. What happened, Lisa?"

"I wasn't ready."

"He wouldn't wait?"

"I told him I didn't know if I'd ever be ready." She'd enjoyed Todd's company. And he'd been willing for a long time to share that company all on her terms. But marriage? Spending her life with him? That was the biggest decision there was. And she'd failed so miserably in New York at judging the two most important men in her life. No, she hadn't been prepared to take that risk.

"Did you hope he'd wait anyhow?"

She closed the empty container her sandwich had been in and tossed it into the open duffel. Then she met his eyes. "No."

"Any regrets?"

"No."

"Doubts?"

"No."

He gave the slightest nod, then put his hands behind his head and lowered himself to the blanket, closing his eyes. A man totally relaxed. Probably this close to dropping off for a nap.

And she was grateful, because it left her to deal with the thoughts whirling through her mind.

No doubts. No regrets.

Totally unlike the aftermath of her time in New York.

Until this moment she'd accepted that she'd turned Todd down because her mistakes in New York meant she lacked the judgment to make such a decision. But if that were true, wouldn't she have had doubts? Maybe even regrets? Instead, she'd never once questioned her decision to refuse Todd's proposal.

She hadn't turned him down because she didn't trust her own judgment. She'd turned him down because she *had* trusted her judgment that she didn't love him and didn't want to spend her life with him.

Shane didn't know how much longer he could keep his eyes closed. He wanted to see what she was thinking. Hell, he just wanted to see her...and feel her...and smell her.

Every day she dropped a little more of that overcautious facade. Yet what appeared from behind it wasn't simply the girl he'd known. She had more sass now, more edge. She was a woman. Very much a woman.

And if he kept thinking along those lines, the G rating on this picnic would be gone in a few more pulses of heat.

"Don't you want to know about me?" he asked without opening his eyes—using that bit of self-denial to prove he was still in control.

"What?"

He opened his eyes. "About my love life since we knew each other."

No! But...yes. Oh, yeah, he could see each response in her eyes. And he wanted to grin big-time. He didn't. Another point for control.

"No."

"I dated one woman for nearly two years," he started, as if she'd given the opposite answer. "I thought maybe, eventually, we'd get married."

"I'm sure she was thrilled to hear that romantic declaration."

He sat up. "You aren't as sweet as you used to be."

"Tough."

"I like it."

That shut her up. Shane had noticed that a while ago. Most people had something they had no answer for—Lisa's was compliments. At least from him. He wasn't sure how he felt about that.

"Anyway, you're right. After a while Julianne wasn't thrilled about me in general. Toward the end she kept complaining that I didn't pay enough attention to her. I suppose she had a point. It took me a month to realize she'd broken up with me."

Her eyes narrowed, checking to see if he was kidding. He wasn't. When she saw that, her eyes widened. "How— A month?"

Her voice rose. Mostly with astonishment, but a dash of amusement and sympathy—no doubt for Julianne—mixed into the brew.

"I knew we hadn't seen each other for a while," he started in his own defense. But was there any defense? "I didn't know how long a while it had been. And when I saw my key on the table, I thought it was a spare. She didn't leave a note or anything."

"How inconsiderate of her. So how did you finally get the news?"

"I was on a case. Homicide. The first twenty-four hours after a killing are the most important for closing the case. My partner and I were on hour twenty-three, frustrated because we weren't getting far on the murder of a thirty-eight-year-old mother of two with a steady job in banking and no bad habits. Found out later the guy broke in, winged her with the first shot. She struggled, got the gun away from him, but she didn't shoot—she didn't know how. He backhanded her, took the gun and killed her. Ann Kaleski. That was her name."

The sympathy quotient in her eyes had shot up, and the amusement was gone. He gave himself a slight shake and went on.

"But we didn't know any of that then—we were still hitting brick walls. And I don't suppose I looked any too fresh. We came out of this building after finding the ex-husband's alibi held about playing poker, and there was

Julianne coming down the sidewalk wrapped around another guy.''

"It must have been horribly awkward for you."

"We were all incredibly civilized."

"It must have been horribly awkward for you."

She gave the repetition enough emphasis to be a mild reproach of his passing this off as nothing. But nothing was exactly what he remembered feeling.

He'd stood there watching Julianne walk away, and he'd known he should feel something. But nothing came to mind. He'd felt empty. Empty and this little nudge of something deep in his gut. Something…

"I was relieved."

He looked toward the stream gurgling away like it had something caught in its throat. Like maybe the truth. He hadn't told anyone he was relieved at Julianne's exit. Hadn't even let the response in his gut take the form of words.

"It was like an anchor pulling me one way when I wanted to go another. I can't say I'd resented her taking up my time, because I didn't let that happen."

She twisted around to smooth a corner of the bedspread that a breeze had flipped up. "Of course. Your job came first."

"Homicide is pretty intense. I've seen people in the department—men and women—have long-term relationships fold under the pressure."

He and Julianne had looked good together, but they'd never been a good fit beneath the surface. Not like his parents, not like other couples he'd seen that withstood the pressure. If Lisa asked him about the end of his relationship with Julianne, he would echo her: no doubts, no regrets. Although Julianne's departure had made him wonder about his life. And himself.

But Lisa obviously didn't want to hear it.

"That makes sense." She said it like her mind was on other things. He watched her making a show of looking up at the sun, then at her wristwatch. "It's getting late, and I have a lot to do."

"I still have two hours on the clock, and we have another stop to make."

She didn't argue, but she didn't look toward him while they tossed the containers back in the duffel and he folded the bedspread. That was okay. It made it easier.

"Look what I found." He held out the stem of the single flower that looked a little like an all-yellow daisy.

She took the flower, but frowned. That wasn't the reaction he'd been aiming for. "That's weird."

"Isn't that the bur marigold that White was always calling you? It grows in Wyoming, right?"

She raised her gaze from the flower to his face. He had the uncomfortable feeling that she would ace a test on reading him at this moment. Was this what witnesses felt like when he interviewed them? Was this how she felt when he was asking about the necklace?

"Yes, it's a bur marigold."

"So what's so weird?"

"It appears to be wilting. As if it was cut some time ago."

"Maybe a deer tore it off its stem, you know? I heard there're lots of deer up here."

"That would be possible, except for a couple things. To start, it hasn't been torn, it's been cut." She held up the stem for him to look at.

Now he felt less like a witness and more like a suspect. "Whaddya know. You'd be good at forensics, noticing something like that."

"There's something odder."

"Yeah?" For the first time he understood why suspects fell back on such lame answers.

"Bur marigold usually grows at lower elevations. More important, it grows at the edges of ponds. Still water. Not moving water like this creek."

"You used to say the seeds stuck to anything passing by

and could be dropped off miles and miles away, right? So maybe this is from a particularly adventurous bur marigold seed.''

She shook her head. ''It can travel great distances, but it still needs the right environment to flourish.''

He had no answer to that.

She rubbed the stem between her thumb and index finger, making the bloom twirl.

''Was the idea that I would remember some never-before-remembered detail if you sprung this reminder of Alex on me? That the location of the necklace would pop into my head and out of my mouth.''

He closed the duffel and slung it over his shoulder. ''It works sometimes. No harm, no foul.''

She stared at him a moment longer before saying. ''Sorry, Shane. I can't remember what I never knew.''

''It was worth a try.''

She didn't sound angry. Better to quit while he wasn't behind. Better to let her think he'd tried an asinine ploy than to let her know how he'd worked his connections to get a bur marigold to give her. When a woman didn't even realize you'd given her a flower, definitely better to drop the whole damned thing.

She hadn't been the only one. He'd also chosen the job over Julianne, whom he'd thought he might eventually marry.

That moment before he'd said he was relieved that Julianne had walked out of his life, Lisa had felt suspended. Waiting for something—anything—to break through the stillness of another of his nonreactions.

Would she have had Julianne's courage to leave him?

She was afraid she might not have. In that case the way things had ended for them had been for the best—a quick, sharp, clean cut.

She'd recognized the case he'd discussed from one of the news accounts she'd read on the Internet as a murder.

from earlier this year. He'd given details of it—the victim's name, her age, her occupation, the ex-husband's alibi. Yet, what he'd said about Julianne had been nearly as vague as his impression of her walking out on him.

Maybe nothing ever made an impression on Shane except for cases. Even going to the extent of finding a bur marigold from someplace and producing it like that. And after all that setup—

"Is that sleet?"

She straightened in the passenger seat and looked around to be sure they were where she thought they were. They'd turned off U.S. Alternate 14 and she'd been so absorbed in her thoughts it hadn't registered. But now it did. Her heart skittered with anticipation.

Shane leaned forward to peer up through the windshield at the cloud that had enveloped his SUV as it climbed the slope approaching one of the highest spots in the Big Horn Mountains—the Medicine Wheel.

"It *is* sleet."

"Uh-huh." She smiled. "But not much."

He grumbled something about August, then added, "And this is one of your favorite places?"

She didn't bother to ask who'd told him that—there were too many possibilities.

"Hey, you're the one behind the wheel—you're the one who's deciding where we're heading."

He looked over at her. "Am I?"

She sidestepped that by announcing, "Here's the parking lot. We'll walk the last mile and a half."

"Oh, good."

But on the climb toward the summit, he sounded genuinely interested when he asked about what they were going to see.

She told him the Medicine Wheel, whose rocks had been dated from 1200 to 1700 A.D., was recognized as a sacred site by several Native American tribes. Theories abounded about the origin of the wheel—formed by rocks, with 28 spokes spreading from a hub to a rim like a giant wagon wheel eighty feet across—including that it was an ancient astronomical observatory. There were also legends that the first men in the area had made signal fires there that could be seen all the way across the Big Horn Basin to the Rocky Mountains.

"What do you think?" he asked, as they paused to draw in air thinned by nearly 10,000 feet of altitude.

"The twenty-eight spokes match a lunar calendar and astronomical features align with the formations, so…" She shrugged. "You'll see for yourself."

When they reached the protective fence that encircled the wheel, the wind, accustomed to flowing unfettered up here, snapped and pushed at them. Instinctively she moved closer to Shane, watching his chest expand as he took in more air.

"What do you think?" she asked.

He looked over the formation that ancient hands had created on the mountaintop scoured by wind and weather. "It feels like the roof of the world, doesn't it? It makes sense that they'd build here for astronomical sightings, with nothing between them and the heavens. But it feels…it's more…"

"Like a great cathedral," she said. "Like the reason we're breathless isn't only because of the altitude and the climb."

She should have regretted revealing how she responded to the Medicine Wheel. She should have considered it a mistake. She didn't.

Especially not when he said so softly that the wind nearly took it away, "Yes."

She didn't know how long they'd stood there when they both took three steps back before turning away. And she refused to analyze the synchronicity.

"Let's go over there." She nodded toward the west. "You have to see this."

She stepped onto a ledge of rock with a raised lip that

formed a natural balcony. The world fell away at their feet, sinking into the broad Big Horn Basin.

A cold, wet missile stung her cheek. Then another and another.

More sleet.

There was something magical about standing here so high, looking down on the shifting patterns of cloud and sun on the earth stretched out in front of them, yet being reminded with each miniature missile of sleet that she wasn't so high-and-mighty after all.

Beside her Shane made a sound caught midway between amusement and disbelief. "You're smiling. It's sleeting in August and you're smiling."

"We don't have to stay, Shane."

"Sure we do. It's one of the things I like about you—you find pleasure in sleet on a mountaintop. But we do have to do something about you shivering."

"I'm okay." She couldn't swear her shiver had been from the cold.

"Come here."

He didn't wait for her to follow his low-voiced order. He stepped behind her, opened his jacket, drew her back snug against his chest, pulled the open sides of his jacket around them both and crossed his arms at her waist, encasing her in warmth and strength.

Her lungs felt as if the mountain they stood on had suddenly zoomed up another 5,000 feet, cutting her oxygen supply to practically nothing.

Shane's body and jacket protected her from the elements, but not from the elemental. His chest was hard and warm behind her. The weight of his arms across her ribs felt so right. With his chin against her temple, she could hear the quickening of his breath and see the puffs of frosted air just before they disappeared. All around her, holding back the raw cold that swept the mountain, was the scent and warmth of a man—this man.

If his hands moved, slid up her rib cage... *No, be honest*

with yourself Lisa, you're not thinking in hypotheticals, you're wishing. She wanted his hands to move up her rib cage. She wanted his warm, hard palms to cover her breasts. She wanted the sensation of his fingers exploring her flesh. Flesh she could feel filling and tightening at the thought alone.

And then she felt something more. A hardening, growing pressure against her right hip. She closed her eyes and released a slow breath through her barely parted lips—it was that or moan.

Shane shifted his weight to the opposite foot, breaking the contact. But she could still feel the heated tingle in her flesh.

A faint sound told her he'd moved again, and she looked over her shoulder. He'd dropped his head back to let the sleet beat on his face, and somehow that was even more compelling.

"We better go," he growled.

The silence of their touches had been a universe cut off from the world, but words brought the real world rushing back.

She started away from him, looking around. "Looks like everyone else had the sense to get in out of the sleet."

"Yeah, that's another reason."

Chapter Nine

If every witness were half as hard to figure out as Lisa Currick, his case-closing record would be zero for his career. Zero. Zilch. No clue.

In the sun-warmed meadow, she'd gone from sass to chill. In the freezing sleet, she'd let him hold her.

Now, she glanced around when he followed her through the open garage to her kitchen door as if she felt hunted, and then, after unlocking and opening the door, she turned back and gave him a smile—small, almost timid, but real. Figure that out.

"Thank you again, Shane."

He took a step forward, she retreated a step.

"Going to Medicine Wheel was…it meant a lot to me."

Another step and the door closed behind him. For an instant they were less than arm's length apart. She backed up again.

"And for lunch. Thank you. It was…nice."

He couldn't take his eyes off her mouth.

"You're welcome."

Ten seconds. He'd give her ten seconds, and then if she didn't move he was kissing her. Thaw. Freeze. He didn't give a damn. Five seconds.

The phone rang.

It barely nicked his concentration. Phones were always ringing in the detective section. He had no trouble ignoring one that couldn't possibly be anything of interest.

But she started, as if the sound had been a mild electric shock.

"The phone." She wetted her lips, and his gaze followed the motion.

She jerked into action, snatching the receiver up, and getting out a "Hello."

There was a momentary pause. Her gaze flicked toward him. "Alex? Is that you? Is everything all right?"

Shane had the portable extension from the living room to his ear to catch the tail end of the response.

"...my bur marigold."

"Alex, how are you?"

"Perfectly well, of course. You know I've never had a day of illness. And how are you? Are you at the studio?"

"No, Alex," she said gently. "You called me in Wyoming. Where my family lives, remember?"

Shane remained in the living room, giving her space, but able to watch her expressions.

"Of course, of course. Your family. Do remember me to your charming mother. I should love to see her Spring Beauty blooming again—I so enjoyed that. And your father is well, I hope? But what are you doing there when there's work to be done at the studio?"

She started to correct him again, then stopped.

That's right, Shane mentally coached, go along with his view of how things are, and you might be able to draw more information out of him.

"I'm visiting."

"Ah, of course, of course. Back to your roots, my sunny

bur marigold. Back to the lessons you have stored away in the trunk of your first efforts. You can stick to whoever passes by, and travel a long, long distance, but those are your roots.''

''Yes, they are.'' Her gaze touched Shane, then skidded away. ''Alex, there's someone else here. Someone you might remember—Shane Garrison. Detective Garrison.''

''Garrison? Oh, yes, of course. Your young man.''

''My...? No. He was never—''

''Now, don't be that way, Lisa. He's perfect for you. I knew it the first time he came into the studio. My, my, my—the way he looked at you. If you'd been a diamond, he'd have had you cut and polished in no time.'' He chuckled. But when he spoke again his tone was serious. ''But I could see that he recognized your special qualities—so much more interesting than a cold diamond. And he didn't rush. I like that in him. Yes, an estimable young man, most definitely.''

''But, Alex...''

Shane suspected she was wrestling with how to convey to Alex in his strange netherworld between the past and unreality that the man he'd been lauding had played a role in putting him in prison.

''Come now, you're not worrying about that foolishness of his saying I am stealing, are you? Because you shouldn't worry about that. I can handle him without any problem. I slide him a little this way, the other way, and then back again. Don't you worry, I'm keeping him on the board, so you two young people will have plenty of time to get to know each other.''

''Good Lord.'' She sounded stunned. Shane suspected she'd forgotten his presence. ''I've wondered why you didn't keep Shane at more of a distance.... Are you saying—do you mean you gave Shane access to the studio in order to play matchmaker?''

She had that backward—White had played matchmaker in order to throw him off.

"Play matchmaker? You make it sound as if I have failed. I do not accept defeat, certainly not so soon. In addition, I found the young man engaging for his own sake." A faint rustling came across the telephone line, then Alex's voice again, abruptly querulous. "I'm in prison you know."

"Yes, Alex, I know." How gentle her voice was. "Because of the pieces you kept."

"Rescue. I rescue pieces. My God, those people—Philistines."

"Yes, Alex. But there's one necklace we've never found. The diamond and platinum swag that's pierced and miligrained, with the emerald pendant. Do you remember?"

"Of course I remember," he said with some of his old snap. "It's a magnificent work. And I saved it especially for you, my bur marigold. I remember the first day you came in—"

"Yes, Alex." A layer of desperation seeped in now. "But the thing is, I can't find the necklace."

"Well, of course not. Not yet."

She put a hand to her forehead. "Not yet? But you said you saved it for me, so if you'll tell me where it is—"

"That's all taken care of. You shall have it when the time is right. All in due time, my dear, all in due time."

"But, Alex, I need the necklace now."

"You need it, or young Garrison wants it?"

Shane had seen the doctors' reports, but could White be faking this after all?

"Alex, please—"

"I'm sorry, my dear, but the gentleman in uniform at my elbow informs me, as they say so colloquially, that my time is up. I can spare only a second to tell you I cherish your letters. Please give my regards to your young man."

"Alex—"

The line went dead.

He returned the handset to its base. Moving much more slowly, she hung up the kitchen phone, delaying the mo-

ment she faced him. He knew the instant she realized that
was what she was doing, because she immediately turned
to him.

"You heard. I tried."

"I heard."

"He's…he's very confused."

"Why are you still so loyal to Alex after everything he
did?"

"Why are you so angry at him?" she retorted. "You
won. You beat him. You put an old man in prison."

"I put a criminal in jail."

"And I helped convict a man who'd never been anything
but kind to me, who'd given me the greatest opportunity
of my life. I betrayed a sick, old man."

"He never felt that way."

He watched her certainty trip, then right itself. "How
could you possibly know what Alex felt? I—"

"He told me."

After a stunned instant, she said, "When? And why are
you smiling?"

"I'm smiling because you're not a half-bad detective
yourself. Didn't take you long to recognize the hole in my
statement."

"When?" she demanded again, ignoring the rest.

"Several times, as a matter of fact. Before the trial—"
he caught her gaze and held it "—and after."

"After? You visited him in prison?"

"Yes."

"Why?"

Her questions were getting tougher. "I wanted to know
more than came out at the trial."

"Like what?"

Like why she'd cleared out so abruptly after the trial.
For a moment it was as if he could feel the coldness of the
receiver against his ear that night after the guilty verdict.
He'd stood outside and tried to call her—and the coldness

that had seeped inside at the mechanical recording inform-
ing him the number was no longer in service.

But before he could decide whether to tell her any of
that, she was going on. "How foolish of me—you wanted
to know where the necklace was. He couldn't tell you. You
just heard the evidence of that."

"Maybe he can't now—though some days I'd bet he still
could—but he definitely could have told me at the start.
Those first couple years, his mind was as sharp as ever."

"And that protects you from worrying that putting him
in prison was what made him..."

"It didn't. The doctors said so. And so did Alex. He told
me both his grandfather and his mother had symptoms of
what doctors now call dementia. He said it must be in his
family's genes."

She studied him, trying to decide whether to believe him
or not. "How many times did you go back?"

"Several."

"You've been that determined to find that necklace?"

He hesitated. But not long. "Did you ever doubt it?"

"No."

Lisa was heading for her car to leave, having decided
her twilight trip to Taylor and Cal's ranch was a bad idea,
and it was a good thing they weren't home, when the dark-
green pickup crested a hill from the west and came toward
the cluster of buildings where she stood.

As it neared, she could make out Sin's pointy collie nose
catching the wind from the passenger window. Cal was
driving, and Taylor sat in the middle.

"Ah, I see Sin rates the window," she said when the
truck stopped beside her and they all got out with hellos.

"Actually, the window's second choice. Whenever we
go somewhere, Sin and I *discuss* who gets to sit in the
middle next to Cal."

A grin tugged at Cal's mouth. An expression that suited
the ease that had transformed his manner these past several

months. Everyone in Knighton knew he'd had another life before he came here, knew he had another name he used for legal situations. But to everyone here he was still Cal Ruskoff.

"Uh, Taylor, could I talk to you?"

"Sure. Let's get something to drink and sit on the porch." They headed toward the house, while Cal departed for the barn with a four-legged shadow.

They'd been seated in the rockers on the porch with glasses of soda for a few minutes before Taylor said, "What's bothering you?"

Shane's lean face came into her head. But she didn't even have words for all the doubts and uncertainties there.

"I feel guilty about Alex," she said instead. "Like I betrayed him."

He never felt that way.

Shane's confidence had been so complete. Could he be right...? But he and she saw what he referred to as "the Alex White Case" so completely differently.

Yet they had shared it.

The rocker pitched forward under the impact of the realization. It was a little like former war enemies swapping stories many years later about a battle they'd both fought. As different as their experiences were, they had a link others did not share.

Odd, she'd never thought about Shane being the only person she could talk to about those times, now that Alex... No, even before. Because such a large part of those times had been what happened away from the studio.

Part of the reason she'd never told her family or friends about those experiences was that she'd been certain she never wanted to be reminded of them. She'd certainly never wanted to talk about them. She'd tried to get Shane Garrison kicked out of town for the same reason...well, mostly for that reason.

And now she realized that along with the pain, she'd buried wonderful memories. Memories Shane's questioning were forcing her to unearth. Memories simply being with Shane were unearthing.

"Why do you feel you betrayed Alex?" Taylor asked.

"I told you—I testified against him."

"You were subpoenaed."

"I could have fought it harder. I could have—"

"Ignored the subpoena? Refused to answer? You'd have gone to jail for contempt. Lied on the stand? You'd have gone to prison for perjury. No, Lisa, as hard as it was, you did the right thing."

"What if I didn't do it because it was right? What if I did it because...because I was trying to win favor with Shane?" It was her greatest fear.

"Did you?"

"I don't know." And that was her greatest shame.

"Did Shane ever...?"

"He never once touched me. I made it appallingly clear that all he had to do was lift a finger. He never did, but even that wasn't enough—I had myself totally convinced that I could read him better than he knew himself. Just like I was so sure Alex White couldn't possibly be doing anything wrong, so there was no case and therefore no reason for Shane and me not to get together. No reason except I was a naive idiot who'd built a castle out of air and was shocked when I managed to turn it into a tornado."

Taylor's frown deepened. "*You* turned it into a tornado? All by yourself? How about what Alex did? He hurt not only those he stole from but the people who'd worked for him."

"I'm not saying it wasn't wrong. I know he's never said he's sorry for taking the jewelry, because in his mind those owners didn't have the right to those amazing pieces. But he has apologized to his employees—he helped a group set up a new studio."

"And Garrison? He had a hand in that tornado, too."

She shrugged. "Like you said the other day, he was just doing his job."

"Bull."

Lisa goggled at her.

"You heard me, that's bull. You say you were obvious enough in your interest for a stupid man to see. Well, I've met this man, and he's not stupid. Quit taking it all on your shoulders."

"He...but..." She pressed her palms to her temples. "God, what a mess!"

Taylor tilted her head. "Lisa, I want to ask you something, and I want you to think about the answer."

She braced herself. "Okay."

"Do you truly think Shane Garrison would try to use Cal's past as leverage."

It surprised her. "If he doesn't find the necklace—"

"You're hedging. Do you truly think Shane Garrison would try to use Cal's past as leverage? Is he that kind of man?"

"I...no." She quickly added, "But if I'm wrong—"

"We'll deal with it. You know something I've learned from being with Cal—to fall in love you have to trust—"

"Whoa! Who said anything about love?"

"—the other person," Taylor continued smoothly. "To let someone love you, you have to trust yourself. Trust that you're a good enough person to be loved, trust that your judgment is good enough that it's safe to let that person love you. That's 'good enough.' Not perfect. There are no guarantees. Just reasonable hope."

Taylor wore a half smile that made Lisa get up from her chair. "I better go. I didn't intend to stay so long."

Taylor called her name as she opened her car door.

"Sounds to me like you've forgiven Alex. Maybe even Shane. So that leaves you. It's time to forgive yourself, Lisa."

Lisa didn't think Taylor expected an answer, which was a good thing, because she didn't have one.

Taylor watched Lisa drive away, gathered their empty glasses and headed inside. She picked up the phone, glanced at the clock and hit a speed dial. Matty answered on the fourth ring. From the background noise, she was in the barn.

"Matty, brace yourself. Our theory just got stronger."

Taylor listened for a second, then replied, "You've seen them together. Besides, I just had a visit from Lisa."

Another pause to listen. "I'm not going to do *anything* about it. And neither are you." Then she added, "Not yet, anyway."

Shane sat on the steps outside the apartment door in the fading twilight, serving up a feast for the mosquitoes.

Sometimes he could outrun voices he didn't want to hear. But seven miles of more hills than valleys hadn't done it this time. Sitting back and taking the memories would be better than sitting here wondering what it would have been like to kiss Lisa. Even the memories of a man in a sterile prison interview room. A man looking faintly amused yet sympathetic—both at his expense.

"Why do you think you come here to see me, Detective Garrison?" The voice hadn't changed. The white hair was neat, though no longer as finely shaped as when an expert had worked on it. But Alex White made even a prison jumpsuit look vaguely urbane.

"I want to find that last necklace."

"You want to find something, but it is not that necklace."

"Well, just for the hell of it, tell me where the necklace is."

"It is where it will do the most good."

"Are you saying you broke it up and pawned the pieces?"

"I am not! I would not commit sacrilege. It is the work of an artist, the balance of weight and color and scale, the flow of workmanship—"

"All right, all right. So if you haven't converted it to

cash and nobody's wearing it because it's too notorious to go unnoticed, how is it doing the most good?"

Alex had leaned back and stared toward the ceiling as if he could envision a smoke ring lingering from a fine Cuban. "There is an expression I have heard rosy-cheeked cherubs use in play with their fellow innocents that applies here. Where the necklace resides is for me to know and for you to find out."

"That's what I'm trying to do—find out."

"Ah, but you're doing it so clumsily. Truly, Detective Garrison, I thought better of you when our paths first crossed."

"No you didn't. You thought I'd never catch you and that you could go on playing your version of Robin Hood, with you being the sole recipient of the goodies stolen from the rich."

"Money is a tawdry motivation. I reassigned pieces of art to a suitably appreciative owner. It was the only sensible course of action. I fear I did somewhat underestimate your detective perspicacity. Although in another regard I sadly overestimated you, I fear."

"Your opinion of my abilities doesn't interest me. Just tell me where the necklace is."

"Your lack of conversational range pains me, Detective. Let's talk of something more pleasant. For instance, my erstwhile intern, the lovely Lisa Currick. Surely you remember her—ah, yes, I can see by your singular lack of expression that you do, indeed, recall her. Of course you do. You two were thick as thieves those months before you arrested me. You don't mind that phrase, do you? Thick as thieves. It has a certain piquancy in the circumstances, I do think.

"But it appears you do not find the amusement in the memories that I do. What a shame. *Que lastima! Quelle dommage.* What a useful phrase in so many languages. And it sounds so lovely, doesn't it. Ah, but I fear I am boring you. What was it I was talking about…yes, of course, Lisa.

Lisa Currick. She writes to me, you know. I have her address right here. If you should be interested…''

"Tell me where the damned necklace is."

White hadn't. And Shane had refused the offer of Lisa's address in Wyoming. He'd already known it, anyway. Had checked it after the recording said her New York phone had been disconnected.

White's offer of it was part of his game. Throwing Lisa in Shane's path to try to distract him from his duty. Just as he'd tried that spring. And had succeeded.

Was that what the old man was trying to do now, too?

Shane shook his head. He was losing it. That made no sense. Because this time White hadn't thrown Lisa in his path. This time Shane had come after her.

With her eyes closed, Lisa sighed as she settled into the passenger seat of Shane's SUV a week later.

She felt as if she'd been juggling a half dozen lobsters. Each time one passed on its way up or down, she was sure it was going to reach out and grab her nose. It had been that kind of week.

Each day had been hotter than the previous, culminating in today's scorcher.

Work was busy: three wills to finalize, another one in probate, plus Taylor's pro bono work on obtaining a restraining order for a woman who's ex-husband found the "ex" difficult to grasp. Come to think of it, the jerk hadn't grasped the "husband" part, either.

Matty had decided they needed to do as much for the double party as possible before Ed and Donna Currick arrived this coming Wednesday. As her share, Lisa had taken on a major shopping trip to Sheridan.

The earrings for Ruth were coming along well. When she was working on them, time disappeared. She would look up from soldering, buffing or polishing, and it would be an hour past time to go to bed.

She'd made both sessions of her classes, but was behind in the reading and had made no progress on her project.

What bothered her the most was how little it bothered her.

And now Shane had insisted she set aside a few hours for him on this hot Sunday afternoon. She'd put her foot down, though. As much as Taylor and Cal had appreciated his work and as much as she'd enjoyed the trip to Medicine Wheel last weekend, that wasn't why he was in Knighton. So today was going to be strictly business. Although letting her head loll back against the headrest while cool air flowed over her skin was relaxing.

She just wished she could persuade herself that anticipation of relaxation had been the reason a pulse of heat had suffused her body like a flush from the inside when she'd opened the door to Shane minutes ago.

He'd be damned if he let a whole week go by again.

Especially since she looked tired.

If he concentrated on the shadows that her lower lashes brushed instead of on the ruby-red sleeveless blouse she was wearing he'd be a lot better off. The blouse wasn't see-through or tight or blatant. It fell from her shoulders, skimmed the curves of her breasts, then fell from their points to just below her waist. Falling loose like that, it made a man think how easy it would be to set his hands at her waist, then slide up under it. Slide up her smooth back, feeling the curve on either side of her spine. Or slide up her ribs to the undersides of her breasts, letting his hands form to their shape—

Lisa shifted, her eyes still closed, and Shane gave a brief, fervent prayer of thanks that the roads in Wyoming were so lightly traveled.

Even so, he sternly kept his eyes off his passenger until they'd turned into the road he'd been told to look for. He got out of the SUV to open the gate. When he got back in, Lisa was looking around.

"This is Slash-C land."

"Yup." He got out again to close the gate behind them.

"What are we doing here? And I should have opened and closed the gate—that's the passenger's job."

"So I gave you a break—sue me."

A small smile lifted the corners of her lips. "Thank you. But you haven't answered—what are we doing on Slash-C land?"

"You talked about it all the time, and I've only seen that one corner of it, so it seemed like a good idea."

"You promised no picnic. All business today."

"And I keep my promises."

She opened her mouth—to protest or to ask more questions, he'd wager—but he spotted what he'd been told he'd find and announced, "Here we are."

He parked in the shade of three cottonwood trees beside a trickle of a stream. A bluff rose ten feet high, roughly parallel to the stream and about forty feet from it. A fence split the distance between bluff and stream.

"Oh, Lord," Lisa groaned, stepping into the heat.

"Don't tell me you think this is hot." He'd opened the back of the SUV, using the floor of the storage area to arrange the items he'd brought. "All I've been hearing all week is how this is a dry heat so it isn't really that hot."

She cut him a look. "It might be better than that boiling soup New York can get, but when it reaches a certain point, dry or not, it's just plain *hot*. What on— Guns? I know I said the Slash-C's posted for trespassers, but I wasn't serious about your being shot. You didn't have to bring protection."

He chuckled at her dry tone, but kept working. "This isn't for me. It's for you. I'm going to teach you how to shoot."

"You're going to what?"

He shifted the shotgun he'd borrowed from Sheriff Kuerten and reached for the box of ammunition. He'd been thinking about what she'd said about bur marigold. *It can travel great distances, but it still needs the right environment to flourish.* If security would give her the right environment to flourish once more in New York, he'd give her a personal guard 24/7. Knowing how she'd feel about that, he'd decided this would have to do.

"I know some people don't like guns, and I'm not saying you should carry one, but you should know how to handle one if you have to. Simple stuff. Mostly common sense. But it can make a woman feel a lot more confident in the city—or the country for that matter. Cal told me some guy has been making noises about the work you and Taylor are doing for his ex-wife."

That was the upside of an area where everybody knew everybody else. The downside was that his afternoon riding with Cal and Matty had left him wondering how much they had picked up from him. He wasn't used to having other people read him, but he'd gotten the uncomfortable feeling that if he'd pitted his poker face against those two any bluffs would have failed.

"Cal told you?"

"Yeah, I was out there a couple times this week. Fascinating place. Interesting guy, too." He took the bag of tin cans in one hand and the board sized to extend between fence post tops under the other arm. "I'd prefer a shooting range, but Matty says this rock is soft enough not to ricochet, and it's kind of nice to have the traditional tin cans for targets. Fitting."

Only after he'd set the last can on the board balanced between two posts and started back toward her did Lisa comment.

"Matty knew you intended to bring me out here to teach me to shoot?"

"Yeah. Don't get on her case, though. She only agreed to help when she couldn't talk me out of it. Cal was showing me around his and Taylor's place, and Matty stopped by."

"That sounds like Matty."

The cryptic remark confirmed his suspicion: she had mixed feelings about this. Before she could rally her objections, he wanted to give her a basic familiarity with guns. If she ever was in a situation like Ann Kaleski had been, he was going to make damn sure Lisa had a chance.

"First and always, you treat every gun like it's loaded. Even if you just unloaded it. No exceptions. Ever. So you never point it at anything you don't want to shoot. No exceptions. Ever." She listened with close attention as he addressed more safety issues, then covered the basic types of guns. "Any questions?"

"No. You explained it very clearly."

He started her with a single-action revolver, figuring it was the least likely to intimidate. It looked simple, and the necessity of cocking the hammer before squeezing the trigger gave learners an added sense of control. He went over sighting, the grip and the stance.

"Now, let's try this."

Barely resisting the temptation to stroke, he put his open hands on her hips to position her, her right foot slightly behind her left one. Temptation's power tripled, because that position brought her right hip against his groin for an electrifying instant that pushed the temperature into record range.

He gave himself breathing room when he reached around to pick up the gun and put it in her hands.

"Shoulders at the same angle." He moved his hands to her shoulders, and shifted them. "Both hands on the grip."

He slid his hands down her extended arms. His own reach was long enough to cover her hands, making sure her thumbs didn't cross. But not long enough to keep from having the back of her body brush against particularly gleeful parts of the front of his body.

Oh, yeah, temptation was having a hell of a good day.

"Line up the sight with the target." He could smell her shampoo.

Hell, he could do more than that. With his chin over her

shoulder and her arms together, he could see down the opening of that little blouse to the ivory-smooth curve of her breasts over the lacy edge of her bra. Another inch, or a jostle or even a breeze, and through the lace he would see the nipples that even now pushed the fabric of her blouse to enticing, rounded points.

"Focus on the front sight first, then line it up with the rear sight. Now cock the hammer. Good. And squeeze the trigger. Firm and steady."

"You mean like this?"

She squeezed the trigger solidly. No jerk, no hesitation. Then coolly cocked the hammer and did it again. Six times in steady succession. And each time the little bit of kick sent her deeper into his arms. He absorbed her body's reaction to the recoil into his muscles without retreating from it—in fact, part of him was definitely advancing—so their contact was stronger and more complete with each shot.

By the sixth and last shot, he thought he might be able to rival a bullet for speed in exploding out of the barrel.

He drew in two deep breaths, grabbing for control by concentrating on something else. Like what they were supposed to be doing. Right. Teaching her to shoot.

He took the gun from her unresisting hands, checked the cylinder to be sure it was empty, left the cylinder open, pivoted to place it in the SUV, then pivoted back.

His eyes focused on the tin-can targets he'd set up.

Correction. They focused on where the tin cans had been.

Gone. Every last one of them. Because she'd hit every last one of them. Okay, it wasn't exactly Olympic distance, but still, he knew a ringer when he treated one like a rookie.

"I think it's safe to say those tin cans will never bother you again."

She made a sort of choked sound that produced a feathery friction of her shoulder against his chest.

"I couldn't resist. Sorry, Shane. But I'm a ranch girl, you should have—"

She turned as she spoke, deviltry in her eyes and on her

lips. And then her gaze met his, and a whole new definition of deviltry rioted in his mind.

She shivered. Close to 100 degrees and she shivered. And it wasn't fear.

"Lisa."

It wasn't quite a question. But she could have said no. She didn't.

Chapter Ten

At least he didn't just grab her and kiss her.

Oh, yeah, he grabbed her. His hands gripping her shoulders like this was his last hold on a world suddenly deprived of gravity.

But he held himself in check enough to brush his lips against hers. Twice. Then he raised his head to look at her. He couldn't see her eyes. They weren't closed, but the lids were partially lowered—he couldn't see the color or the expression. Then she stretched up and put her mouth softly against his, and he had his answer.

He slid his hands under her arms and around to her back—partly to urge her arms to circle his neck, just the way they did, and partly so he could spread his hands wide across her back and pull her firm and close.

Shane had known he would kiss Lisa someday. He'd wondered too long about his mouth on hers not to experience it, even if it was a goodbye kiss the moment before he walked out of her life for good. Given a choice, though, he'd imagined discovering her taste, her textures, her timing in a leisurely voyage of exploration.

This was no leisurely voyage of exploration. He flicked his tongue between her lips, and it was ignition on the blast sending a rocket to Mars, all power and fire and roar. So strong and so loud that his mind could barely keep up to collect the evidence that this Lisa was real, not in his dreams. Her back under his hands, pliant yet strong. Her fingers threading into his hair, gentle yet certain. Her hips cradling him, welcoming yet mysterious.

He plunged his tongue into her mouth with a desperate hunger and left his mind behind.

Kisses turned ragged, even frenzied on the edges of their contact, but settled into slow and deep and strong when they came back together.

His hand glided over the shoulder of that little blouse, finding the heat and heart of the flesh below. She turned her opposite shoulder into him, giving him access. At the same time her mouth left his to touch his jaw, then below it, then his neck.

She murmured something while her tongue rode the ridge of his collarbone. He nearly staggered. Holding on because he wanted so damned badly to touch her. *Her* not the blouse. He flipped open the first four buttons he could reach. He dragged his palm gently down her throat, then into the opening, his widespread fingertips feeling her heartbeat and the pulse at the base of her throat.

She'd opened his shirt. And now the soft heat of her lips covered his heartbeat, and he felt the answering kick in hers.

The stuff of dreams. His dreams.

His fingers followed the sleek curve of her breast, sliding under the fabric of her bra, reaching for the tip. *Yes.*

She sucked in a breath, her breast seeming to swell to his touch, the nipple beading and pushing.

He wanted to taste her. To take her into his mouth and—

A prickle up the back of his neck was the first warning.

Instincts warred for one balanced second, then the one to protect her made him break the kiss, angling to see behind him at the same time.

"Shane—" She sounded warm and tousled and unwilling to end this.

That gave the first instinct a little jolt, but he pushed it down as he turned her so he was between her and the approaching rider. "Someone's coming."

She went up on her toes to look over his shoulder. Her breath, in small uneven puffs, caressed the side of his neck and he mentally sent the intruder to perdition.

"Oh, Lord. Dave and Brandeis."

Lisa had her head down, busy with the buttons he'd undone. He felt a pang of loss as the material covered her.

"Shane—your shirt."

He shook his head, even though she wouldn't see it. "Too late. He knows what we were doing." Her head snapped up, and he was immeasurably relieved to see that the memory of what they were doing was hot and potent in her eyes, undulled by regrets. "But you take your time."

He dipped his head to touch his lips to hers, then faced the nearing rider, blocking any view of Lisa with his body.

Lisa's brother's cold, steady gaze didn't budge from Shane's face. He didn't mind, because that meant the other man wasn't taking in the full extent of Lisa's situation.

Of course it had to be her brother.

Lisa focused on that aspect, ignoring all others.

Dave stayed astride Brandeis and stared down at them. One glimpse as she tried to finish buttoning her blouse with fumbling fingers showed he was wearing the expressionless stare Westerners gave strangers that could be more intimidating than the worst glare, because it gave away nothing.

"Lisa. Everything okay?"

At last the final button slipped into place. As she moved past Shane, she saw that he wore that no-reaction look of his—the east-of-the-Mississippi cousin of Dave's look. Men!

"Everything's fine."

"Didn't know anybody was going to be out here today, especially not my sister." The last word had an edge to it.

Brandeis sidestepped and shook his head, picking up the vibes.

"Matty knew we were coming out here." Shane said.

"Yes, well… Time for us to get back. I have studying." Lisa took a step toward the SUV's passenger door. Neither man moved. Neither man looked in her direction.

"Coming out here to do what?" Dave demanded.

"Just seeing the ranch—" Lisa started.

"Shoot."

"Shoot?" Dave looked around, as if noticing anything besides the two human beings for the first time. "Why?"

"I was teaching Lisa to shoot," Shane deadpanned.

"We've got to go now—"

"You were—" Ignoring her attempted diversion, Dave broke off repeating Shane's words, and whistled.

"That's right," Shane acknowledged with a grin of self-mockery. "I thought I'd teach Annie Oakley here the basics of handling a gun. So she wouldn't be afraid of them."

"That's not a very nice way to treat a friend, Lees. Nothing makes a guy feel more like an idiot than trying to teach a woman something and finding out she's an expert at it."

She'd been enjoying showing up Shane. There was no sense pretending she hadn't been. He'd been so adamant…. Dave doing it wasn't nearly as much fun.

It didn't seem to bother Shane, who was saying something more about Annie Oakley. "Like that musical you told me you used to watch with your mother as a kid— what was the name of it? The one about Annie Oakley."

"Annie Get Your Gun," she murmured. Only because she was so surprised he remembered that conversation about her mother's penchant for musicals.

"Yeah, we used to watch that one," her brother said. "But Mom always says she's like another Annie."

"Dave—" Lisa warned.

"Which Annie was that?" Shane egged him on. As if Dave needed encouragement.

"Lisa's favorite song was from *Oklahoma*. The one Ado Annie sings about 'With Me It's All Or Nothing.' Never does anything halfway, that's Lisa. So when Dad started teaching her to shoot—the basics, so she'd be safe around the ranch—she went all out. Actually, she missed—"

"I need to get back home." Neither of them was listening.

"—the first target and she glared at it so hard the thing should have burst into flames. After that it was a sure thing that she'd practice and practice and practice, because if there's one thing Lisa's always hated it's being outside the bull's-eye." As if he hadn't already rubbed it in enough to Shane, Dave asked, "Did she tell you about her marksmanship awards?"

"We hadn't gotten to that. I suspect that would have been next."

Heat suffused Lisa's body. What would have happened between them next if Dave hadn't arrived would have had nothing to do with her awards.

And she would have welcomed it. Throwing self-preservation to the hot breeze without another thought. All or nothing.

"Shane. I have to get home. Now. If you're not ready to leave I'll ride behind Dave to the house and get Matty to drive me."

Lightning exploded the sky and rain thundered down, punishing the hard earth.

The heat wave was over.

Lisa ran a polishing cloth over the pad for the earring post one last time, even though it didn't need it. The box was waiting. She was idiotically delaying putting them in the box and wrapping it. Being stupid and sentimental and emotional.

Just the way she'd been Sunday at the Slash-C with Shane.

She had played by the rules. She had built a safe life and stayed carefully within its lines. Not once had she allowed herself to leap before she looked. Not once had she let herself be lost in the hopeful fog of creativity. Not once had she strayed into the uncharted realm of leading with her heart. Not once. Not one damned time.

Then Shane Garrison walked in the door.

And none of it had done any good. It had not protected her. Not from confusion. Not from making mistakes. Not from feeling. Not from wanting.

She'd let him position her to shoot, absorbing the sensation of his hands through her clothes, through her skin into somewhere deeper than her bones. The sensation of his hands sliding down her arms, covering her hands, made it harder to sight and shoot than she could ever remember.

And then when he'd turned back from putting the gun down, she'd watched his shadow coming nearer and nearer, had felt it touch her face as he bent to kiss her. She shivered now as she had then. Not from chill and not from the heat of the day. Heat and goose bumps.

Lisa, talk to me, he'd said when he brought her home.

I've got to go.

If you want me to back off you're going to have to say it.

Could she say it? If she wanted to hold together the shreds of her orderly life, she had to, but—

But maybe this time was different. Maybe...

No! Whether ordered by his bosses or driven by his own need to set things right, Shane Garrison was here on an investigation. And that was his priority.

If he wasn't staying as distant as he had before, well, this wasn't an official case, she wasn't nineteen anymore, and she was probably giving off strong enough signals to alert an airplane control tower.

The phone rang at her elbow in the spare room she'd set

up as a temporary workshop. She jumped so hard she knocked the receiver off, and had to reel it back up by the cord.

"Hello, dear."

"Mom! Where are you?"

"At the ranch. We just pulled in."

"Today? You weren't supposed to be here until Wednesday."

"Yes, dear."

"Oh, God, it is Wednesday, isn't it? I'm so confused."

"Now, that's promising."

"What?"

"Your being confused—it's definitely a step in the right direction. You've been much too certain for much too long."

"Thank you, Mother."

Her mother answered her sarcasm with a pleasant, "You're welcome, dear. Now come out to the ranch and let your father and me get a look at you, not to mention a hug."

It wasn't sleeting this time, but the driving rain was still damned cold for August. Shane didn't care. He sat on a rock where he could see the Medicine Wheel, and he wished to hell he could line up its stones somehow so they'd give him an answer to Lisa.

To himself.

What the hell was he doing in Wyoming looking for a necklace nobody but him cared about finding? What the hell was he doing these past couple weeks *not* looking for the necklace?

Before Lisa answered the knock at her door, she slid her latest sketches under the class reading she hadn't been doing. She'd promised herself she'd do that reading first thing after work. But when she walked in she'd caught sight of a partial sketch. The knock had probably saved her from another lost evening.

Shane Garrison stood on her doorstep. The breeze that had followed yesterday's heat-breaking thunderstorm ruffled his hair, a frown pressed down around his eyes.

"Check who it is before you open the door, Lisa."

"If you're here to yell at me over my safety habits, you can turn around and leave."

He opened the screen door and stepped in. He was right about one thing—she should have kept the screen door locked. She backed up, like the morning he'd cooked breakfast, but this time she wasn't in a robe, she wasn't fresh from a shower. She wore a baggy T-shirt, leggings and socks. Why didn't it feel any different?

Because he's looking at you the same way, and you like it.

"It's only part of why I'm here."

He stepped toward her. She stepped back, bumping against the lamp on the sofa table. "Shane—"

"Don't look like that." His face grim, he held his open hands to his sides, gesturing that he posed no threat to her. *Right.* "I kept a leash on myself when you were nineteen, I'll do it now. But you're not going to pretend this is because I tried to teach you to shoot when you already know how."

She jumped on it. "And told me how to kick when I didn't want to know, and gave me lessons on using my elbow I didn't want." And the earlier lesson that her mentor was a thief. And that the man she'd thought she was falling in love with saw her only as a witness to a crime. "You're always teaching me lessons I don't need and don't want."

"If you weren't scared of New York, I wouldn't—"

"I'm not scared of New York." The lightbulb clicked on. His trimming the bushes to the comments on her sandals to the tale of the break-in's effect on his father to the self-defense lessons—all revealing his concern with physical safety. "Is that what the shooting and all of it was about, because—"

"If you're not scared, why are you hiding out?"

Hiding out. The words hit a blow to her solar plexus. Was that what she'd been doing?

"I'm not scared." At least not the way he meant it. "And I don't need or want self-defense lessons."

He was shaking his head, his eyes narrowed. "You haven't been avoiding me because of that."

"I haven't been avoiding you at all."

"That's bull—" She watched him swallow something stronger. Watched the slow, deep working of his throat. She'd felt that motion under her lips. She'd tasted the skin there. "You've been avoiding me, and it's because of Sunday. Because I want you. And that scares you. It was a lot safer when I didn't show I want you, wasn't it, Lisa?"

Yes.

"Too bad." His low voice had no softness in it. "I want you, and you want me."

Oh, God, he was right. It did scare her. But could that jump of the muscle by the turn of his jaw mean it scared him, too?

The creak of a door opening cut into her awareness.

"Hello? Lisa? I can only stay a minute, because your father's chomping at the bit to ride the ranch, and I promised Jack that I'd go with him to keep him in line. But I have something I forgot to give you last night, so—"

Lisa shook herself at the first sound of the familiar voice coming from the vicinity of the garage door. The sound indicated her mother was crossing the kitchen. Lisa glared a warning at Shane, gave her shoulders a second small shake then imposed a smile on her lips.

"Hi, Mom. We're in here."

"Ah, I thought you had a visitor, but I didn't recognize the vehicle—" Donna Currick came around the corner talking, and with a warm smile. "Hello!"

"Mom, this is Shane Garrison, a...uh, an acquaintance

from New York, who's passing through town. Shane, this is my mother, Donna Currick.''

Shane's eyes flickered to her, and Lisa knew he was registering her similarities to her mother.

When she'd been younger, Lisa had been told over and over that she looked exactly like her mother. That wasn't entirely true. Donna's delicate features and lithe grace had mixed with Ed Currick's strength to make Lisa taller and stronger featured. But the proportions had remained nearly the same. And the similarities used to be strengthened by mannerism and expressions. These days she seldom heard comments about being a dead ringer for her spritely mother.

''It's a pleasure to meet you, ma'am.''

Shane put his hand out. Donna met it with both of hers, enfolding his hand more than shaking it.

''And it's wonderful to meet you, Shane. Are you the detective everyone's talking about?''

''I'm a detective.''

She beamed at him. ''Then you're most definitely the one everyone in town's talking about. They seem to think that you think my daughter can solve some mystery for you.''

''Mom—!''

''Do you?'' she insisted with bright interest but no apparent animosity.

Lisa prevented any answer. ''Shane was just leaving.''

With her back to her mother, she gave him a commanding stare. He clearly understood her message, and after a half beat of consideration, she saw that he wasn't going to argue.

''I have an appointment in town.''

A small breath of relief escaped Lisa.

''Oh, what a shame! Well, we'll have to make sure to see each other again when we have time to talk. Perhaps you could come out for—''

''We don't want to make Shane late, Mom,'' Lisa interrupted ruthlessly before her mother could have Shane lined up for family meals through New Year's.

"Yes, I'd better get going. It was nice to meet you, Mrs. Currick."

"Donna," her mother corrected.

But before she could say more, Shane had turned toward Lisa, and she saw her relief had been premature.

He wrapped one large hand around her upper arm, sliding his warm palm up under the loose short sleeve, and gave her a pointed, intense look that promised they weren't done with *this*. The temperature of that look telegraphed to anyone attuned to such undercurrents that a major ingredient in *this* was sexual.

Donna Currick was attuned enough to undercurrents to track a submarine in the Pacific Ocean all the way from Wyoming.

"I'll see you later."

It was promise, threat and proposition, all rolled into one. Even as the withdrawal of his hand left an odd impression of coolness, Lisa felt a rush of heat rising across her belly, over her breasts, up her throat and into her cheeks.

The kitchen door *thwacked* closed, and Lisa jumped.

Oh, Lord, she'd been staring after him. What would her mother think? What would she—

"So that's Shane Garrison."

Lisa barely stopped herself from spinning around and demanding what her mother meant by that tone—thoughtful, intrigued, speculative. But even her self-control couldn't stop her from giving her mother a sharp look and demanding, "Someone told you about him? About his being here?"

Her brother. Had to be. Her protective, concerned, sure-he-knew-what-was-best brother. She would apologize profusely to Matty for making her a young widow, and then she would tear Dave apart piece by piece.

"Oh, I heard a stranger was in town, of course. But I

hadn't put it together until now with what you told me about him a long time ago.''

''What *I* told you? *I* told you?'' Her voice slid up. She grabbed calm before it deserted her for good, and she shook her head. ''I never told you anything about him. I never even mentioned Shane Garrison to you. Not ever.''

At first the hopes had been too fragile and precious to voice—she'd barely allowed them to form in her own heart. Afterward, the pain had been too intense—and, yes, the embarrassment. She could admit that now. She'd been embarrassed to have been so wrong about Alex, whom she'd believed in, and to have been so wrong about Shane, whom she'd let herself weave hopes about.

''Not by name,'' Donna said with a characteristic flip of her hand. ''You never said in so many words that the man you were falling in love with was Shane Garrison, but you did say there was someone in your life that last spring before you came home.''

''Falling in love—I didn't. No, I *never* told you I was falling in love with anyone. Never. Not in any words.''

''No, dear,'' her mother said. ''You never said you were falling in love. You didn't need to say it. My children do seem to have a knack for falling in love young but needing time to settle into it. Now, I'd better go join your father or he'll be interfering with everyone's work. Oh, here's something I picked up for you.''

''Mother—''

But Donna Currick was already gone, leaving a book on the history of jewelry design.

Some time later—Lisa didn't know how much time later, because she'd been sitting under the umbrella on her deck watching the sun settle behind the mountains, with no sense of time or conscious thought—her brother came out the French doors carrying two glasses and the pitcher of iced tea from her refrigerator. She really was going to have to talk to her family about just walking into her house. Or maybe she should invest in a security system. That would make Shane happy.

Oh, God. *Making Shane happy*—when had that become part of her thinking?

"Go away, Dave."

"If he's bothering you, I can have it taken care of," he said grimly.

She didn't even pretend not to know whom he was talking about. "Good grief, you sound like a mobster."

"All right then, get him to leave town."

"I tried that," she admitted. "Ask Duane Jessup. I had no idea Shane would make Sheriff Kuerten his best buddy."

"You thought Jessup could do any good? I only met this Garrison twice, but I can see that was no even match. So Garrison won over Sheriff Kuerten, huh?" That obviously gave Dave pause. But after a moment's consideration he shook his head. "Doesn't matter. I can get Kuerten to get him out of here if you want."

She opened her mouth to sidestep the entire topic, but Dave's concern was genuine, the offer sincere. And tempting.

A voice whispered how easy it would be to let Dave send Shane on his way. No more sessions of unending questions. No more self-defense lessons with his guiding touch on her arm or leg or shoulder. No more shooting lessons with the heat and power of him wrapped around her so she could hardly—

Her mind skidded away from that like a newborn foal on a patch of ice.

"Lees?"

Yes, Dave. Please, make him go away. Let my life get back to its safe, sane routine.

What came out of her mouth was, "No. Thanks, but no. This is a situation I need to take care of myself."

"Lisa, are you—"

"Yes, I'm sure." *No, I'm not. But I'm going to do this, anyhow.*

She got up, leaving the umbrella's shade to retrieve that glass of iced tea.

Her brother took one look at her and let out a whistle. "Mom said she was coming over here, but—if I didn't know better, I'd say you've been run over by a truck named Donna Currick."

"Yeah? What would you know about that? You've always been her golden boy."

"No different from you, kid. Lisa's so smart, Lisa's so talented, Lisa's so ambitious. Besides, they let you get away with murder because you're younger and a girl. So, what did she say? Did she call you an idiot?"

She gave him a scathing look. "Right, like Mom would call her kids that."

"How about a jerk? She's called half of her kids that. She as much as said I was a *real jerk* when I was younger. Then, when Matty and I had trouble a couple years back, she said a lot more. It wasn't easy to hear, but it did make me think. Made me see things with Matty from a different perspective. It helped. Don't shut out what she says."

She could only take so much advice in one day. "When it comes down to it, this is my life, and my business. I'm the one who has to make the decisions."

"Which reminds me, I never have given you hell for calling Mom and Dad wherever they were at the time and—"

"New Zealand."

"—telling them about my business. My personal business."

"You were on the verge of blowing it with the woman you've loved all your life," she said without sympathy.

"Yeah, I was, and that's pretty much what Mom said. But I still wasn't thrilled to have my kid sister blabbing away about my business. It was my life. I'm the one who had to make the decisions."

She grimaced at his use of her own words. "All right, all right."

"Good. I have a couple more things to say."

"Dave—"

"The first thing is that Mom told me my problem was I wasn't believing enough—not in Matty and not in myself. Not in *us*. And I wasn't believing because I was scared. Now, I don't know what you're scared of, but I do know you've been scared ever since you came back from New York. No—let me finish. You were different when you came back. It's like somebody who's been thrown from a horse and now every move they make is guarded, cautious. You and I both know that's the fastest way to get thrown again. Seeing you like this makes me want to take whoever or whatever did this to you and—"

"Dave—"

"Don't say it—I know. Leave you alone. Don't butt into your life. And don't lay a finger on Garrison. Fine. For now. But if I see you unhappy…"

He swallowed and cleared his throat, and somehow the choked-up feeling transferred to her. Finally he stood.

"The last thing I'm going to say is, Thanks."

She blinked back tears. "Thanks? For what?"

"For calling Mom and Dad when Matty left me. For butting into my life. For caring about me, and about Matty."

The French doors closed behind him as he left through her house. Tears made warm splashes on her hands.

Lisa's job the afternoon of the party was to get her parents to her house for an emergency, then return them to the Slash-C by six o'clock. They would think that was plenty of time to get ready for the surprise party for Hugh and Ruth, which they'd been told would start at seven-thirty. They had seen many of the party preparations, but that was okay as long as Matty had time for the final touches that indicated this party was also for them.

Taylor and Cal were seeing to it that Hugh and Ruth, who would be expecting to help with preparations for a surprise party for Donna and Ed scheduled to start at seven-thirty, also arrived at six.

In the meantime, all the guests would have arrived by five-thirty, with their vehicles tucked out of sight. And when the two couples were brought in—the Curricks through the office door from the back, and the Moskis through the front door—there'd be the double shout of ''Surprise!''

So, at three-fifty, Lisa called the Slash-C in tears, saying her oven had stopped working in a puff of smoke and a flash of flame—circumstances sure to spur her father to action—and that the twelve-egg-white angel-food cake she was slated to bring to the party was a disaster—a cry for help her mother wouldn't be able to resist. After reassurances from Matty and Dave that they could continue the party preparations without the senior Curricks, Donna and Ed left the Slash-C and arrived at Lisa's house right on time.

Her father set down his toolbox, gave her a big hug, then got to work turning off the power so he could check out this danger to his daughter.

Her mother brought a toolbox of another kind. She grabbed her daughter, some equipment, and the pan with the ruined cake—it had taken a half-dozen strong whacks on the counter for Lisa to get the darned thing to fall, because naturally this time the cake had turned out perfectly—and headed for the kitchenette of the mobile home Ed had parked in Lisa's driveway.

Donna soon had everything ready to make a dessert out of layers of small pieces of angel food cake, strawberries, vanilla pudding, ice cream and nuts.

Lisa sat at the tiny table shredding angel food cake into the bottom of a rectangular pan, while Donna sliced the strawberries. They constructed one layer and were well on their way with the second when Donna's desultory conversation about the travels she and Ed had been on took an abrupt turn.

"Why did you leave New York, Lisa?"

"Ready for the strawberries," Lisa announced, buying herself time. "I came back to all the nice people here in Knighton. To the warmth."

"You'd always had that warmth. You'd always had these nice people around you. You'd always had a steady, predictable life. And you wanted something different. From the time you were a little girl you dreamed of going to New York and making your beautiful jewelry. Here, pour the pudding mix over it now."

"And when I left, you cried."

"Of course I did. That's what mothers do—now more cake—but I was happy for you, because you were going after what you wanted."

"What I'd thought I wanted." What I'd thought I could handle.

Suddenly her hands were empty. She'd shredded the final third of the cake in record time.

Her mother chuckled as she topped that layer with strawberries.

"Oh, my dear, dear daughter. There was never any doubt that what you wanted was what you *wanted*. When I was pregnant with you, I had cravings that would not be ignored. Your father wouldn't even ask if I was sure I had to have root beer and apples—he'd go get them. When I started having labor pains, and Doc Johnson said I was being overanxious, your father took the phone and told Doc that if this baby had decided to be born now, it was going to be born *now!* And you didn't change a bit after you were born."

Her mother's smile faded. "Until you came back from New York, and started living from your head instead of your heart. And you never talked about why."

Lisa sighed. She'd seen it with Dave, but it was even

stronger with her mother—how much her silence had worried them and hurt them.

"Let me put this in the fridge. And then I have a story to tell you."

She edited the version she'd told Matty and Taylor, playing down Shane's role in her life even more than she had for them. But she did tell her mother how Alex's arrest, trial and conviction had convinced her that she was not suited to life beyond the safety and security of Knighton.

"So I finally understood why you left New York," Lisa concluded. Then she jumped up. "Look at the time! We better collect Dad and get back to the Slash-C if we're going to help Matty before the party."

But her mother stayed seated until Lisa met her eyes. "You didn't understand at all, Lisa—I wasn't ever running from something, I was running *to* something."

Shane watched the proceedings from a corner of the porch that gave him a wide view but left him in the background. After the initial "Surprise!" and exclamations, they'd moved the main event outside, with three grills going, an impressive spread of side dishes, and a sheet cake for each celebration.

Matty Currick was a marvel. Everything went off like clockwork. And Shane would stake his reputation that neither couple had had an inkling of the part of the surprise aimed at them.

Everyone had been friendly to him. That included Donna Currick, who had introduced him to Lisa's father with a flick of intensity in her look. Ed Currick had clearly caught that flick because he gave Shane a long, measuring look and an extremely neutral hello.

Shane congratulated Hugh and Ruth, who'd surprised him with a hug. Taylor talked with him for a while, Cal said hello, Dave made sure he had a drink, and Matty zoomed by for a quick chat.

And Lisa…Lisa knew exactly where he was at all times.

He was sure of that because she arranged to be on the opposite side of the group. The one compensation was he got to watch her move in a simple jade-green dress with buttons down the front.

Now, with folks fed, sparkly lights turned on against the deepening twilight, and the mood mellow, Dave Currick clanked a spoon against the neck of a beer bottle to get everyone's attention.

"Hugh's got something to say."

The crowd milled down to silence, with Hugh and Ruth in the center.

"I've done one really smart thing in my life—and that was snag this gal fifty years ago." Cheers and applause greeted his words. "Next smartest thing I ever did was havin' neighbors like all of you. There's one of you who's got special talent in her fingers, and I'm proud to let that talent show my Ruth what these years have meant. I, uh… Here."

He held out a small package beautifully wrapped in gold paper with white and gold ribbons cascading from it like tiny waterfalls.

Everyone pressed in as Ruth unwrapped it. Shane could see that most people were straining to see what was in the package, but Lisa was watching Ruth's face.

The older woman looked inside, gasped liked women did when they were thrilled, and held the box for others to see its contents. Lisa's shoulders eased as if she'd released a long-held breath.

"Oh, Hugh!" said Ruth Moski, before that practical, levelheaded woman burst into tears.

"Hey, Ruth. No, don't cry, Ruth."

Hugh took his wife in his arms, while Donna patted him on the back and said, "Don't worry, Hugh, that's a good thing." And everyone laughed.

The crowd condensed around Ruth like a building imploding. Lisa slipped out to the fringes. Moving quietly in the darkness beyond those fringes, Shane came up behind her.

"It's good to see your work again."

She spun around, her eyes wide. "This was a one-time situation. It's not a return to jewelry design for me."

"You can't deny you've started sketching again after a long time away from it."

"Just because I didn't sketch a few times, doesn't mean I'd given it up. It doesn't mean—" She got a good look at his face then, and her expression changed. "Oh, hell. Ruth?"

"Yup. And Hugh. But now you are sketching again, and I'm thinking my coming here had something to do with that."

"If it did, it was as a way to soothe my nerves and—"

"What nerves are you trying to soothe? Maybe I could help."

"—because Hugh asked me to help him out," she concluded, ignoring his interpolation.

"There you are, missy!" Hugh was beaming as he patted Lisa on the shoulder. "Told you Ruth would love the earrings. And you—" He took Shane's hand and pumped it. "Can't thank you enough for putting me onto the idea."

Lisa's head snapped around to Shane. "You?"

"Sure," Hugh said. "I had a whole speech about how Shane here gave me the idea, then how you made 'em better'n I coulda imagined—meant to thank you both proper, in front of everybody, but every word went clear out of my head. So I'm saying thanks again for myself and for Ruth. Though I know when I tell her about this—" He clapped his palm to his forehead. "For crying out loud—I haven't told her yet. I'll be right back."

He was gone as suddenly as he'd burst upon them.

"Why did you do that?" Lisa asked in a small voice. Stunned was the only reaction he could read in her face.

"You mean besides thinking it would make a great gift for Hugh to give Ruth?" A roar set up in his head, like he was standing right next to cathedral bells that were ringing. "Remember when I asked if you wanted to know why I was here?"

"I remember, and I told you I didn't want to know. But you told me anyhow—for the necklace. What I don't understand is why you aren't off looking for it somewhere else by now. Why you're still wasting your time in Knighton when it's obvious you aren't going to find what you're looking for here."

Maybe he had found what he was looking for. So screw the necklace, screw the investigation, screw everything but the way she looked right this instant

"Maybe I needed to find you."

Her eyes were wide, her face fragile. He'd seen her look like this before...when? "But..." She shook her head, as if to clear it. "You mean for the necklace. I've told you everything I can remember. I've answered all your questions—"

"Oh, Lisa!" Ruth burst upon them this time, enveloping Lisa in a hug.

Shane never knew if he voluntarily stepped back deeper into the shadows, or if the recognition of a memory blew him back.

He knew when he'd seen that expression on her face before. The day he'd confirmed he had the evidence to arrest White and had gone to the studio, planning to do it right then. She hadn't known that of course. But when he walked in, he'd seen by that fragile expression that said she'd sensed his withdrawal and he'd wanted to wipe it away. So he'd let the arrest of Alex White slide for twenty-four hours so he could spend an evening with Lisa.

How many times had he asked himself if all the stolen pieces would have been recovered if he hadn't waited that extra day? It sure hadn't made any difference in how Lisa looked at him when White was arrested. It had gained him nothing, and it had cost him nights of sleepless wondering.

And now he recognized the clamor in his head for what it was—sirens. Clanging and howling and bellowing at him.

Here he was, letting a pair of wide eyes and his own weakness take priority over tying up a case. Did he think it would make any difference in how Lisa felt about him? Hadn't he had it drummed into his head during the weeks here that she wanted him as far away as he could get?

So, they'd had a few hot kisses. She'd run in the opposite direction, hadn't she? Just like before.

But he wasn't going to make the same mistake as before.

Lisa finally disentangled herself and looked around for Shane. Ruth's thanks and excitement had segued into a string of friends and family expressing their joy that she was back to designing jewelry. She'd sidestepped with vague murmurings and smiles until she could break free.

Shane was no longer where he'd been. But she knew he wasn't far away.

He'd been so...

Her breath caught as she remembered the glittering intensity of his eyes as he'd looked at her. A tension—and something more—seeming to come off him in waves that reached out and surrounded her, as his shadow had that day they'd kissed. But he'd never even touched her tonight.

And yet she had been touched. He'd urged Hugh to get her to make the earrings. In the second after Hugh's revelation had sunk in, she had understood that Shane had done it for no reason other than he thought it would help her.

Maybe I needed to find you.

The words had barely registered at the time, but now they reverberated in her head. What did he mean?

Urgency caught her like the push of the strengthening breeze. She had to find him. To find out...to finish what they'd been talking about.

What was it they'd been talking about...?

A cloud slid off the moon and she saw him leaning against the corral fence, watching her.

Oh, yes, the necklace.

Of course. Suddenly weary, she walked to him. "Shane, I can't imagine there is another syllable I can tell you, but if you think more questions—"

"No. We're done fooling with that. I want the letters."

"What?"

"White's letters to you. All of them."

It was like a bucket of ice water in the face.

"Let-letters?" She sputtered from weariness to fury in an instant. "Those are private. Personal."

"You want me out of your town, out of your life? That's the price."

Chapter Eleven

This time self-preservation had nothing to do with cowardice. It was self-preservation, pure and simple.

It took the form of cold precision as she drove from the Slash-C to Shane's apartment. He'd followed his edict by striding into the darkness while she'd been temporarily frozen. When she retrieved her keys and got in her car, it was with absolute clarity that she needed to pay attention to her driving—and only her driving. No other thoughts or reactions were allowed in. As soon as she turned off the car engine, however, anger swept in like a blast furnace firing up.

She slammed the car door and headed up the steps in the dark, so intent on pounding on the door that she almost stepped on Shane sitting on the top step.

She backed down one, still at eye level with him. "I want to talk to you, Garrison."

"Talk to me? You mean lay down more rules? Forget it."

"I won't forget it. I—"

"Dammit, Lisa." It wasn't a shout but it was loud enough to stir a bird sleeping in the tree that shaded the porch. He stood, towering over her, and turned around. "Get inside before this hits the Knighton grapevine and I have another visit from Jessup."

He jerked the door open, and she marched through, turning back to look at his face now that there was light. The tight lines in his face stoked her blast furnace another notch.

"*You're* angry! What reason do *you* have to be angry? I—"

"Reason? You want reasons? Try this—I don't appreciate being thanked for having the basic decency for not taking advantage of a nineteen-year-old kid. Forget about professionalism. God knows I did. Hell, if I'd had half my brain on what White was doing instead of my whole brain below my belt and—" He swore low and vehement, turning away.

She grabbed his arm trying to swing him back around. She added a second hand to her hold and budged him enough to see his profile.

"Instead of what?"

From the day he'd walked into Taylor's office he'd been pushing her into this ocean of emotions, and she was not about to let him leave her adrift now that she was in the middle of the deep waters.

"Instead of lusting after you." He turned his head toward her. "I was so tied in knots that I don't even know if I stuck with that investigation for so long because I had a gut instinct White was up to no good or because it was an excuse to be around you."

She shook her head. "You didn't let anything come between you and arresting Alex."

"You did. Even after I had the evidence. Just to have one more day—God, a kid."

"Quit saying that. I was not kid. I was—"

"Nineteen! And I was twenty-seven. I reminded myself

of that fact a hundred times a day. Would you have been happier if I'd come after you?"

"Yes!"

Her own voice shocked her into silence. Or maybe it was the blue blaze from Shane's eyes.

"Yes, I would have," she said, quiet now. "Instead everything you did was calculated, thought out ahead of time—*thought* being the operative word. Not felt."

He winced. She was sure of it. But he faced straight ahead again so she couldn't read any more of his expression.

"And now?" he said low. "You want me to act on my feelings now?"

Nothing anyone ever says or does is going to change the past, it's only going to change the present and the future.

Matty's theory.

Both sides…have to say we're here now, where do we want to go and how are we going to get there?

They were here now. Cut away the past, and only this moment existed. What did she want?

"Yes."

Again he turned only his head to look at her. For four burning breaths, she saw that stillness. Then his gaze dropped to her mouth, and the burn flashed down through the core of her body and into her soul.

"I'm not asking again," he warned.

But he still didn't turn toward her, leaving her the maximum freedom to break away. And he lowered his head slowly, forming its own kind of question.

She relaxed the fingers still gripped around his arm, running one hand to his shoulder, then across it until she could reach up and touch her fingers to his cheek.

There was no tentativeness, no brush of lips to lips. His mouth came down on hers hot and possessive. Yet it was only their mouths at first. Sliding, opening, pressing, tasting.

Then his tongue stabbed into her mouth, and they turned

into each other, her arms wrapping around his neck, his around her back.

He picked her up, carrying her in two strides to the sofa, and settled her on the cushion beside him, her legs across his lap. He drove both hands into her hair, his long fingers supporting her head as his mouth took and gave, sought and found.

Heat dissipated. Any grade-school science student knew it. She knew it for a fact from years of using heat to mold and meld metals.

So the heat from Sunday had to be gone. The sun had set, the storm had broken the heat wave, the blast of desire between them had been cooled by days and doubts.

Yet the first touch and it was there. Shimmering, dancing between, around, inside them.

Showers of embers skittered across her skin as he unbuttoned the top of her dress to rub his prickled jaw in the valley between her breasts. Her blood turned molten at the draw of his mouth on the hardened tip of her nipple. Fire surged through her veins at the touch of his hand delving just under the hem of her dress.

She met the heat in him, with her mouth to his throat, her fingers opening his shirt, her palms absorbing the resilient texture of the hair sprinkled across his chest, then following it down between his ribs. Lower. To where her touch caused a rippling in his muscles that gave her the opening to slide lower, beneath his zipper.

"I want to hear it."

"What?"

"That you want me."

"I want you, Shane Garrison." Eight years ago, now and probably every day in between.

His hand slid over the outside curve of her thigh. Reaching the elastic edge of her panties. Closer, but not yet where she wanted his touch. She squirmed to ease the wanting, felt the evidence of his ever-expanding pleasure and wanted even more.

"Lisa. Are you on something? Birth control?"

Heat did something to the words. They contracted and expanded like on a tape left too long in the sun. It took concentration to abstract the meaning from the noise. It took willpower to answer.

"No."

He held totally still for a moment. Then he sucked in air with breaths so deep the movement of his chest rocked her. He rearranged them, subtly closing her open dress, scooting her hem to upper thigh. His lips to her temple, he stroked her hair.

"You…you don't have anything?" His actions gave the answer, but she hoped…

"Are you kidding? The way things have been between us, I thought being tarred and feathered and run out of town on a rail was more likely."

She chuckled.

He pulled back enough to meet her eyes. "I could use a good laugh right now. Want to share?"

"Matty once volunteered for that duty."

He dropped his head back with his lips to her temple. "That figures."

"Shane…" She spread her hand inside his shirt, her fingers feathering across one flat brown nipple. The tightening of the nub and the jump of his heartbeat under her palm gave her the courage to continue. "There are other ways…"

"Not for us. Not the first time. I want to be inside you."

Heat stabbed through her so hard and fast that she shuddered with it.

He muttered a curse, kissed her hard once on the lips, then set her beside him on the sofa, one arm still around her shoulders but otherwise not touching her.

"I know you don't like lessons, but this should be one for both of us about starting something we can't finish."

"How did this start?" Her voice sounded as throaty as if she'd been caught in smoke.

"You mean like the first time I saw you in New York?"

She shook her head. "Tonight. To get us here, sitting like this thinking…"

"What? What are you thinking, Lisa?" He sounded raspy, too.

"I'm thinking there's one hell of a business opportunity for the right entrepreneur for we-deliver condoms."

He chuckled as he stroked her shoulder. "It would have to be We Deliver Damned Fast."

Her mind started kicking in again. At least enough to trace back the conversation that had brought them to this point.

"This doesn't change what I said before, Shane. About the letters."

"They're personal," he quoted, pushing her hair behind her ear. "Private."

"I owe him, Shane. I won't cheat him of the little dignity he has left. I have to do this my way. I'll look at them again. If there's anything I didn't see before, if there's anything…I will tell you. You have to understand."

He stared straight ahead, yet his expression reminded her of that moment at Medicine Wheel when he'd thrown back his head and let the sleet hit his face.

"You haven't left me a choice." He still didn't look at her. "If I don't accept your conditions, you could close the door on me."

He didn't say if he meant only on his chances of finding the necklace or on something more.

And she didn't ask.

Lisa opened the box of letters she'd taken from the shelf in her linen closet.

She'd considered waiting until the morning, tackling them after a good night's sleep. But she wouldn't sleep. Not with her body thrumming with both pleasure and frustration. Not with her head spinning with questions.

The earliest one was at the back, with each letter Alex

White had sent her placed in front of the previous one. She ruffled across them with her hand, setting the deterioration of his handwriting into motion.

Oh, Alex.

But she didn't let the tears that burned her eyes fall. There were emotions in this box—her emotions about Alex, as well as about Shane and about herself. She'd kept them walled off all this time. Afraid to feel the painful ones, forgetting the healing of the others. Shane had forced her to take this box down from the shelf. As his conspiring with Hugh had pushed her to design and make jewelry again.

But she had to take this next step by herself. As her hands alone had shaped the gold, selected the stones, soldered, buffed, washed and polished.

She opened the first letter and began reading.

The afternoon sun was warm at Lisa's back. She shifted the box to her left hip, freeing her right hand to knock on the door of Shane's apartment. She drew in a deep breath.

She knew what she was going to do. She'd known it from the moment she woke close to noon, curled on her bed with the last few letters left to read beside her. She'd finished those, showered, dressed in shorts and a shirt and headed here.

It was harder this way than being caught in the moment…harder and more important.

She knocked on the door.

A call of "Just a minute" came immediately, then sounds of motion.

When the door jerked open it caught her by surprise. But it was the sight of Shane that made her suck in her breath.

He had clearly just come out of the shower, with his hair half-dry, beads of moisture glinting in the T of hair on his chest, and wearing only shorts. And those appeared to be a last minute addition.

"I brought…" She couldn't get out more than that, silently holding up the box.

His gaze flicked to the box, then pinned on her face. He opened the screen door. When she offered the box again, he didn't take it from her or even look at it, instead tipping his head toward the desk.

A towel was draped across the bathroom threshold as if it had been discarded on the run. It must have been around his hips. He'd pulled it off and… Placing the box on the desk she squeezed her eyes closed to keep the image from swamping her need to say this.

"I read them all again. Maybe you'll see something in them, but there was nothing about the necklace. Nothing to help you…" She swallowed and started again, looking down at her hands still resting on the box. "But they helped me. I've been hiding out. I know that now. It's time to stop."

Brave words from a woman who still hadn't turned around to face him.

He came up behind her. She could feel the moist heat from his body at her back, even more potent than the afternoon sun.

He rested his hands at her waist. She could see the tips of his fingers against the turquoise of her shirt.

Slowly he lowered his hands, resting them on the flare of her hips. If he'd tried to turn her to face him, she might have stood firm. If he'd tried to draw her back against his chest she might have resisted. If he'd tried to control, she might have broken free. But he simply rested his hands there, his palms communicating heat. The heat grew. Or her sensitivity to it grew.

"I do want you, Shane."

His hands flexed, ever so slightly. The thumbs nudging into the flesh just below her waist. Again. And again. He lowered his hands another inch, then another, then began to climb. A massaging so seductive—no, she wasn't being seduced. She was a participant, a most willing participant.

But for now accepting this sensation was so…so very satisfying.

Neither forward nor back. Inexorably up, never letting his hands slip around to her breasts. She wanted them there…but she didn't want to forfeit the sensation of this moment.

His hands kneaded across her shoulders until his thumbs met at the base of her neck. They started a path of almost imperceptible progress. She wanted to let her head fall forward, but didn't.

Why not? Would it show weakness? So what. She wasn't perfect.

She dropped her head forward, changing, deepening his touch along her spine. Still without letting their bodies touch, he'd come closer…how did she know that? Ah, yes, from his heat radiating across her back.

Recognition of a tension point seeped into her. Finally localizing it, she became aware of her hands gripping the edge of the desk. She released her hold. That left only one coiling tension and its release was not nearly so simple a matter. She moaned, swaying slightly.

Shane waited for her to regain her equilibrium, then slowly drew her back to bring her in full, heated contact with the front of his body.

She hadn't brought just the letters to him. She'd brought herself. She wouldn't stop this, and she prayed he wouldn't, either.

He slid his hands over her shoulders, spreading them across her collarbone and urging her head back against his shoulder. His head bent, pressing his lips to the side of her throat.

All the touching had been his, and she had cherished it. But she also needed to touch, to give. She reached, found the slick material of his shorts and slid her palm down the back of his thigh, stretching her fingertips to full extension. She knew her power in the surge of his erection against her. The knowledge and the contact brought a flush of shivers across her chest and down into her core.

Goose bumps and heat.

"What?" His hoarse rumble in her ear was another friction of delight.

But she couldn't concentrate on just one delight because his long, blunt-tipped fingers were at the buttons of her shirt, brushing against her skin, stroking it and exposing more with each motion.

"So good." Her murmur turned to a sigh as her shirt opened and he stroked his fingertips across her breast.

Watching his hand on her breast twisted the coil of tension deliciously tighter. The power and strength of that large hand, the delicacy of her own skin only partially covered by lace and softness.

She stretched both hands behind him to stroke there. Her position gave him free access to her breasts and he took full advantage. He slid his hands into the cups, covering her breasts, and pushing down the material to free them. Yet they were not free, for they were captive to the exquisite torture of his touch.

She turned, her arms going around his neck, feeling the press of his aroused body against hers, the hair and muscle of his chest against her sensitized nipples.

"Lisa?" He pressed his forehead to her forehead. "I don't want to rush you."

He thought she'd turned to him in shyness? In a need to slow down. No, definitely no.

"You don't think eight years of foreplay is enough?"

His eyes flared to blue heat, but he also produced a grin.

"You pick a hell of a time to show you've got your sense of humor back—we-deliver condoms and eight years of foreplay."

Get it back? Had she lost it? She didn't care. She had a stampede going on in her senses that had nothing to do with humor.

She tipped her head to look at him as she unhooked her

shorts and let them drop. She shrugged off the open shirt and reached back for the hook of her bra. But his hands replaced hers.

She stepped into him to make it easier and to slide her palms down his back and under the elastic of his shorts, over the muscle-hardened curve of his buttocks.

He made a sound so low in his throat it seemed to come from his gut. The rest was a blur of sensation and elation. He jerked off his shorts, maneuvered them both to the bed and had them side by side. She barely caught her breath while he opened the bedside table drawer for a foil packet and put on its contents with more speed than finesse. Then he rolled back to her, dragging down her panties with her help, and there was no time or thought or desire to spare for breathing.

He opened her legs with gentle hands and the urgency of his body. He touched her, so lightly. Her hips came off the bed, pursuing the fuller contact she craved. His fingers delved where she was already wet and hot. He made that sound again, and then positioned himself and pushed into her. She felt her body's resistance and wanted to scream.

"Okay. It's okay. Take it slow," he murmured to her.

"I don't want to take it slow."

She pressed her feet flat on the bed to lift her hips, and he adjusted, finding the right angle with a driving motion he couldn't hold back. She wrapped her legs around him, drawing him in, pushing his slow consideration to frenzied strokes.

He tensed, muscles bunching, cords tightening in his neck, the pressure of his body inside hers pulsing hotly.

Everything released at once, with her name escaping his lips on an exhalation. He collapsed onto her. She wrapped her arms across his shoulders and held him to her.

Shane dragged in air, expanding his chest so it pressed even tighter against her breasts. It set up a new friction that mixed with her wonder that she had created such a response in him.

He expelled the breath in a rush on the tail of a "Damn." Then sucked in another breath before he could say. "I wanted you to— Sorry."

"It's all right. Better than all right. This feels so good…"

"It's not all right." Still inside her, he levered his upper body, looking at her. Balanced on one forearm, he stroked her hair back from her face, kissed her softly.

She was smiling as he pushed his upper body farther away, opening space all the way to where he entered her. To where they connected. Lisa gasped at the clutch of her inner muscles at the sight. He brushed across her hardened nipple and the clutch came harder, rocking her hips.

He growled, and dropped his mouth to her nipple. Sucking, stroking, licking, drawing.

Two times more her muscles clutched against the fullness inside her. Three, four times. Was that six? No, seven. Then no counting, no keeping track, not even of the molecules that made up her body most times of the day. They were spinning, wildly expanding…and then they flung themselves, wide and glorious, into the universe.

She didn't realize she'd drifted off until the motion of his getting out of bed roused her. He grabbed the towel from the threshold as he entered the bathroom.

She was glad they hadn't made love last night. If they had it would have been about the heat between them. Not that she had any wish to deny the heat. It was spectacular. But until she'd read through the letters again—more important—until she'd brought them to Shane, there would have been no heart behind the heat.

A few minutes later he returned, wearing nothing but a thunderous expression.

"What's wrong?" The words felt raw because her throat had constricted.

As he crawled back into bed beside her, he muttered something that sounded like "fast on the trigger" then "like a randy teenager."

She relaxed, stroking his side. He shifted, and when she saw his face she knew he was still wrestling with this.

"Shane, I didn't fake— I mean you do know I really— When you…I, um…"

How stupid to stumble over the word considering the intimacy they'd shared, and their continued nakedness.

"Yeah, I know."

His eyes never left hers, and the heat gathered again deep in her stomach.

Her breasts rose and fell faster, her nipples hardening. He watched the motion with concentrated attention, and the more he watched, the faster the rhythm. He pressed a soft, almost sweet kiss to one. Her response was neither soft nor sweet.

He grabbed another condom from the drawer.

"Not the way you're going to come."

Shane left her alone in the bathroom with the blow-dryer.

Would she leave when she came out? Would she pull back into her cautious mode? Would she regret these hours? Would she look at him like a stranger?

Hell. Whatever she did, he wouldn't make it any better by hovering like a buzzard around the bathroom door. He took the box of letters from the desk, cleared off the coffee table and set to work.

He hadn't left her alone much since she had shown up twenty-five hours ago. Just now she'd been in the shower and he'd invited himself in to wash her hair—and other parts.

She hadn't objected, but he didn't fool himself. Reaction was going to set in anytime and she'd be itching for some space. Someone who'd spent so many years being cautious and orderly didn't let it all go without a backward glance.

Hunger had forced them out of bed around eleven last night. She'd declared her clothes irretrievably wrinkled, so she'd worn one of his Wisconsin T-shirts, trailing down to her midthigh. They'd foraged for food in his refrigerator.

He would have settled for a cheese sandwich or scrambled eggs, with ice cream for dessert. She'd produced French toast and split bananas grilled with lemon and cinnamon.

They ate in bed, with some old movie on the TV. If he'd been quizzed five minutes later, he wouldn't have recognized a single scene. He was too busy enjoying her animated commentary.

They made love again. Slowly this time, almost as slowly as he'd wanted to make it for her the first time. With a lot of exploring and touching and holding. Sometime before dawn he woke up with Lisa in his arms and an idiotic smile on his face. Sometime after dawn he woke up with Lisa touching him. Hours later they had microwave popcorn in bed for breakfast. They didn't get into the shower until an hour ago.

When he heard the bathroom door open, he kept working. She stood behind him for a full three minutes before she spoke.

"What are you doing?"

He didn't turn around. He figured staying behind him was one way for her to have a little space. He wouldn't take it away.

"Dividing the letters as I read them. I figure the date's not as important as White's state of mind when he wrote each letter. So those are the piles—" He gestured to the six divisions, most with only one letter so far. "Mostly about the distant past. Mostly about the time when he was stealing the pieces. Mostly about your future. Mostly about the present. Elements from all the above. Not really with it."

"Oh."

She drew in another breath, and he braced for her to announce she was leaving.

"I suppose that makes sense. I'll leave you to it."

He worked through the letters while listening to her moving around. At one point he thought she opened the envelope of her sketches that he'd left out. Good.

He finished the last letter and dropped it on the Mostly Her Future pile. Alex White had a lot of problems, but he recognized talent when he saw it, and he wanted the best future possible for Lisa.

Shane heard the drawer on the bedside table open and a choked sound between a laugh and cough. He twisted around and saw her—still wearing his T-shirt—with her hand over her mouth.

"Sorry, I didn't want to interrupt your reading."

"I'm taking a break."

She looked down into the drawer where he'd put the condoms and back at him. "You got quite a supply."

"Uh-huh. Had to go to Sheridan for them, so I figured I should make the trip worthwhile."

"Sheridan? But they have them at the—" She met his raised eyebrows. "Oh."

"Right. I was raised in a small town, too. First time I bought condoms, my mother knew about it before I got home. I hadn't recognized the clerk, but she knew I was Molly Garrison's boy, and there I was—busted."

"Going to Sheridan was very considerate of you." Without closing the drawer or looking at him, she changed the subject. "Where'd you go last night?"

That surprised him. "I didn't think you'd realized I'd left."

"I had other things on my mind when you came back to bed."

His body surged at the memory. "I noticed. I took your keys and moved your car to the lot by Taylor's office and walked back. I figured you would prefer questions about what was wrong with your car to questions about why it was here all night."

Her eyes widened as he spoke. By the end a faint smile had formed, too. "You have learned a lot during your time in Knighton. Thank you."

"You're welcome, now why don't you come sit by me and take a break, too?"

"Will you tell me about seeing Alex in prison?"

"Okay." He faced forward, spread his arms across the top of the cushion, dropped his head back, closed his eyes and waited.

He heard the drawer close, her coming around to the far corner of the couch. Then came a sound he couldn't identify. He opened his eyes to find her dropping the last of a handful of condoms on the coffee table. His eyebrows shot up.

She met his look with humor and something a lot hotter sparkling in her eyes.

He groaned. "Has the possibility that you're overestimating my stamina occurred to you?"

She kissed his left eyebrow as she sat beside him. "These aren't a hint. They're insurance. Just in case our recent track record continues. Now, tell me about Alex."

He told her about White refusing to say anything about the necklace's whereabouts except that it was where it would do the most good. He answered her questions about how the man had looked and sounded. He told her everything except White's prodding him about her.

"I don't understand what he means by 'where it will do the most good.' Is he thinking of preserving the necklace?" she asked.

"Maybe. Or of preserving something else he might think was important."

"Like what?"

"You. He—"

"Me!"

"—thinks very highly of your talent, and of you. Almost as highly as I do."

She gave him a look he couldn't decipher. That wasn't good. "Let's get our minds off the necklace for a while. Talk about something else. Tell me about Julianne and the new job."

"Whoa, why put those two things together?"

"Because they're related. According to the news report,

Ann Kaleski was killed in late winter, and you said that's when you realized Julianne had left. You chewed over your reaction—your nonreaction—a while and then you took the new job.''

The knowledge that she was right surfaced from his gut as if it had been waiting for him to see the light:

"Guess I need a break. It's gotten so I have an easier time talking to witnesses and suspects than ordinary people. Maybe it's seeing too much.''

"That's why you skipped going home to Wisconsin this past Christmas?''

He wanted to shut off her questions; even more he wanted to shut off his answers. But she was looking at him, expecting more of him.

"The year before was stilted. Better to stay away last Christmas than to see their confusion again. Then, when Julianne left, and everybody was saying they were sorry, and I wasn't, I realized I hadn't felt anything for a long time, but I couldn't pin down exactly when. That bothered me. So I started working it like a case. Looking at the evidence, working it backward—until I came to you.''

She had her head tipped, studying him. But her eyes held no judgment. "You felt. You just didn't want to show it. So you developed that no-reaction reaction when you shut everybody out. I remember flashes of it eight years ago. Only it gets to be such a habit that it clamps down over you even when you might like to show your feelings. Like—''

"That's—''

She talked over him. "Like I'd been doing since I came back from New York.''

He saw it right away. He didn't like it. "Another unwanted lesson I taught you?''

She reached across the space between them and touched her fingertips to his throat as if she knew of the rawness there.

"If you taught it to me, you also helped unteach me, Shane. I just hope you've untaught yourself."

He cupped his hands around her neck, his thumbs overlapping on the soft underside of her chin, the ends of her hair tickling the back of his hands. He kissed her.

He kissed her again and again. They were making out on the couch like a couple of teenagers, and he couldn't believe how fast and hard he got turned on. Touching her through the material of the shirt was as thrilling as if he'd never touched and kissed and tasted every inch of her.

Then he discovered she wore his shirt and that's *all* she wore. And the condoms she'd brought over *in case* turned into a necessity. He pulled her across his lap to straddle him, and other than that thin plastic protection, neither of them wore anything but each other.

She woke the next morning with the idea fully formed.

As if she'd gone to sleep with all the pieces in her head, and unseen hands had put them together while she slept.

Still, she didn't move. She considered the idea from every angle, testing the fit of this piece and that. All snug. All contributing to the overall design.

And so like Alex.

After a foraged supper last night, she and Shane had spent several hours reading the letters from each pile aloud to each other. Digging hard for any shred of a lead. There hadn't been much.

Then they'd both forgotten about the letters and the list and the necklace when he'd kissed her. She'd fallen asleep an hour later, her muscles sore and sated.

Now she dressed silently, not considering the alternative—not until she stood at the open door and looked back at Shane still sleeping in the bed they'd shared. It felt strange to be leaving here after all these hours.

She could wake him....

No, let him sleep. And she would find out. It might be nothing.

In another two minutes he was going to say the hell with surveillance, and he was going in there to find out what was taking her so long.

When she'd gotten out of bed and dressed so quietly, he'd figured the most likely reasons were to get away from him or to get to the necklace. He'd hoped when she stood at the door…but she'd closed it and left.

Her note said she'd gone home to get ready for work; she'd talk to him later. She'd had to walk to the office to get her car, so he'd had plenty of time to dress and pick up her trail. He'd seen her leave a note at the office, too, then followed her to the Slash-C.

He'd told himself she might have come out to this barn for a hundred other reasons. A cop couldn't afford to forget other possibilities. Sure, the pieces of what had happened might add up to her having figured out where White hid the necklace and deciding to go after it without telling him. Without trusting him, even after…

Maybe she'd needed to clear her head. To take a ride the way some folks took a walk. To let what had happened settle into place. If he was honest with himself, it had rocked him—and he'd been half expecting and wholly hoping for it. So the effect on Lisa, who'd been so sure for so long there was nothing left between them, had to be like seeing the Big Horn Mountains collapse.

So he'd waited. And tried not to wonder. Tried even harder not to rerun the scent of her with every breath, the taste of her against his lips, the pulse of her all around him.

Then, as the second hand on his watch advanced as if it were powered by molasses, new possibilities crept in.

What if she'd gone up into the hayloft and fallen? Or one of those horses could have turned mean on her. There must be a couple hundred ways a woman could get injured in there. She might be lying on the cold barn floor right now, in pain.

The hell with giving her another two minutes—

Lisa came out of the barn with something white in her hands.

He couldn't see what it was, but he could see that she wasn't bleeding or limping. He breathed in that reality for a second before grabbing his binoculars.

Somehow they ended up trained on her face instead of examining what she held. The powerful magnification brought her expression close enough to see the tuck between her brows, the hint of excitement in her eyes. He was a hell of a lot less certain about what else he saw there.

Secure the package. That's what every bit of training told him to do. When there was no danger to bystanders, no danger to the officer, no danger to the evidence, and no danger to the subject, securing the evidence was the necessary step.

But how about the danger to something else—to the trust that had built up between him and Lisa.

Built up thin, delicate layer upon thin, difficult layer. Until they stepped back and looked at all those layers piled up and realized that what they'd built was the first floor of a damned palace.

A palace in danger of having its foundations pulled out from under it right now.

He could move in and take the package. He'd have his perfect career record. Nothing to nag at the back of his mind at night. Nothing to play what-if about or to second-guess himself about.

But whatever he did he had to do right now, because she was opening her car door.

Shane secured the binoculars, backed out of his viewing spot and half-skidded down the hillside, with his heels digging into the soil.

He started the SUV and came to the Y in the rough track. One leg led toward the barn, Lisa and the package; the other leg led to the main road that would take him back to the apartment. To wait. And hope.

Chapter Twelve

Shane was frying bacon, his shirt hanging loose, his feet bare.

"You know, you really should be more careful." Lisa had walked straight into his apartment because the door was unlocked, just the way she'd left it.

He'd given no sign of hearing her come in, but he didn't turn around at her voice.

"You mean about leaving doors unlocked? You're the one who keeps telling me this isn't Manhattan."

"Actually, I was thinking of these ranch-hand breakfasts." She moved aside the grocery bag that announced he'd been to the market since she'd left earlier this morning. "You're starting to make them a habit."

"So, it's cholesterol, not crime you're worried about."

"Oh, I worry about crime."

She was surprised her voice didn't shake when she said that. She was even more surprised her hands didn't shake when she walked up to his side and held out the package wrapped almost casually in once-white paper, now yellowed, but otherwise intact.

"I believe this is what you've been looking for."

He glanced at the package, then his eyes came to her face.

"Is it?"

Maybe I needed to find you.

She thought that was in his eyes, but could she be sure?

The spit of bacon grease made her jump, and she realized her hands were trembling. He turned off the burner and wrapped both his hands around hers and the package.

"The necklace?"

She nodded.

Instead of opening the package he looked at it, sitting in a nest of their hands.

"Shane." He met her eyes. "Thank you."

"What for?"

"I saw you." It was the simplest way of saying something that wasn't simple at all.

"You couldn't have."

"You're right. I didn't see you—I saw the evidence of your leaving. You must have gone down that hill like a bulldozer. You left a plume of dust as high as a house."

He swore under his breath. "Don't have to worry about that in New York."

The urge to laugh died under the weight of the other issues between them. She slipped her hands free, removing them from between the package and his hold.

"You trusted me to bring you the necklace. Thank you."

His head came up, and his eyes met hers. The flecks of black seemed to glitter against the blue.

She pulled in a steadying stream of air. "So, now what?" She was surprised at how much asking the question hurt, when it was the answer she dreaded.

"First, let's take a look at this thing."

He put the package on the counter, took a table knife from the drawer and used its tip to pull back the layers of paper she'd loosened.

"I didn't think about fingerprints. Mine are all over it now."

"This is more force of habit. I don't think there'll be any doubt that White took this along with the others. There's a note here."

"A note? From Alex?"

"I sure as hell hope so," he muttered, grabbing a second knife and, using both together, smoothing out the folds in the heavy paper enough to read it.

The note was dated April 6 from eight years ago.

"You'd just started investigating Alex then."

He shot her a look—too fast to categorize it—then back to the note.

My dear Lisa,
If you are reading this, my preferred line of action has not borne out. Quelle dommage! Still, great minds prepare for contingencies, so here we are.

As you are aware from having worked with me, I am the master at envisioning the perfect assemblage of line and color.

"Modest, too," Shane muttered.

If a piece has fallen short of the perfection of my vision, it has invariably been the result of the stones failing to match that vision. In you and Shane Garrison I recognized strong—though not yet perfectly polished—stones, which taken together bring out the depth of color and clarity in each other. I knew from the first the perfect design for you both, intricate yet simple and durable. And so I set to work drawing you gradually toward your destinies.

You have cooperated quite well to this point. But Shane Garrison is a more obdurate stone than I had first thought. This has produced unfortunate consequences.

I might not be able to pursue my life as I choose for too much longer. I have addressed that contingency by leaving this breadcrumb here with the assistance—unwitting though it might be—of your charming mother. I am certain that if other circumstances should conspire to push you and our granite-willed young swain apart, that this breadcrumb will lead him back into your orbit. Then, my dear, it is all up to your magnetism.

If I am being overly pessimistic in that regard, I shall retrieve this necklace and find another way to ease young Garrison's stubbornness.

His rigorous standards have not allowed him to fully explore the feelings he has toward you. He dances around those feelings with the elaborateness of a minuet, yet still holds back.

Never fear, my dear, sunny bur marigold. I shall prevail!

It ended with the interlocking flourishes of his signature.

"Oh, God." A whisper was all she could manage. All this from Alex's matchmaking!

Shane said nothing, intent on lifting the lid of the box with the knife tips. He placed the lid on the counter and began meticulously pulling back the layers of tissue until emeralds and diamonds and platinum glowed out of the box at them.

He whistled but never looked up, as he methodically

used the knife to close the box, refold the note and draw the outside papers back into position.

Then he straightened and faced her.

"I have to go back."

The pain stunned her. What had she expected? He had the necklace, that was the end of it. "Of course."

"I have to," he repeated, as if she'd argued with him. "It's not like I can put this in a box and ship it to New York."

"No. How soon will you leave?"

His gaze went over the room, as if estimating how long it would take him to pack his belongings. How long to get out of her life.

"I should get a statement from you mother, but that shouldn't take long."

"You don't know my mother."

"Alex White arrived quite unexpectedly that weekend. He said a friend had flown him in from Denver on his private plane. We were astonished, but made him welcome, of course. He said he wanted to talk to your father and me about your career prospects."

"You never told me this!"

"He asked us not to. He wanted us to understand how incredibly talented you are—as if we didn't know—and talked of sending you to study in Italy and of introducing your work in major shows. But he didn't want to lay out that plan to you yet to avoid putting pressure on you."

"And the package, Mrs. Currick?"

"Please, call me Donna." She gave Shane a warm smile, as if this were a social call. "After Lisa's father left to check on flood damage—and I suspect to lick his wounds over the idea of his baby daughter growing up—Alex told me he'd left a package for Lisa in her old trunk in the barn, which apparently she had described to him in some detail.

He asked that I not give it to her or tell her where it was unless she asked about it.''

"And you agreed, Mother? Didn't you ask him what was in it? Or—''

"Certainly not. He was a guest in our home. He'd asked me to do him a favor, and I agreed. I knew later about Alex's arrest, of course, but—''

"What? But—you've never said anything—''

"You've never said anything, either, Lisa. Not until Friday, and then with the party and…'' A flicker of her eyes made Lisa wonder if her mother knew where she'd spent the rest of the weekend. "Your father felt that until you brought up the subject, neither should we. So, how did you know to look in the barn, dear?''

Lisa sank back against the chair cushion. "It was a hunch. I thought maybe there'd been a second visit I didn't know about—Rainie said something about my white-haired friend from New York, but Alex was never in the café on the first visit. Plus, he said he'd like to see your Spring Beauties blooming again, but he was here with me in September. Alex mentioned something about the trunk with my first efforts on the phone. And if Shane's theory about Alex's motivation was right…''

She glanced over at Shane. He immediately looked away from her.

Pulling out his cell phone, he stood. "I better check on flights.''

"Of course, dear,'' her mother said. "The number for the Sheridan airport is on the bulletin board by the back door.''

Lisa stared at her mother in silence until she heard Shane's muffled voice coming from the kitchen.

"Mom, you had to have had suspicions about Alex and that package. Why didn't you ever tell me or Shane about it? I know you had to have put it together.''

For a moment she thought her mother would ignore her questions. "It was your mystery to solve."

"But that necklace could have stayed out there—"

"Oh, I'm not talking about the package. If it had looked like Shane was leaving without you two getting around to going out there, I would have mentioned Alex's trip. That's not the mystery I meant."

"But that's—"

"No flights until 6:00 a.m.," Shane said as he came into the room and stopped beside her chair. "We better go now. Thank you, Mrs. Cur—Donna."

She rose, taking his hand in both of hers. "You're welcome, Shane." She stretched up and kissed him on the cheek. "Take good care of yourself until we see you again."

He looked both surprised and pleased.

They drove toward Knighton without speaking. But not in silence. A chorus drummed in Lisa's head.

Six o'clock. He was leaving at six o'clock. Barely half a day, and he'd be gone.

She'd wanted so desperately for him to leave, and now he was. Why did she have to get what she'd wished for only after she'd stopped wishing for it?

He pulled into her driveway and stopped. "I have to make calls, pack, settle up with Hugh and Ruth—"

"Of course. I understand. I hope everything goes well for you, and—"

"I should be back by seven."

"Seven?" She repeated it as if her familiarity with numbers stopped at six.

"If it's okay with you."

Eleven hours was so much less than enough. And so much more than she'd feared she'd have.

"Yes. I'll make dinner."

He hooked one hand around the back of her neck. He

kissed her hard and deep, but not long. Not nearly long enough. Then he was gone.

Shane had learned to push back sleep when he needed to. It was a useful ability for a detective. It was a necessity for a man leaving too soon.

Lying on his back in Lisa's bed, with his arm around her, her head pillowed on his shoulder, he had no intention of letting either one of them sleep tonight. They'd eaten and made love. He was content at this moment to hold her like this and to have his left hand held up as she massaged it with both her strong, talented hands.

There was a nick near the nail of her right index finger and redness across the thumb's knuckle. He drew their hands close enough to kiss each spot, then gave control back to her.

"What happened when you went in the barn? Were you looking for the necklace all that time."

She linked her fingers through his, holding their hands up as if examining the effect.

"Not really. I saw the trunk where Mom's kept everything I ever made when I retrieved my tools to make Ruth's earrings. When I came back from New York, I threw everything in that trunk. I never even looked at it. So I had to go through my sketches from my time with Alex to get down to the package. I got distracted...I know looking at old sketches instead of just digging through them for a fabulous necklace wouldn't make sense to most people—"

"And what did you see?"

"I was good."

He jackknifed up, then bent to kiss her rib cage below her breasts. "You're still good."

"Hmm." Her sound of satisfaction vibrated under his mouth. "Actually, I'm better."

He raised his head to look at her, smiling. "Oh?"

"Yup." Her eyes were serious, but a smile lifted her lips, too. "The sketches I've done these past few weeks—the ones you took from the trash and the ones for Ruth's earrings—are better than the work I was doing at the end with Alex. My technique is rusty, and I'll need to get updated on the new alloys and—"

He kissed her, a sweet contact of mouth to mouth. "You're going to design again."

"Maybe part-time, while—"

This kiss was firmer, and he snared her bottom lip between his teeth.

"You have too much talent for part-time. Besides, now you have an MBA, all that business and legal background—hell, you should run your own studio."

"I can't just leave Taylor," she protested.

"She'd be thrilled. Especially—" he slid lower in the bed, dragging his body along hers in a friction so delicious he felt like singing hallelujahs "—since you're better."

And then—to make sure she understood the context had changed from designing jewelry—he raised her left knee and slid his tongue along the remembered track of a water drop that he'd so envied four weeks ago.

Some time later as she nestled against him, he murmured, "Yes, definitely better."

He was a man who set things right. He had found the necklace and would return it to the rightful owner, setting that final piece right.

And he'd set her right.

He'd destroyed the orderly, cautious routine she'd smothered herself in and made her breathe again. She wouldn't go back to either the girl she'd been or the robot she'd tried to be. Discipline and experience would now temper the creativity she'd once let run wild...the creativity and the emotions.

Oh, yes, he'd definitely returned her to the world of the emotions.

She loved Shane Garrison.

At nineteen she'd been so totally and completely unprepared to love him. The first time he became absorbed in a case she would have felt it as a rejection. Now she had context for that absorption, she had understanding of it, she'd even shared it the past few days.

And she knew what she had to give him. To keep him from becoming an exile from the world of emotions, too. He'd risked the necklace by trusting her. Could he risk more? Could he accept her love? Could he love her?

Taylor had said that to love you needed to trust the other person, but to let yourself be loved you needed to trust yourself. She'd faced both those obstacles. But Shane had pushed and prodded her past them. Could she do the same for him?

"Lisa." Shane spoke into the darkness as if he knew she was awake. "I asked Hugh to get the SUV back to the rental company. I told him unless I called, I'd—" He made a rough sound low in his throat. "Take me to the airport. Come see me off."

No. She wouldn't stand there and watch him fly away. She couldn't.

"Okay."

Yes, she would. Because he'd asked it of her.

She didn't cry.

The burning at the back of her eyes never eased. The brick that had lodged in her throat never softened. But no tears fell.

Not even when they'd turned over his suitcase to the single ticket clerk and headed toward the tarmac. He put his hand to the small of her back and guided her out of the small building. A tremor of goose bumps and heat spread from that point.

Shane glanced toward the waiting sixteen-passenger plane, then turned to her. "Lisa—"

"Let me, Shane. Let me say thank you."

"Thank you?" His voice sounded strained.

"Yes, thank you. I fought you every step of the way, but I do thank you for making me let go of the ghosts. For making me see that living a cautious life isn't safe or sane when it's not who I am. Thank you for making me return to myself. No—better. No longer all or nothing, but some of each—the best of each, I hope."

He took her face in his hands, sliding his fingers into her hair. She thought he was going to kiss her. Instead, his gaze stroked over her features as if he were memorizing them. Returning again and again to her eyes.

"Lisa…?"

She heard the questions piled into the voicing of her name. *Are you really okay now, Lisa? Okay with what happened? With me and White and you?*

"Yes." Still within the embrace of his hands, she nodded, emphasizing her answer to all his concerns.

"God, Lisa—"

"You have to go, Shane. They're boarding the plane."

"Did I ever tell you I like your hair cut this way?"

"No, you never did."

"I do. I can see your face better. Your beautiful face."

He dropped his hands, turned and boarded the plane, never looking back.

She'd intended to drive to her house, get dressed and go to work, as usual. She ended up at the Slash-C.

Dave, her dad and foreman Jack Ralston were mounting up in the corral. They waved, and she waved back, relieved they were too far away to see her clearly.

She wasn't that lucky with Matty.

As Lisa entered the kitchen door, her sister-in-law, dressed for ranch work, was putting her breakfast dishes in the dishwasher.

"Hey, Lisa. How're you doing? I was heading over to the Flying W, but I could put it off a while if you've come to visit. Pour yourself some coffee and—" She slammed the dishwasher door. "That son of a—"

Lisa averted her face, a case of closing the barn door well after the horse had bolted.

"I'll kill him."

"He's gone." She poured herself coffee.

"I'll still kill him. And he'll be *glad* I killed him, because it'll save him from what Dave would do to him if he knew Shane Garrison had made you cry!"

"I haven't cried."

"Maybe not on the outside, but—"

"Matty, dear," came Donna Currick's voice, and Lisa realized her mother was sitting quietly at the breakfast table, "if making their women cry now and then was a death sentence for men, you and I would both be widows."

Lisa and Matty exchanged a look, and the memory of Lisa being a witness to Matty shedding a great many tears over Dave was clear between them.

"Come to think of it," Donna went on, "there might be few men left at all."

Matty looked from Lisa to Donna and back. "I'm going to leave you to talk to your mom, Lisa, but if you decide you want action instead of talk, you come find me."

Lisa almost chuckled at her sister-in-law's fierceness. Almost.

Matty gave her upper arm a pat and called out goodbyes before slamming out the door. Lisa pitied any cow that crossed Matty Brennan Currick today.

She took her cup of coffee around the end of the counter,

leaning back against it instead of sitting at the table. It was a futile effort to keep her mother from examining her.

Her mother tsk'd. "Lisa Louise, what am I going to do with you?"

"Don't go lecturing me, Mother. You should have told me everything you knew about Alex and that package. Anytime in the past eight years would have done, but especially when you heard a New York detective was here."

"I told you, you and Shane have bigger mysteries to solve."

"I don't know what you're talking about." But she did know.

"Have you solved that mystery, dear?"

"No. It's...I don't know." She looked up and met her mother's eyes. "But I'm going back. To New York."

Donna let out a contented breath. "Well, that's fine, then. And Shane?"

"I'm going back for me, not Shane. I have things to accomplish there. Things to learn there. I'll always have roots here, and I'll come back to visit—probably more than you and Dad do—but I'm not done with New York."

Her mother simply repeated, "And Shane?"

"I...I don't know."

Less than a week ago her mother had said her confusion was a good sign. Her life was littered with those good signs now.

"Well, you have time. Lots of time. And with you living in New York again, maybe I'll finally get your father to spend time in The City."

Lisa laughed. She was still laughing when her mother folded her into her arms and stroked her hair. Only then did Lisa realize she was crying.

"You can crow over this one, Garrison. I never thought you'd find it."

Tony Prilossi set a glass of scotch in front of Shane. His words should have been sweet. Prilossi rarely admitted to being anything short of infallible.

Shane picked up the glass but didn't answer. Tony kept talking about the news conference the department brass had set up for tomorrow. "With that necklace and you as prime exhibits for show-and-tell," Tony added. "Guess I should be there as your new boss, right?"

With that new track for Prilossi to consider, Shane was free to look out the office window. With the midnight lights of the city shining through, it appeared even dirtier now than when he'd left. He supposed he wouldn't win any prizes for freshness, either. Airplanes, airports, a car to the police lab to have the necklace examined. And when the lab guys confirmed it was the real thing, then reports left, right and sideways. Not to mention interviews with the brass. Always keeping Lisa and her family far in the background.

He'd called the prison before coming by here, as Prilossi had ordered, "no matter how late." But Alex White was having a bad day, and Shane had to be satisfied with leaving a message.

Odd. He hadn't talked to the man in nearly a year, yet his voice sounded louder in Shane's head at the moment than Tony's clarion tones as he justified his presence at tomorrow's news conference.

You want to find something, but it is not that necklace.
It is where it will do the most good.

Where it would lead him to Lisa—that's what White had meant. And it had.

To seeing Lisa, being with her, touching her, arguing with her, kissing her, holding her...loving her.

But now he was back in New York, and she was still in Wyoming. And the necklace wasn't one damn bit of good in dealing with that reality.

Lisa had her back to the door, putting away files from the morning and pulling out two that Taylor wanted to check after lunch. Tomorrow the first applicant would come. She'd offered to stay until she could train her replacement, but Taylor had insisted that Lisa leave whenever she wanted—she would fill in with temps, and she could get Ruth to train the new office manager.

The door opened behind her, and Lisa said, "I'll be with you in a moment."

"Don't take too long."

She spun around, spewing the contents of two folders. "Shane! What are you—"

"I know. It took me longer than I expected. Knighton needs better airline connections. I feel like I've spent thirty-two of the past thirty hours in airports or airplanes."

"But—"

"No, you had your say at the airport yesterday. It's my turn now. But I'm starved." He hooked her arm and tugged her toward the door. Just before it closed, Lisa saw Taylor's smiling face watching them. "C'mon, let's go to the café for lunch."

Less than two days apart, and there was something different about him. Although she couldn't define it.

Certainly no one else seemed to notice. Not as they walked to the café and several passersby included Shane in their hellos. Not as they passed down the line of stool sitters who each greeted Shane. They hadn't even realized he'd left. She could hardly believe he was here.

"Rainie, could you give us a few minutes?" he asked as they headed for the back booth.

"Sure thing, Shane."

Automatically Lisa slid into the back bench. Shane slid in right next to her, his left arm curling around her shoulders, his hip against hers.

"This way we both get to sit with our backs to the wall."

"Shane, can't we go someplace and talk—someplace private?"

"Like I said, I get my say now. And I figured you couldn't get too rough with me in front of all your friends and neighbors."

It hit her then. What was different about him was he was nervous.

"I sat out there two days ago waiting for you to come out of that barn and I thought about all the possible ways it could go. And the one thing I knew was if giving up finding that necklace meant I'd be with you, it could go down a well for all I cared.

"I've got nearly a month before I'm due to report to the D.A.'s office. I'm going to stay here until then. It's all set with Ruth and Hugh—they picked me up at the airport, and we settled that. And after that I'll have vacations. I'll come back. And I'll keep coming back. Maybe I could find a job out here."

"Oh, Shane." Her voice wobbled; he looked like he'd had the breath knocked out of him, or maybe the heart.

"I'm going to say it whether you want to hear it or not. I love you, Lisa."

She put her hand to his cheek, feeling the stubble there of a man who'd been in the air more than on solid ground in the past day and a half.

"You don't want to give up your work in New York. Maybe someday, but not now. You need the challenge. You even need the stress."

"I need you. You make me feel."

"Yes, you do. And I need you. I love you, too."

His eyes flared, but his mouth remained grim. "So, that's settled. I'll keep coming back here as long and as often as I can."

"Does that mean you're not ready for me to come back to New York?"

His gaze touched her mouth, her hair, and came back to her eyes.

"You're serious."

"I've been told on good authority that I've been too serious for too long, but I think this is one time when no one could disapprove of my saying, yes, I'm serious."

He gave a whoop that must have been heard all down Main Street, then put his mouth over hers. They opened to each other, exploring and reassuring and confirming all at the same time.

It was the second break for the tedious necessity of breathing that opened Lisa's consciousness enough for the oddity of silence to sink in. With one hand to his chest and the other to his cheek, she stopped Shane as he was about to reclaim her mouth.

"Shane, listen."

She felt four strong beats of his heart under her hand before her words seemed to sink in. Then he turned his head, also giving her a view of the rest of the café.

Ruth stood a half dozen feet away, her back to them, her hands on her hips, and her posture clearly daring the lineup of stool sitters—including her husband—or Rainie or the kitchen help who'd appeared at the door, to make a sound. None of them dared.

"They'll tar and feather me for taking you away." He sounded willing to pay that price.

"Not as long as I'm happy." She turned his face so she could look into those blue eyes. "And I'm very, very happy."

Epilogue

Four years later

Lisa Garrison, known professionally as Lisa Currick, fingered the bur marigold pendant of gold and amber that Alex White had sent as a wedding gift. His note had said it was for her and her alone, since he'd given Shane the opportunity to meet and win her, and that was the greatest gift.

Even as she teared up, she smiled. Alex was at peace now. Six months ago he'd died in his sleep. She was glad the last visit she and Shane had made together had been on one of Alex's increasingly rare good days.

The flight attendant appeared to remove their breakfast trays, and Lisa blinked back the moisture in her eyes before her husband spotted it.

She slid her right hand into Shane's left, feeling the smooth gold band there, warmed as always by his heat.

"Why don't you try to get some sleep, Shane? Did you get any rest last night?"

It was their first opportunity to relax after the rush to the airport, getting settled in, then takeoff, and breakfast service starting as soon as the plane leveled.

"Not much." He shifted in the first-class seat. "I swear Tony Prilossi tries to make me work so hard before I leave on vacation so I'll stop taking vacations. If you didn't have him wrapped around your little finger, I think he'd refuse to let me go."

They were headed back to Wyoming for what had become an annual gathering. Dave and Matty, of course, with little Brennan now nearly three and Matty expecting again. And Taylor and Cal, with Cassie two months older than Brennan and three-month-old Rob. But also the elder Curricks, as well as most of the Garrisons, along with Taylor's parents, and sometimes one or more of her brothers and their families.

Although Matty and Dave had adopted a mixed-breed puppy from the Rescue League three years ago and the elder Curricks took in an older spaniel, Sin ruled the canine roost. Sin was still intensely loyal to Cal, but reveled in all the children, occasionally displaying his collie traits by herding the various toddlers into a compact unit if he felt anything threatened them.

This wasn't the only vacation for Lisa and Shane, either. She made sure he didn't pile up weeks upon weeks of vacation by working without a break. There were visits to his family in Wisconsin and long lazy weekends in New England at the shore or cuddled in their apartment with the phone turned off.

"Tony's afraid every time we go that you won't come back," she said.

He grunted. "Maybe sometime I won't—we won't. You miss home. You'd like to be closer to your family."

"New York's home, too." She didn't even try to deny what he'd said about family. Although family could grow anyplace.

"You can design in Knighton and take a few trips a year

to New York to see how the studio's handling your pieces. You're hitting your stride now. Another year and you could support me.''

"That would only be fair after you've supported us both while I got established. But what would you do in Knighton? No offense, darling, but I've seen you work cattle, and I don't think ranching's in your future. So that leaves what? Joining the stool sitters at the café?''

"I can think of worse things. Or maybe give the sheriff a hand.''

But he wasn't ready. Not yet. He still had things to do in the wild, amazing city they called home, and she was happy to be there, too. As long as he was there.

"Maybe someday we'll make a permanent home in Knighton. But right now's not a good time.''

His attention focused immediately, in that uncanny ability of his to home in on a mystery. "Why's now not a good time?''

"Well, as wonderful as it is that Ruth and Hugh's granddaughter is working with Doc Johnson to take over his practice, I don't think this is the right time to be changing doctors.''

"Doctors? Is something wro—?''

And then he had it. But she could see he was afraid to say it. Disappointments had piled up over the past year and a half. She didn't blame him for being wary. Even with the nausea she'd been experiencing she hadn't wanted to get his hopes up. But this time…this time, even before the doctor had given her the test results yesterday, she had known.

She put her palm to his stubbled cheek. "Something is very right. We're going to have a baby in a little over seven months.''

Tears came into his eyes, and if it had been possible, she would have fallen a little deeper in love at that moment. Then he kissed her. Slow, hot, sensual and tender, and she found out it was possible.

"I want you," he whispered, his lips brushing hers as he formed the words.

"Tonight, when we're settled in—"

"Not tonight—well, maybe tonight, too. But first, now."

"Now?" She pulled back enough to see his face. He was serious. And the heat deep in her belly pulsed through her body. "But…but…"

"They say the lavatories are a tight fit, but they work."

"Shane, we can't. If we got caught…"

"We won't get caught."

"But…" The possibility of touching him, having him inside her had awakened the need that never seemed to sleep very deeply. She blurted out the first thing that came to mind. "Matty and Taylor will take one look at us getting off the plane in Sheridan, and they'll know what we've been doing."

"Honey," he drawled, "they've got to suspect, since we've been married nearly four years, and when you tell them our news, their suspicions are going to be confirmed."

She looked at his face for another twenty seconds— mostly for the pleasure of looking at him, because her decision was already made—before whispering, "I'll go first, then you come right after."

He grinned. "My plan exactly."

Dave and Matty, and Cal and Taylor were the welcoming contingent at the Sheridan airport. Matty stared at them as they came down the steps from the small plane they'd transferred to in Denver. Lisa avoided eye contact.

"Shane's parents are with all the kids at the Slash-C this time," Dave said as he took the carry-on bag from Shane and clapped him on the shoulder. "How does it feel coming in second to the charms of a smelly diaper?"

"Not so bad. Grandparents are entitled to those priorities." Shane's voice was remarkably normal.

But Taylor's eyes widened and she spun around and stared at Lisa. "Are you?"

Dave and Cal caught up a couple beats later, looking from Shane to Lisa, with growing grins.

But Matty, clearly intent on her own quest, wasn't paying any attention. She propped her hands in the vicinity of her hips, which emphasized her eight-months belly and announced, "You two have that look. What have you been up to?"

"I don't know what you're talking about." Lisa tried to walk past her.

Matty took her arm, looking from her to Shane and back. "Okay, you two decadent New Yorkers—where?"

Dave groaned. "I don't want to hear this."

"Matty," Taylor started, "did you catch what I asked—"

Matty continued her own line of questioning. "I want to hear—where?" She slanted her husband a look. "Could come in handy."

Dave's face brightened. "In that case…where?"

"We got a hotel room during the two-hour layover—" Shane started.

While Lisa was saying, "It's not an urban legend about those lavatories—"

Cal burst out laughing.

"Okay, which one of you is making this up—" Matty stopped abruptly, then joined the laughter. "Both? I don't believe it—yes, I *do* believe it. You two *are* decadent. It's a good thing you're married."

"Yes, it's a very good thing they're married," Taylor said with emphasis. "Makes it so much nicer for your niece or nephew, Matty."

"My niece or ne— Oh. Oh!"

The hugs all around significantly slowed their departure from the airport. But that was one of the joys of vacationing in Knighton—there was no hurry.

Once in her brother's car, seated snug against Shane with his arm around her, Lisa asked, "Dave, could you do me a favor?"

''Sure. Pregnant ladies definitely get favors.''

''Let's stop by the café for a late lunch. I have a craving for a BLT.''

Shane groaned, but he was smiling. He kissed her and groaned again.

''This time,'' she said softly. ''I'm asking for what I know I want.''

* * * * *

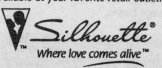

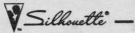